Ann Cleeves

KILLJOY

BELLO

First published in 1993 by Macmillan

This edition published 2014 by Bello
an imprint of Pan Macmillan, a division of Macmillan Publishers Limited
Pan Macmillan, 20 New Wharf Road, London N1 9RR
Basingstoke and Oxford
Associated companies throughout the world

www.panmacmillan.co.uk/bello

ISBN 978-1-4472-5322-8 EPUB
ISBN 978-1-4472-8911-1 POD

Visit www.panmacmillan.com to read more about all our books
and to buy them. You will also find features, author interviews and
news of any author events, and you can sign up for e-newsletters
so that you're always first to hear about our new releases.

Chapter One

At seven o'clock on November 30th the Grace Darling Arts Centre was busy. The fog seeped inland from the Tyne and hung around the horse chestnut trees in Hallowgate Square but the building had a light in every window and the car park behind the house was full. Hallowgate had once been a prosperous Victorian suburb. The wealthy middle classes from Newcastle who made their money from ships or coal built houses there. Then the conurbation spread and Hallowgate became part of the North Tyneside sprawl. Its fortunes declined. It had never been as smart as Tynemouth or Martin's Dene to the east and was too far from the metro line and the main road to be taken up by serious commuters. From attic windows in the solid red-brick houses there were views of the cranes along the river, a rope factory, the remaining skeleton of a boatyard. Hallowgate was close to the Tyne but this part had an identity of its own: quiet, shabby, forgotten.

The rest of the square was quiet. Most of the residents were elderly. Recent news reports of skirmishes with the police on the Starling Farm, a nearby council estate, kept them inside. The talk in the pubs was of joy riding, ram raiders. The streets seemed dangerous. On the corner of Anchor Street the Bengali grocer's shop was still open but the languid teenage girls behind the counter had no customers to serve and spent the evening reading magazines and sucking sweets. By then the fog was so thick that even with the street lights they could not see the visitors to the Arts Centre in any detail. Even if the visibility had been perfect they were unlikely to take any notice.

Evan Powell drove into the Grace Darling car park, saw that it was full, and drove out again to find a space in the square. It would not have occurred to him to cause inconvenience by double parking. The manoeuvre took longer than he had anticipated and it was just after seven when he opened the door to the small music room where the other members of the choral society were arranging chairs and music stands. Punctuality was important to him and he had been faintly anxious that they might have started. It came as a relief to see that three other people came in after him. Before the conductor called them to order he wondered briefly if his son John had remembered that he would be here tonight to give him a lift home. It was a bad time for youngsters to be out on the streets alone.

In the main hall the Tyneside Youth Theatre had just begun its rehearsal. The teenagers were limbering up to loud rock music. The windows were covered by blackout curtains and the room was dimly lit by coloured spots. They moved barefoot across the wooden floor, jumping and twisting, dressed in cycle shorts or Lycra leggings and loose, sexless T-shirts. Prue Bennett, sitting on the stage and watching them, admired their youth and energy, with a trace of envy. She switched off the large cassette-recorder.

'OK everyone,' she said. 'Relax.'

Then she turned to the theatre's director, who was too grand, it seemed, to take the exercises but who came in now once the real work of the evening was to begin.

Gus Lynch was a local man. His dad had been a draughtsman at the Swan Hunter boatyard and he had been to school in Wallsend. The trustees of the Grace Darling thought it was local pride that had brought him back to run the Centre and direct the Youth Theatre but he was too canny for that. Soon after drama school he had starred as a token Geordie in an ITV sitcom. The series had run for years to a dwindling audience and when it came to an end Gus was virtually unemployable. He had no experience of the serious stage and in its final years the series had been something of a joke; advertisers and the producers of the new, slick comedy programmes were not interested in anyone associated with it. Gus was an ambitious man and although he had played hard to get he

Ann Cleeves

Ann Cleeves is the author behind ITV's VERA and BBC One's SHETLAND. She has written over twenty-five novels, and is the creator of detectives Vera Stanhope and Jimmy Perez – characters loved both on screen and in print. Her books have now sold over one million copies worldwide.

Ann worked as a probation officer, bird observatory cook and auxiliary coastguard before she started writing. She is a member of 'Murder Squad', working with other British northern writers to promote crime fiction. In 2006 Ann was awarded the Duncan Lawrie Dagger (CWA Gold Dagger) for Best Crime Novel, for *Raven Black*, the first book in her Shetland series. In 2012 she was inducted into the CWA Crime Thriller Awards Hall of Fame. Ann lives in North Tyneside.

had welcomed the approaches from the Centre's trustees. He recognized the potential the post had for reviving his image. It made him the North-East's most prominent media man. He was invited on to late-night television shows to discuss provincial theatre. The money was crap, he had to admit, but in the scheme of things the Grace Darling Centre was performing a useful function. The situation comedy had almost been forgotten and he was already looking forward to something new.

He cultivated the part of the famous actor. Despite middle age he wore a lot of denim and he swore at them all. The teenagers thought he was wonderful. They gathered together to listen as he joined Prue on the stage.

'Let's do some work on the last scene,' he said, 'when Sam Smollett rescues Abigail from the crowd around the gallows, don't forget I want real menace, not just a lot of shouting and abuse.'

He was very thin and his head was the shape of a skull, Prue saw now, prompted by talk of the gallows.

The group had devised the play—*The Adventures of Abigail Keene*—from stories they had grown up with since childhood, and from a folk song performed still in clubs and pubs all over the region. Abigail Keene had been an eighteenth-century rebel, the daughter of a Hallowgate merchant who had run away from home to travel and see the world. She had taken up with a robber and highwayman, then been caught and sentenced to hang, rescued only at the last moment by her lover. There was no real evidence of her existence but her story had survived in the area through song and myth. The group had turned it into a roistering melodrama, full of black humour and sexual innuendo, interspersed by music. Prue Bennett described it to her friends as Richardson's *Clarissa* crossed with *Monty Python*.

Gus looked down at the expectant teenagers and felt the sudden exhilaration of power. This might be a small pond, he thought, but he was a bloody big fish in it.

'OK,' he said. He moved restlessly over the stage. 'Let's set it up. John and Gabby to their positions, the crowd over here. We'll try it without the music first. Don't forget we've our first dress rehearsal next week.'

The young people were using the stage and the front of the auditorium below it. They had placed blocks to separate the space and give a variation in height. They milled around to find their starting positions.

'Right!' Gus said. 'Now, can we have more light?'

The hall was suddenly lit by a series of white spotlights. In one, on the stage stood a dark, muscular boy in a track suit. He held one hand to his face to shield the glare from the light.

'Gabby's not here,' the boy said flatly. 'I haven't seen her all evening.'

'Bloody hell!' Gus Lynch said. 'We can't do much without her. Prue, where the hell is Gabby? She lives with you, doesn't she? What have you done with her?'

'I haven't done anything with her,' Prue said calmly. 'I'm her landlady not her minder.'

'Well, we can't wait any longer for her. Anna, you can play her part for tonight. Let's get on with it.'

Prue Bennett watched her daughter move from the shadow, sensing her nervousness. In the circle of light John Powell stood, moving his feet and shaking his hands as if he were some athlete warming up before a big race. She wondered if Gus Lynch had hoped to cause her some awkwardness by choosing Anna as Gabby's understudy for Abigail Keene. He knew that the girl worked well as part of a group but became shy and diffident when she was the centre of attention. Was this an attempt to give her confidence, or just an opportunity for him to exert his authority over Prue?

Gus produced in Prue, as always, mixed feelings. She knew he was an arrogant bastard, but she enjoyed her work in the Arts Centre. She had been there for three years and still thought she was fortunate to have the job, that Gus Lynch had in some way been kind to employ her. She had applied for the job at the Grace Darling with enthusiasm but with little hope of success. She had little enough experience—a year in rep between university and getting herself pregnant. She had had no real work since then. First there had been Anna to look after, and just as the child grew more independent her elderly parents had begun to make different and more cruel demands. Even now, three years later, she felt a remnant of gratitude to Lynch for not choosing one of the eager and attractive young actresses she had met at the interview. She was still uncertain why he had gone for her.

Prue watched John Powell put his arm round her daughter. She knew it was acting. John was Sam Smollett, the highwayman, hero of the piece. But still she felt a twinge of possessiveness. Something about the guarded tension of Anna's face made her anxious, reminded her of the turbulence of her own teenage years. She fancies him, she thought suddenly. She's excited by the physical contact. Then, almost immediately: I hope nothing comes of it. Not with John. He's too reckless. He's more Gabby's type. Then: What has it got to do with me anyway? I always promised myself I'd never interfere.

Thought of Gabby produced her to more irritation. Where was the girl? She could be unreliable at home but usually took the Youth Theatre seriously. She had never been this late before. For the first time she began to worry, influenced despite herself by the lurid news reports. Perhaps Ellen knows something, she thought without much hope. I'll speak to her after the rehearsal. Then she felt resentful. She had responsibility enough without having to take on someone else's child. She forced herself to concentrate on the teenagers in the body of the hall.

Ellen Paston was Gabby's aunt, her dead father's sister. She had worked part-time in the cafeteria in the Grace Darling Centre since it had opened, had worked there in fact before that, cleaning for the old lady who had owned the big house. On November 30th Ellen Paston began her shift at six o'clock. She got a bus from the Starling Farm to the end of Anchor Street and walked the rest of the way, staring in at the shop windows. Most of the shops were shut but the windows were bright with gaudy Christmas decorations. Outside the pub a thin-faced man sold flimsy sheets of wrapping paper twisted into tubes. He smoked roll-up cigarettes and his eyes were alert, all the time, for the police. Ellen was heavy, big boned, and walked with a slow, lumbering gait. She took in all the details of her surroundings.

By seven o'clock Ellen Paston was pouring coffee for the Hallowgate Writer's Circle. They met in the cafeteria then moved on to the small lecture room to share news of rejection slips and to massage bruised egos. The membership was composed mostly of middle-class women who drove in from the more affluent suburbs. Ellen Paston listened to their conversation without apparent interest. Despite her size she managed to be unobtrusive and though they met her each week the Writers' Circle hardly noticed she was there. The women's competitive boasting about their grandchildren's achievements left Ellen cold, but she listened just the same. You never knew when you could pick up something worthwhile. She was single, always had been, and realized that being single put you at risk. There was a danger that you would miss out on what was due to you. Ellen knew instinctively that information gave you power and she was determined always to know what was happening in Hallowgate.

It had been inevitable that John Powell would be chosen to play Sam Smollett, the hero of *The Adventures of Abigail Keene*. He had been given a leading role in every production since he was fourteen. Even then, sullen and covered with spots, brought by his father who thought it would be good for him, Gus had recognized something special about him, something moody and reckless. He saw that John would not be afraid of taking risks. The character of Sam Smollett suited him down to the ground.

Tonight John's performance was not up to its usual standard. It lacked the pace and swagger needed for the part. His mind was not on the role. Gus blamed Gabby's absence for the lack of energy, but John knew that his inability to concentrate was at fault. He was ashamed of some of the trivia which distracted him. The lousy mark he'd got for the last history essay, for example. He couldn't hide it from his father any longer. The old man was already asking about it—not angrily but with that hateful, compassionate interest that made John want to hit him.

'How did you get on with that project you were researching?' his father had asked the night before. 'Cromwell, wasn't it?' He had come in from a late shift and looked tired, but still made the effort to take an interest in his only son's work. When he was eleven John's form teacher had said he was Oxbridge material and Mr Powell had never forgotten that.

'I don't know,' John had muttered. 'Haven't had it back yet.'

And Powell had shaken his head in disappointment. 'I suppose they're overworked,' he had said, 'but all the same. . .' He wondered if they should have sent John to private school after all. Jackie had been all for it, had offered to go out to work to pay the fees, but Evan hadn't been keen on that. In his work he saw too many kids allowed to roam the streets without proper supervision. That wasn't going to happen to his son.

John stood, waiting for the crowd to move back to their places so they could rehearse the movement again. It was the climax of the play, a piece of comic melodrama. He appeared, disguised as the hangman, and at the last moment pulled Abigail to safety through the crowd. Usually, he enjoyed the scene but today he was preoccupied, wondering why his father bugged him so much. He wasn't unreasonable, not compared with some other kids' dads, but he left John always with a sense of vague and uneasy aggression.

And there was the same unease whenever he thought about Gabby. . .

Anna Bennett touched his shoulder to move him back to their starting place, and he jumped with a start. He was getting nervy. That wouldn't do. In his game he needed to keep his nerve. He breathed deeply into the pit of his stomach as he did in the relaxation exercises Prue set them before they started rehearsing.

'Are you all right?' Anna whispered. 'Is anything wrong?'

'No,' he said, smiling, super cool. 'It's just a drag, isn't it, Gabby not being here?'

She turned away and he saw with irritation that he must have offended her. He should be more careful, keep his feelings under control. It wasn't her fault. He saw himself as a modern Sam

Smollett, gallant and daring, a gentleman of the road. He flashed her a smile.

'I'm sorry,' he said. 'I didn't mean that. You know what it's like when you get used to working with someone. It's bound to make a difference. Let me buy you a Coke later, to show there are no hard feelings.'

Gus Lynch looked at his watch and saw gratefully that it was a quarter to nine. He felt like giving the whole thing up now.

'We'll go through it just one more time,' he called, unenthusiastically. 'Try to be aware of each other. We need a co-ordinated movement. It's not a rugby serum. God knows how we'll be ready for performance. And what happened to you, John? Let's have a bit more dash and pace.'

'Sorry, Gus!' John shouted. 'I'm feeling a bit off tonight.'

Gus Lynch shrugged and gave the cue to start them off. He watched the dispirited, disorganized performance with annoyance. This play was important to him. For God's sake he needed a bit of media attention. Especially now. He wouldn't allow the bloody kids to let him down. If John Powell didn't pull his finger out he'd be replaced with someone more committed.

The rehearsal rambled on to its close. The lights were switched up and the young people stood in groups, blinking and shame-faced, expecting an angry lecture from Gus. The old lecture about how he'd given up a good career to come and work with them and he expected some guts and energy in return. But he let them go in silence and they wandered through to the cafeteria where Ellen Paston stood, hunched and unresponsive, behind the counter.

John Powell, haunted by the old worries, forgot immediately about the easy promise to buy Anna a Coke when the session was over. He left the Centre, ignoring the porter's greeting, and stopped at the entrance to the car park. He'd always liked cars and it had become a habit to stop there to admire the smart vehicles left by the Centre's patrons. But the fog and the smashed security lights meant that visibility was poor and he hurried back to the square. The pavement was covered with sodden leaves and his footsteps made no sound. Through the mist he saw his mother's car parked outside the grocer's shop. He remembered his dad had said he could borrow it because his was in the garage for a service, and was pleased, it would give him an excuse for not waiting for a lift home. He would say that he'd forgotten about the service and when his father's car wasn't around he'd presumed that he had missed the choral society because of some emergency at work. His excuses to his father grew more elaborate every day.

In the cafeteria Anna Bennett pretended not to notice that John had left without buying her a drink, without saying goodbye. The place was busy so she could chat to her friends and ignore her mother's glances of anxious sympathy.

'Gabby wasn't here tonight,' Prue said to Ellen as she collected her coffee.

Ellen looked up, said nothing.

'She told me she'd be here,' Prue said, trying to contain her impatience. 'You don't know where she might be?'

Ellen shook her head then seemed to realize that some contribution was expected.

'Perhaps she's poorly,' she said.

'She didn't say anything this morning,' Prue said. 'But perhaps that's it. Perhaps she didn't feel well at school and went straight home.'

'You don't want to worry about that one. She can look after herself,' Ellen said unhelpfully. She began to serve the next customer and added as an afterthought: 'No need to fuss.'

'All the same,' Prue said, 'I think we'd better go home and check.' She imagined Gabby in the house at Otterbridge, alone, seriously ill. She drank her coffee quickly and called to Anna who was standing at the edge of a group of girls, smiling too brightly, pretending too hard to be interested in what they were saying. With a relief that was only obvious to Prue, Anna gathered up her coat and bag and followed her mother into the lobby.

At an impressive wooden desk sat a short, thick set, bald man, reading the *Sun*. This was Joe Fenwick, retired boxer, porter and security man. He looked up from the paper and smiled.

'All right, Miss Bennett?' he said. 'Finished for the night, then, pet?'

'Yes,' said Prue, then, contradicting herself, 'no, I'd forgotten. I must see Gus before I go.' She turned to her daughter apologetically. 'He's worked out a final draft for the programme and I want to check it before it's printed. I'll take it home with me.'

'Go on then!' said Anna, long suffering, tolerant of her mother's middle-aged absentmindedness. 'I'll wait for you here.'

Prue ran up the stairs and paused outside Gus's office door to catch her breath, then knocked and went straight in. She saw first that Gus had a visitor then that she had interrupted some silent confrontation. Gus was sitting behind his desk facing a middle-aged woman who sat squarely in a leather chair inherited with the house. The woman was well dressed, confident, classy. Prue recognized her as Amelia Wood, Deputy Chair of the Grace Darling trustees. Prue composed herself. Mrs Wood was an intruding presence and she wondered briefly what trouble the old bat was causing now. She smiled.

'Sorry to disturb you, Gus,' she said lightly. 'I'm here for the programme. I was hoping to work on it at home, this evening.'

He jumped to his feet, all tension and nervous energy. He was rattled, Prue thought. Mrs Wood sat with her gloved hands clasped in her lap and smiled.

'Yeah,' Gus said. 'Right. Of course. Look, the draft's still in my car. In a file in the boot. Why don't you help yourself?' He took keys from the pocket of a jacket which was hanging on a coatstand by the window, and tossed them to her. 'Leave them with Joe at reception,' he said. 'Save you coming all the way up the stairs again.'

Mrs Wood watched his agitation with amusement. She stood up, offered one of her hands to Prue and said: 'Miss Bennett! How nice to meet you again.'

Resisting the urge to curtsy Prue left the room and returned to Anna.

When they walked into the car park the Christ Church clock was striking 9.30. Usually the place was brightly lit with security floodlights but they had been smashed by vandals the weekend before and still not replaced. After the warmth and light of the house the car park was chill and uninviting. The only light came from the orange street lamps beyond the trees and from the uncurtained windows of the cafeteria. From the mouth of the river came the distant, muffled sound of a foghorn and the smell of mud. The car park was almost empty. The teachers and solicitors who came to the Grace Darling Centre to sing and write enjoyed its facilities but were nervous about its location. One heard such dreadful stories. At the end of each meeting they were relieved to find their cars still there intact, and drove back with relief to the civilization of Tynemouth and Martin's Dene.

Gus had his own space in the car park. He had insisted that Joe Fenwick should paint DIRECTOR in big white letters on the concrete. The blue Volvo was parked at an angle between the parallel white lines as if he had arrived in a hurry. Prue fitted a key into the lock of the door. As she lifted it a bulb inside lit automatically, and she had no difficulty in seeing the contents. There, on top of the file containing the programme for *The Adventures of Abigail Keene*, lay Gabby Paston, curled on her side like a child at sleep. But her eyes were open and bulging. Gabriella Paston was dead.

Chapter Two

Inspector Ramsay was loaned to the North Tyneside division of Northumbria Police to work on the Gabriella Paston murder because it was desperately under-staffed. The area had seen an epidemic of what was known in the anodyne jargon of the sociologist as auto-related crime. Young people had always stolen cars and driven them dangerously. The offence was so common in the North Tyneside courts that it was hardly taken seriously. But recently the thefts had become more organized. There was a suspicion that they were being co-ordinated by more sophisticated criminals. The situation was complicated too by gangs of ram raiders who drove high-performance cars through shop windows to steal the expensive goods inside, and by the circus-like exhibition of the racing of stolen cars around the district's council estates in the middle of the night.

Nightly street disturbances followed the police's attempts to control these demonstrations of male bravado and there were tragedies: the death of a seven-year-old child as a stolen car chased by the police swung out of control at a school crossing, and the stabbing of an eighty-year-old man who was rumoured to have given information to the police. In the quiet period before Christmas there was little other domestic news and the broadcasters and newspaper reporters gathered in the area in their hundreds, inflaming the locals' bitterness with their cameras and their questions. There was talk of riot and constant criticism of the policing of the area; the Northumbria Police sweated it out defensively, waiting for the situation to calm of its own accord.

The murder of a teenage girl, which in other circumstances might have been seen as a welcome break from routine, an excitement to see them through until Christmas, was only an added complication, a distraction from the important issues. Ramsay was welcome to it. Besides, they soon found that the girl had lived in Otterbridge, the Northumberland market town twenty miles away where Ramsay was based, and that was excuse enough to pass it on to him.

Ramsay arrived at the Grace Darling car park at the same time as the pathologist, a man of ridiculously youthful appearance, consultant at one of the Newcastle teaching hospitals. He was a clean-shaven athletic Scot who spent his spare time climbing mountains and playing rugby.

'What did you think of the game at Murrayfield on Saturday?' he whispered with barely concealed delight as they walked together to the car, managing just to maintain an air of appropriate solemnity. He had Ramsay down as an ardent English fan, perhaps mistaking him for some other colleague met in similar circumstances and always made some comment on the latest Rugby International. Ramsay, who had no interest at all in sport, was never sure what to say.

'She would have been a pretty young thing,' the pathologist muttered appreciatively, peering into the boot of the car. Ramsay resisted the temptation to say that he could tell that, without a medical qualification. The pathologist straightened. 'I can't give you much,' he said cheerfully, 'until I examine her. It looks like asphyxiation. No scratch marks on the neck but I'd say she was strangled. And moved of course after death.'

'Time of death?' Ramsay asked, more in hope than in expectation.

But the pathologist shook his head and refused to commit himself.

One of the attractions for Ramsay of taking responsibility for the Hallowgate murder was the chance to work with a new team. He thought he was getting stale. He hoped, perhaps to find a new enthusiasm for the job. In Otterbridge his sergeant was Gordon Hunter, brash, over confident, with the sensitivity of a cart horse. Ramsay thought that in Hallowgate he would find a more sympathetic colleague, someone less abrasive. There was Evan

Powell, for example; he would find out if Evan was available to join him on the enquiry. They would work well together. He felt a jolt of disappointment then, when he saw Hunter sauntering across the car park towards him. The sergeant wore his usual uniform of designer trainers, jeans, and leather jacket and greeted colleagues from North Tyneside with easy frivolity, using nicknames, making jokes.

'What are you doing here?' Ramsay demanded, then regretted his abruptness. Hunter was a good policeman in his way. There was no point in putting his back up. But Hunter was too insensitive to take offence.

'Knew you couldn't manage without me,' he said. 'Besides, it's as quiet as the grave in Otterbridge. All our bad lads are on this patch joining in the fun.'

Ramsay thought that riot and ram raiding and the death of a child was hardly his idea of fun but he did not want to provoke an argument, especially here in front of strangers. He knew he already had a reputation for being pompous and humourless.

Hunter sensed nothing of Ramsay's disapproval. 'Think of the overtime,' he said. 'It'll come in handy just before Christmas. And it doesn't hurt to volunteer for something occasionally. Makes them think you're keen.' He turned to one of the local uniformed officers who had been first on the scene. 'What's the score, then? Do we know who she is?'

'Her name's Gabriella Paston,' the young man said warily. He was new to the force and unsure of Hunter's authority. 'She's a member of the Youth Theatre but she didn't turn up for the rehearsal tonight.'

'What *is* this place?' Hunter asked of no one in particular. He looked with distaste at the building with its Gothic turrets, at the gloomy garden and dripping trees. This time Ramsay answered.

'It's the Grace Darling Arts Centre,' he said. Diana, his ex-wife, had brought him to the Grace Darling when she was trying to educate him, to see experimental theatre groups and exhibitions by obscure local artists. He had no positive memories of these experiences but remembered what Diana had told him about the place. 'It was a big private house. The old lady who lived here left it in her will to the community to be used as a centre for encouraging the arts. She came from Bamburgh originally and stipulated the name. Eventually the trustees bought up the house next door and extended it.' He stopped, knowing that Hunter hated to be lectured and saw that his attention was already wandering. He was staring at the body.

'I think I may have seen her around,' Hunter said. 'In Otterbridge. In that new night club on the market square. She was a cracker. You couldn't help noticing her.' He paused and Ramsay thought he might express some grief, a reflection on the waste of a young life, but he continued cheerfully, 'I offered to buy her a drink once but it didn't do me any good. She could have had any bloke in the place.' He swung round and faced the uniformed constable. 'Who found the body, then?'

'A mother and daughter,' the man said. 'But it's not their car. Apparently the owner gave them his keys to fetch something from the boot.'

'Where is the owner of the car now?' Ramsay asked.

'In the Centre with the other witnesses. We've got the names and addresses of the people who were here when we arrived but we've let most of them go home. There weren't that many—mostly kids from the Youth Theatre hanging around the cafeteria. Apparently it was very busy earlier on but most people went at about nine. The only people left now are some security and domestic staff, Gus Lynch the director, who owns the car, and the two women who found the body.'

'We'll need an appeal on local radio tomorrow morning asking everyone who used the Centre today to come forward,' Ramsay said, thinking out loud. 'Then we'll need more men to take statements.'

'You won't be popular,' Hunter said, grinning, thinking again about overtime. 'I hear they've already exceeded their budget.'

Ramsay turned away and muttered under his breath. This would be hard enough—working on an unfamiliar patch—without the political pressure of keeping costs down. Perhaps over-work wasn't the only reason why his North Tyneside colleagues had handed the case to an outsider. He shivered, feeling suddenly very cold. The mist was thinning again and above the grey slate roof of the Grace Darling appeared a small sharp-edged moon. In the distance they heard the wailing siren of a police car or fire engine, the sign, perhaps, of more disturbance.

'Come on,' Ramsay said. 'Let's go in and see what they've got to say for themselves.' Then, with an optimism he did not feel, 'This might be a straightforward one. Perhaps we'll have it all wrapped up by morning.'

The sound of the siren came closer.

In the lobby of the centre many of the original features of the old house remained. There was wood panelling, a huge portrait of a stern Victorian, a chintz-covered sofa. How did they survive, Ramsay wondered, these remnants of gracious living, without being stolen or vandalized?

Joe Fenwick recognized the men as police as soon as they came in. Until he was fifty he had worked as a bouncer for one of the roughest clubs in Newcastle. He was a squat tub of a man, known to his opponents in the ring as Popeye, because of his protruding head and his ability to find sudden bursts of strength from nowhere. He had retired from boxing thirty years ago and still missed the excitement. The work at the Grace Darling was steady, without the aggravation of the club, but he found himself perpetually bored. The murder had lifted his spirits considerably. He set aside his newspaper and waited for Ramsay to approach him.

'You heard what happened outside tonight?' Ramsay said.

Fenwick nodded.

'Is this the only entrance?'

'Aye, that's right. The trustees decided it'd be more secure that way.'

'Do visitors have to check in?'

'No,' Fenwick said. 'It wouldn't be practical the number that use the place. But there's always someone on duty here, day and night. It costs them a packet but they reckon it's worth it. I've been here since ten this morning.'

'Do you ever get any trouble?' Ramsay asked.

'Nothing we can't handle,' the porter said. 'It gets a bit rowdy sometimes, especially if they have a rock group in, but not *nasty*. You know what I mean?'

Ramsay nodded.

'They got a consultant in to make it vandal-proof—wire-mesh shutters on the windows, everything with locks on. It's not foolproof—some bugger smashed the security lights last week—but I've never had any real bother. I've been here since the place opened.'

'So you know most of the regulars, at least by sight?'

'I suppose so, but there's often something different going on—one-off shows or concerts, that bring in their own audience. I can't keep track of everyone then.'

'No,' Ramsay said. 'Of course not. Was anything unusual happening tonight?'

Fenwick shook his head. 'No,' he said. 'It was just a normal Monday night—the Youth Theatre rehearsing in the New Theatre, the Choral Society in the music room, and the Writers' Circle in the small lounge.'

'And all the activities started at the same time?'

'Aye. They all run from seven until nine. It doesn't always work out like that. The groups fix their own times.'

'Did you know Gabriella Paston?' Ramsay asked gently.

'Oh, we all knew our Gabby!' Fenwick exclaimed. 'Such a bonny lass. It brightened my day to see her.'

'Did you see her today?'

'No,' Fenwick said. 'And I missed her.'

Ramsay paused and Hunter, impatient as always, hoped that he had finished with the old man. But Ramsay continued: 'You can't see the car park from here. Do you do any security checks out there?'

'No! The trustees are worried about the building, not the punters' cars.'

'So you wouldn't have noticed if Mr Lynch's car was there all day?'

'No,' Fenwick said sadly. He would have liked to have helped them.

'We'd like to talk to Mr Lynch,' Ramsay said. 'Where can we find him?'

'Upstairs in his office.'

'Thank you,' Ramsay said. 'You've been a great help.' He walked up the curving wooden staircase with Hunter at his heels.

Gus Lynch was drinking whisky from a large tumbler. His face was grey and the hand that held the glass was shaking. When they knocked at his door he was speaking, caught in mid-sentence, and when they went in his mouth was open, gaping and ridiculous. Ramsay introduced himself. Lynch half stood to greet them and finally shut his mouth.

'I was just explaining to the policeman,' Lynch said, nodding towards the constable who sat nervously in the corner clutching a notebook on his knee, 'that I didn't know anything about it. How could I? I would hardly have given my keys to anyone else if I were intending to dispose of a body.' He looked around desperately. 'Now would I?'

Ramsay ignored the question.

'How long has your car been parked there, sir?' he asked. The calm question seemed to reassure Lynch. He set the tumbler on the desk and made a visible effort to control his panic.

'Since ten o'clock this morning,' Lynch answered. 'I don't work office hours, Inspector. Most of my active work is done in the evening.'

'And you've been in the Centre all day?'

'All day. Certainly.'

'You didn't go out for lunch?'

'Lunch?' Lynch expressed surprise as if lunch were too trivial a matter for the Inspector to bother himself with. 'Oh, yes, of course. I'm sorry. I should have realized. Just to the Ship in Anchor Street for a sandwich. But I walked. I didn't take the car.'

'And on the way out did you notice that your car was in its usual place?'

'No,' Lynch said. 'Not specially. My space is at the end of the car park, under the trees. I wouldn't see from the front door or the street.'

'Do you usually go to the pub for lunch, Mr Lynch? Was that a normal daily routine?'

'Yes,' Lynch said with some irritation. 'I suppose so. If I'm here. I have other commitments, of course. Radio. Local TV. But if I'm here I like to go to the pub, get some fresh air.'

'When was the last time you looked inside the boot of your car, Mr Lynch?' Ramsay asked.

Lynch answered immediately. 'This morning. Before I left home for work. There was a programme I'd been working on. I put that in the boot.'

There was a pause.

'Would that be a bulky manuscript?' Ramsay asked at last.

'Bulky?' Lynch seemed astonished. 'No, of course not.'

'Wasn't it unusual then,' Ramsay asked, 'to open the boot specially? Wouldn't it be more normal to take the paper into the car with you, to put it perhaps on the passenger seat?' He paused again. 'Unless of course you had a passenger with you.' He looked up from the notes he was making. 'Do you live alone, Mr Lynch?'

'Yes,' Lynch said sharply. 'Of course.' There was a silence which he seemed to need to fill. 'I have been married, Inspector. When I was a drama student. We were both very young. It didn't work out and we parted, quite amicably, twelve years ago. Since then I've lived alone.' There was another pause before he continued. 'My wife was a rather jealous woman, Inspector. She couldn't cope with my success.'

Perhaps he expected then a question about his career in television because he seemed quite surprised when Ramsay said: 'Tell me about Gabriella Paston.'

Lynch shrugged. How can I tell you anything, he implied.

'How long has she been a member of the Youth Theatre?'

'For four years. Since she was fourteen.'

'You must have learned something about her in that time.'

'Look, Inspector, we're not friends, me and the kids. I never meet them socially. I run a workshop session every Monday night and then they go home. There's no time to chat.'

'You don't meet for a coffee afterwards?'

'No,' Lynch said. 'The kids usually meet up in the cafeteria but to tell you the truth I've had enough of them by nine. I'm knackered and I want to get straight home.'

'But not tonight?' Ramsay interrupted.

'What do you mean, not tonight.'

'You didn't go straight home after the workshop finished tonight. You were still here, in your office at nine thirty when Miss Paston's body was found. What was different about tonight?'

'I had a visitor,' Lynch said reluctantly. 'One of the trustees, Amelia Wood. She descends on me occasionally to make sure I'm running the place efficiently. The trustees think I need help with the administration.'

'Was she still here when the body was found?'

'I'm not sure. She might have been downstairs. She'd left my office by then.'

'And there's nothing more you can tell me about Gabriella Paston?'

'You should ask one of the others, Inspector. Her aunt works in the cafeteria here. Her landlady's my assistant. But I'll tell you something about Gabby, I liked her. She was fun.'

During the interview Hunter had remained uncharacteristically unobtrusive. There was no fidgeting, no theatrical sigh to show that he thought the witness was a blatant liar. The stillness was unusual and Ramsay wondered what was the matter with him. He would have been surprised to discover that Hunter was thinking, with some regret after all, about Gabriella Paston.

He thought he had probably seen her three or four times in the night club in Otterbridge. Hunter went there regularly to impress new girlfriends and it was always packed. He had only spoken to Gabriella once. On the other occasions he had glimpsed her sitting at the bar with friends or on the dance floor under the flashing lights, but she had always attracted his attention. On the night he had spoken to her he was on his own, stood up by some woman, determined all the same to have a good time. She had been sitting on a tall bar stool, her legs crossed at the ankles, laughing. He had offered to buy her a drink, and she had laughed again and refused, saying she was waiting for a friend. That was all that happened. There had been no more contact than that, but Hunter felt the result of the encounter all evening. He was excited, suddenly optimistic about the possibility of good times ahead. He wasn't sure what it was about her that had been so special and was trying to find a word to describe her when Gus Lynch provided it for him. Gabriella Paston was fun.

In Lynch's office Ramsay looked at Hunter, giving him the opportunity to ask questions of his own, but the sergeant shook his head.

'That'll do for tonight, Mr Lynch,' Ramsay said, surprised. 'We'll be in touch again tomorrow.'

'Oh!' Lynch said with some bitterness and self pity. 'I expect you will. How will I live it down, do you suppose? What will the trustees think? Even if they don't believe I'm a murderer they'll think I'm remarkably careless. To allow my car to be used as a dump for dead bodies.'

Ramsay was already on his feet but he hesitated at the door.

'Were you careless?' he asked. 'With your car keys for example. There's no indication that your boot was broken into. Could someone have taken your keys without your realizing?'

Lynch shrugged. 'I keep them in my jacket pocket,' he said. 'My jacket's usually hanging up in my office. I don't usually lock my office door. I suppose that's careless.'

He turned his back to them and poured another drink.

In the lobby Joe Fenwick was still pretending to read the *Sun*, but he was looking out for them, hoping to be involved, an insider in the investigation.

'The others are waiting for you in the small lounge,' he said. 'At the end of the corridor and turn left. I can show you if you like.'

Ramsay seemed to consider the offer carefully. 'No,' he said. 'Thank you. I think someone should stay on the desk if you don't mind.'

'Sure!' Fenwick said, grinning to expose a mouth full of crooked teeth.

In the lounge the mock-leather chairs were still set in a circle. Earlier the Writers' Circle had sat and listened with rapt attention to a local author of historical romances talk about the necessity of proper research. The three women in the room had pulled their chairs out of the circle and sat in a corner around a small table which held a tray with a teapot and mugs. The heating in that part of the building must have been switched off automatically because the room was very cold. The women were all wearing coats.

Hunter opened the door without knocking and they turned to face him with the wary suspicion that usually met the police. Ramsay, standing behind him, did not hear the sergeant's introduction and his explanation that they had questions to ask but they would be as quick as possible. He was staring at Prue Bennett, recognizing her immediately, waiting for some sign that she recognized him.

Chapter Three

One summer, more than twenty years before, Stephen Ramsay had been in love with Prue Bennett. He had been a sixth former at Otterbridge Grammar School. She had been a year older, at the same school. There, Ramsay had been considered boring. He was hard working, not terribly bright, never a real member of the arty group which dominated the Common Room. He found the talk of politics, rock music, and pop psychology bewildering. There was nothing in his background or personality to excite interest and the girls who were at that time into long floral dresses and self-expression ignored him. In their presence he was awkward, gawky, quite socially inept. He cared too much what they thought of him, desperate for some contact, some intimate female company. Now, in the Grace Darling Centre, standing in the doorway, trying to catch Prue's eye, he still remembered with pain the desperation of that summer and the occasion that had brought them together.

A trendy young English teacher had organized a trip to the Newcastle City Hall in the school's minibus. The lead guitarist from a famous rock group had recently gone solo and was playing there as part of a country-wide tour. Who was he? Ramsay wondered now. But although he had an image of a fine-featured young man, with long ginger hair, bending over a guitar, could even hear one of the more lyrical tunes which had the girls in the party dancing, he could not remember the musician's name. Had it been familiar to him even then? Or had he gone along on the trip just because he was frightened of being left out altogether, of becoming one of the strange, misfit pupils, the target of jokes, hardly considered as part of the sixth form at all? He had gone, he admitted to himself now, though he would not admit it then, because there would be girls in the party and in 1971 he was obsessed by women. For Ramsay, at that time, almost any girl would have done. He would have been content with a kiss, a touch, a token taste of the sexual activity which was going on all around him and in which he never participated. He supposed that someone fat or particularly ugly would have been an embarrassment but he had the sense that once he made it with one girl the rest would be easy. There was a feeling of time running out.

Prue Bennett was not any girl. She was a calm, dark young woman as tall as he was. She was in the upper sixth and had already gained a place at Cambridge. She was, he knew, way out of his league. Yet because of chance or circumstance, because the trendy English teacher was infatuated with a married woman, Ramsay and Prue were thrown together.

It had been arranged that the minibus would deliver all the girls to their homes, but it had taken longer than the teacher had expected to negotiate the traffic generated by the concert. He had a date with his mistress and knew she would not wait for him if he were delayed. She had a husband to return to. He was a mild distraction to relieve her boredom, not someone to ruin her life for. When he arrived at the town centre with Prue still on board he was frantic.

'Look!' he said, persuasive, chummy, one of the lads. 'I've got an appointment, something I can't miss. You know how it is. Steve, you've got to get the bus home anyway. Can't you walk Prue to her house and get it from the top of the hill?'

'All right,' Ramsay had said hesitantly. Would Prue Bennett want him to walk with her? She was independent. Perhaps she would prefer to walk alone. He was more nervous than he had ever been. More nervous than before 'O' levels, even than before the eleven-plus and then he had been so frightened that he had spewed up in the playground of the village school where he'd been a pupil.

'Prue?' the teacher had said. 'You don't mind, my love? You'll be quite safe with old Steve.' And he had laughed, a little unpleasantly, as if he knew of Stephen's inexperience and was making a joke of it.

'No,' Prue had said easily. 'Of course not. I'd like the walk if you don't mind . . .' She had turned round in her seat in the minibus to face him and put her hand on his arm. 'If you're quite sure.'

Oh yes, Ramsay mumbled. He was quite sure.

'Let's go through the park,' she said as they crossed the bridge. It was still warm but a breeze from the Otter blew her hair, and the skirt between her legs. He looked away.

'I thought it was locked at night,' he said.

'It is. But I know a way. Come on. It's miles quicker.'

And she took his hand and ran with him across the bridge and pulled him through a hole in the hedge. They were alone in the moonlight in the park. The trees threw long shadows across the path and there was a smell of honeysuckle and roses.

'Well?' she said. 'What do you think?'

'It's lovely,' he said. 'Really lovely.' But he was not sure if that was what she wanted him to say. Perhaps they were too corny for her these images of moonlight and roses. Perhaps she expected him to laugh.

He was still holding her hand. He began to stroke her palm with his thumb, expecting her to pull away and make a fuss. He was tensely defensive, prepared for rejection. But she didn't make a fuss and when he put his arm around her shoulder and then pulled her towards him to kiss her she went along with that too, with a kind of amused good humour.

Now, in the Grace Darling Centre, he wondered what she had seen in him. She could have chosen any of the boys: one of the intellectuals from her scholarship group, a musician, an artist, anyone. Perhaps she had picked him through a stubborn perversity, just because he was unfashionable. Walking with her that night through the park, burying his face in her hair, he did not care. He knew he would never be so happy again.

She had lived in a large Victorian house on the corner of a street, with a view over the park to the town.

'Why don't you come in?' she had said that night. 'Meet Mum and Dad.'

'I don't know,' he had said. 'I don't want to disturb them. Perhaps they'll be ready for bed.' His mother would already be in her candlewick dressing-gown, nervously watching the clock, waiting for his return. 'No,' she said. 'Of course not. Don't be silly. It's early yet.' And in her laughter he had the glimpse of a domestic world completely different from his own.

'I'm sorry,' he said reluctantly. 'I should get the bus. My mother . . .' he did not finish the sentence, unwilling to imply that he was in any sense a mother's boy.

'Of course,' she said. 'Well, another time.'

'When?' he had demanded, decisive for the first time. 'When can I come?'

And she had laughed again. She was pleased with him. 'Whenever you like,' she said.

'But when? Give me a definite time.'

'Tomorrow,' she said. 'Come for supper tomorrow. About seven o'clock.'

And she had run up the crumbling grey steps and through the front door, so he was left open-mouthed, staring after her.

He had three months before she would go away to university. He never considered that they would stay together once she left the area. The affair had a natural time scale and he counted the days. He came to know her parents quite well during that time. He was happier in the large, untidy house than he was introducing Prue to his own home. Mr and Mrs Bennett were older than his own parents, in their late fifties, and he thought their age gave them a licence to be eccentric. Although Prue was an only child they allowed her a freedom which he envied. They were wrapped up in their own interests: Mrs Bennett taught piano and always seemed, Ramsay thought, to have music in her head. When she was not teaching the stream of eager middle-class children who came to the door she was playing herself, and even in the middle of a conversation she would break off, and begin to hum absentmindedly. She encouraged Prue in her academic interests without putting too much pressure on her—of course the girl would do well, she implied. Why should *she* fuss about it?

Mr Bennett had been a civil engineer and had taken early

retirement because of ill health. He was a cheerful, unassuming man who held the house together. He took care of all the practical matters—ordering milk and bread, fixing dripping taps, battling with the large, unruly garden.

Stephen was flattered because the family seemed to like him. He was invited regularly to relaxed, chaotic meals, where he was introduced to olive oil, garlic, and wine. It was much easier than taking Prue back to his home in the pit village between Otterbridge and the coast. She was charming, uncritical, but in her presence Mrs Ramsay grew uneasy and threatened. She looked around the small Coal Board cottage where they lived, as if she knew it was not what Prue was used to. She could not bring herself to apologize for it but Prue's style and confidence made her resentful. She was brittle, too polite, and when Stephen's father came home from the pit with coal dust under his fingernails she blushed with shame.

Ramsay standing in the doorway, looking at the three women huddled around the tea tray, thought that Prue had grown to look more like her father. She had not changed so much. Her hair was streaked with grey and she was drawn and tired but he would have known her anywhere. She looked up at him calmly, without apparent recognition, and he thought he must have aged dramatically or that their relationship had meant so little to her that she had forgotten it long ago.

'Good evening,' he said evenly. 'I'm sorry to have kept you. My name's Ramsay. I'm an Inspector with Northumbria Police.'

Then there was a slow recognition, a relief. 'Stephen,' she said. 'It is you. I wondered but I couldn't believe it. It seemed too good to be true.'

Ramsay was uncomfortably aware of Hunter. What would the sergeant make of that? he wondered. What sordid rumour would he start in the canteen?

He spoke formally. 'I'm afraid I have to ask some questions,' he said. 'I'm sure you'll understand.'

'Yes,' she said. Was she offended by the formality? Surely she would understand. Probably she hardly cared either way. If there was a daughter there was probably a husband. She wore no wedding ring but that meant nothing. And many women used their maiden names for professional purposes. 'Yes,' she repeated. 'Of course.'

He was aware of the need to concentrate, to bring his attention back to the case, to treat it as just another investigation.

'Perhaps you would introduce me,' he said briskly, to get things moving. She seemed surprised by his tone but answered readily.

'This is Anna,' she said. 'My daughter. You must realize that she's very upset. Gabby was a close friend.'

He looked at a thin, pale teenager with unusually straight dark hair. He saw a shadow of Prue as a girl in the features, but there was none of Prue's confidence and the shadow disappeared. Anna had been crying and clutched a wet handkerchief in long white fingers. She looked up at him and nodded, then returned to her grief.

'This is Ellen Paston,' Prue said then. 'Gabby was her niece.' Ramsay saw a large middle-aged woman with a permanently curved back, she shape of a turtle's shell, and huge red hands. She stared back at him, blankly, without distress or anger.

'I work here,' she said. 'In the cafeteria.' Then, grudgingly: 'I suppose you'll want some tea.'

He shook his head. He was unsure how he should handle the situation. He should see them all separately of course, take statements, check discrepancies, the small lies and mistakes which would lead to a conviction. But was there any need for all that tonight? Surely it could wait until the morning. Tonight an informal discussion, when shock would make them talk more freely, would be more fruitful. Hunter would disapprove of course. He had the technique of the macho hectoring interview down to a fine art. But Ramsay was used to Hunter's disapproval. He pulled a chair between Anna and Ellen Paston. 'Tell me what happened,' he said, gently.

'We found her body,' Prue said. 'You know that.'

'It was dreadful!' Anna cried. Prue seemed surprised by the interruption and Ramsay thought it was hysteria which had given the girl the courage to speak. 'I was so cross when she didn't turn up tonight, you know. She messed us around and put Gus in a bad mood. I even thought she'd done it on purpose to make us realize how indispensable she was. And then there she was. In the back of Gus's car. Her face all swollen and distorted.'

'You were expecting Gabby at the rehearsal tonight?'

The girl nodded.

'When did you last see her?'

'This morning at breakfast.'

Ramsay looked at Prue for explanation.

'Gabby lived with us,' Prue said. 'She was a sort of lodger, I suppose.' She looked warily at Ellen.

'We weren't good enough for her,' Ellen said sharply. 'We brought her up and when she was sixteen she decided Starling Farm wasn't good enough and she left.'

'We?' Ramsay asked.

'Me and her gran. Her mam and dad were killed in a car crash when she was a bairn.'

'When did she leave home?' Ramsay asked.

Ellen shrugged, not sufficiently interested apparently to work it out.

'About eighteen months ago,' Prue said.

'And she's lived with you since then?'

Prue nodded. Ramsay turned again to Anna.

'You didn't see Gabby at school?' he asked.

'No,' the girl said. 'She still went to school in Hallowgate. To the sixth-form college. I'm at Otterbridge High.'

'How did she get to school from Otterbridge every morning?'

'I gave her a lift,' Prue said. 'Unless I had a meeting in another part of the region. Then she got the bus.'

'But this morning?'

'I gave her a lift.'

'All the way to school?'

'No. We were late. I dropped her here and she said she would walk.' She put her head in her hands. 'I left her here in the car park. We made plans for this evening. She said she had been invited to a friend's house after school and she would come straight here afterwards. I never saw her again.'

'Was that sort of arrangement usual?'

Prue shrugged. 'She was eighteen, as streetwise as any kid I've ever met. I didn't feel any need to check up on her.'

'She didn't seem unusually worried? Or excited?'

'She was always pretty high,' Prue said. 'But perhaps she was even more excitable than usual. I didn't think anything about it.'

There was a pause.

'Did you notice any change in her clothes when you found her body?' Ramsay asked cautiously. The last thing he wanted was a distressing scene with Anna in floods of tears. 'Or was she wearing the same things as when you left her this morning?'

'The same,' Prue said. 'Definitely the same. Black leggings, a long navy sweater, a black leather jacket, and DMs.'

'DMs?' Ramsay asked.

For the first time Hunter interrupted, pleased to emphasize Ramsay's age, to show how out of touch he was.

'Dr Marten's,' he said, with a sneer. 'They're boots.'

'Oh yes!' Ramsay said confused. Weren't Dr Marten's worn by the thugs who kicked policemen at football matches and marched on National Front demonstrations? What was a pretty young girl like Gabriella Paston doing wearing boots that his dad would have worn down the pit?

'They're quite common,' Prue said. 'All the kids have them.'

He said nothing. How could he know what all the kids were wearing?

'We'll check with the school,' Ramsay said at last. 'See if she was there all day. We haven't got a time of death yet. . .'

He paused unhappily, aware that he was passing on ideas and information to which the witnesses had no right. He was treating Prue Bennett as a friend not as a possible suspect in a murder investigation. He should know by now the danger of becoming involved. . .

'Gabby weren't at school,' Ellen Paston said suddenly. 'At least she weren't there late this morning. I saw her.'

'Where did you see her?'

'Hallowgate Market,' she said flatly. 'I don't start here until six on a Monday. I went out and did my bits of shopping before I came.'

'What time did you see Gabriella?'

She shook her head. 'Twelve o'clock,' she said. 'Half past.'

'Did you speak to her?'

'Na!' she said. 'I didn't get a chance. I was queuing by that stall that always has the cheap veg.' She turned to Prue. 'You know the one. I said to the lass behind me: "It's like bloody Moscow waiting to be served here." But it's worth it in the end. You can get a canny bargain. . .I was just about to be served when our Gabby came past, walking very fast, almost running. I shouted out to her but she didn't take no notice. Perhaps she didn't hear me but I think she heard well enough. I wasn't going to lose my place in the queue to go chasing after her.'

'Were you surprised,' Ramsay asked, 'to see her out in Hallowgate when she was supposed to be at school?'

'Na!' Ellen Paston said. 'It's not like a *real* school is it, the sixth-form college. They're in and out of it all the time.'

'Did you see if she met anyone?'

She shook her head. 'I was too busy keeping my eye on the lad who was serving me. They give you all the shite from behind the counter if you don't watch them.'

She sat back in her chair, her feet planted firmly on the floor, her legs slightly apart remembering her weekly triumph in the battle with the market salesman. Perhaps the thought of the victory gave her courage because she went on: 'Well, if that's all I'll be off. I've been here two hours longer than I'm being paid for and I doubt if Mr Lynch will want to cough up the overtime.'

Ramsay was surprised by the woman. He would have expected more reaction. Even if she and Gabby had lost touch shouldn't there have been some grief, the pretence at least of sadness? She seemed not to care what impression she was making. He decided that her lack of response was caused by shock, and her gracelessness touched him and made him sympathetic. He would have taken her address and arranged to speak to her in the morning then let her go. But Hunter wanted to stamp his authority on the interview.

He thought she should have more respect and thought he would show her who was in charge.

'This is a murder enquiry,' he said sharply. 'A serious matter.'

'Go on then,' she said, not intimidated in the least. 'Get on with it. I live with my mam. She's an old lady. She'll be wondering what's happened to me.'

Hunter paused. Having made his point he was having difficulty coming up with a relevant question.

'There is something,' he said. 'Probably not important but I'm interested all the same. Why Gabriella? Why choose a name like that? Not a common name for a Hallowgate lass.'

'Her mother was Spanish,' Ellen Paston said, as if the word was an insult. 'Our Robbie met her when he was working the fishing boats. He had a season down in Spanish waters and brought her back with him. She never settled. I don't know why. Our Robbie spoilt her rotten. I doubt if it would ever have lasted. Mam and I could never take to her. All show.'

She was jealous, Ramsay thought, of her brother's wife. Is that why she expressed so little grief at Gabriella's death? Had her ugliness made her resent the beautiful young girl?

'And they were both killed in a car crash?' Hunter said.

'Aye.' Ellen paused, leaned forward, her elbows on her knees. For the first time Ramsay sensed real pain. She had loved her brother. She seemed lost in thought, then stared up at Hunter defiantly. 'Look,' she said. 'I'll tell you because you'll find out anyway. Or perhaps you already know. They were in a stolen car. Robbie was a bit wild when he was a lad and that wife of his only egged him on. They were coming out of town down the Coast Road when the police saw them and started chasing them. They drove into the back of a lorry. They didn't have a chance.' She snapped her mouth shut as if she had already given away more than she had intended.

'Did Gabby know how her parents died?' Hunter asked.

'Not the details,' Ellen said flatly. 'Not from us.'

So, Ramsay thought, despite what the politicians and the media said, joy-riding wasn't an invention of the nineties. Since the invention of the motor car there had always been foolish young men who drove too fast.

'We won't keep you,' he said to Ellen. 'If you wait in the lobby I'll arrange for someone to give you a lift home. My sergeant will come with you and make sure we have your details.'

He was left alone then, in the cold impersonal room, with Prue Bennett and her daughter. He wanted to say something which would establish some real contact between them, to ask about Prue's parents, to tell her about Diana and the divorce. But Prue had taken his last words as a general dismissal. She helped Anna to her feet and left the room without a word.

Chapter Four

When John Powell arrived home the house was empty. It occurred to him briefly that his mother was out a lot lately, but with the self-absorption of youth he only considered her absence as an effect on his own convenience. He had not eaten since lunch time and he was hungry. He was worried that the house might be cold.

The house was modern, detached, built at the end of a light-bulb-shaped close on a new housing estate. John hated it. His friends at the sixth-form college mocked him for living on the smart new estate. Most of them lived on the Starling Farm or in the terraced houses which spread from Hallowgate Front Street to the river. Some allotments and an adventure playground had been flattened to allow the new houses to be built—the council, poll-tax capped and almost insolvent, had reluctantly sold the land for private development—and feelings in the area had been high. There had been demonstrations and petitions.

Evan Powell had insisted on the move from the three-storeyed terrace house where John had spent his childhood. That part of Hallowgate wasn't a good area to bring up a teenager, he said. There were too many distractions, too many temptations, the wrong sort of influence altogether. The new estate, called by the developers Barton Hill, would attract a different class of family. John would meet new friends, find new interests. And the move would be good for Jackie too. It would give her something to do, planning the decoration and the furniture. They could afford it after all since he had got his promotion.

As John approached the mock-Georgian front door the security light was switched on automatically. The white light threw a shadow behind him and made him blink. Its brightness still surprised him. He unlocked the door and went immediately to the downstairs cloakroom to switch off the burglar alarm. Bloody security, he thought. His father was obsessed with it. What have we got that's worth stealing anyway? It'll all be insured.

He threw his coat and bag on to the floor at the bottom of the stairs and prowled through to the kitchen looking for food. The house was, as always, immaculately tidy. The thick-pile carpet in the living room still lay in strips where it had been hoovered, like a closely mown cricket field, the glass-topped coffee-tables gleamed, the Dralon-covered sofa stood square to the wall. He thought again about his mother and wondered how she stood it on Barton Hill. At least in the old street there had been a bit of life and bustle. This was like a grave. And she wasn't dumb. She had been training to be a teacher when Evan Powell, fresh from the valleys, had exerted his Celtic charm and swept her off her feet. So how did she put up with the tedium of housework? Her only social life seemed to consist of charity coffee mornings and parties organised in neighbours' houses to sell imitation perfume. Soon he would be going away to college and then there would not even be his mess to clear away.

In the kitchen there was a note on the table and a meal for him to microwave. He studied the note with more interest than usual, hoping that his mother had found something more challenging to do with her time. But it said only: *Babysitting at Joan's.*

Joan was his mother's younger sister. She had two primary-aged children and it seemed to John that the cycle of domestic drudgery was simply continuing in a different place.

He had just put the meal into the microwave when the telephone rang. John felt a rush of adrenalin. He was expecting Connor to call. When he picked up the receiver his hand was shaking.

'Can I speak to Evan, please?' John recognized it as a colleague of his father's and relaxed.

'No,' he said. 'He's not in yet. He'll be back any time. He should be here by now.'

'Ask him to phone work as soon as he gets in. It's urgent.'

John replaced the receiver and heard the sound of his father's car pulling into the drive.

He could tell as soon as his father came in to the room that he was irritable and he moved immediately to the offensive.

'Where have you been then?' he demanded. 'I didn't see your car at the Centre. I had to walk home.'

'I was there!' Evan Powell said, but he was relieved that his son had an adequate excuse for not meeting him. He always wanted to believe the best of him. 'I had to park round the corner. I was in your mother's car. You know that. I waited for you in the cafeteria. I thought you usually went for a drink after rehearsal.'

'Yeah!' John said. 'I usually do, but not tonight ...' He played his trump card. 'Too much homework.'

He saw his father relax, proud that his son made time for homework, glad that he wasn't one of the young tearaways who stole cars for kicks.

'There's just been a phone call for you,' John said, pressing home his advantage, hoping to avoid further questions. 'It was work. They want you to phone in as soon as you can.'

'Right ... Well ... OK. I'll not keep you from your homework.'

His father used the telephone in the sitting room so John, eating lasagne and reading the evening paper in the kitchen, did not overhear the conversation. But his father, shocked by the coincidence that a body had been found at the Grace Darling Centre, returned immediately to tell him the news. He was surprised by the boy's reaction to Gabriella's death. John said nothing. He disappeared to his room and Evan did not see him again all evening.

The police offered Gus Lynch a lift home—of course they would need to keep his Volvo, they said, for forensic tests. He declined the offer and took a bus, going the long way avoiding the Starling Farm estate. It was a precaution he had taken since the disturbances began. He was terrified of physical violence and had nightmares about it. He lived by the Tyne in a building that had once been a chandler's shop. The fog lingered over the river softening the outlines of the ice factory and the new fish market. Gus was pleased with his flat on the quay. He had been lucky to get it. With the decline of the fishing fleet, the chandlery business, which sold everything from creosote to jerseys, had gone bankrupt and an enterprising architect had bought the building and converted it to flats. The area was not as fashionable as the Newcastle quayside where warehouses had been transformed into luxury apartments and wine bars had appeared on every street corner. It still smelled of fish. All the same Gus thought the flat was an investment and it would not be long before other developers discovered the fish quay too.

As he drew closer he looked up and saw that there was a light in his flat.

Shit, he thought. He should never have given her those keys. He had presumed that when he was late she would go away. His flat was on the first floor, up wooden steps from the outside of the building. Jackie must have been looking out for him, or she heard his feet on the steps, because she had the door open before he reached it.

'Well?' she demanded. She was blonde, very thin, attractive in a feverish neurotic way. 'Well, where have you been? Where's your car? I was looking out for it.'

'Look,' he said. 'I've had a hell of a day. Aren't you going to let me in first?'

She stood aside and let him in to the kitchen. His breakfast plates were still in the sink and he thought wryly that she was slipping. She must be anxious not to have washed them up for him.

'I need a drink,' he said. 'A bloody big drink.'

He walked through to his living room and stood by the uncurtained window and looked out at the boat moored against the quay. When he was young he had haunted the quay on Saturdays, picking up casual work gutting fish. In the boats' romantic names he had imagined adventure. Now he was back here, only a couple of miles from the house where he'd been brought up. It didn't feel much like success.

Jackie had been watching the television and Lynch heard an announcer on the late local news talk about a ram-raid attack on the Metro Centre in Gateshead. He stopped to switch off the television and the silence was broken immediately by the foghorn at the end of the pier.

'You're so late,' she said, following him into the room with a drink. She stood close beside him. 'I was worried. You hear such dreadful things. All this violence . . .'

'Oh,' he said automatically. 'You listen too much to your old man.' Then he realized what he had said and how close he had been to violence and he started to laugh.

'It's not fair,' she said. 'You know how hard it is to get away. I need to talk to you . . .'

He looked down into the street and watched two drunks stagger from the pub two hundred yards away as they made their way along the quay, stumbling on the cobbles.

'What's the matter with you?' Jackie cried. 'Did you speak to Mrs Wood? What did she say?'

'It's no good,' he said. 'She wouldn't listen.'

'What are we going to do?'

'I don't know,' he said. 'It hardly seems to matter now.'

'Of course it matters!' She was beside herself with frustration. 'We're talking about your future. Our future.'

He turned back to her, suddenly sad and calm, he saw with detachment that she was a nuisance, that he could never be happy with her.

'Look,' he said. 'I can't talk about it now. Gabriella Paston's dead.'

Amelia Wood's husband was an architect. When she had married him as a young woman this had seemed a promising career, glamorous even. She had imagined him as an artist, creating brilliant designs in glass and steel. She had been working as a secretary in a solicitor's office and saw marriage as a romantic escape. The reality had been rather different. The loft conversions and garage extensions which comprised her husband's bread and butter work did little to inspire her and she soon decided that if she wanted glamour and excitement she would have to provide them herself.

She had few qualifications—the small private girls' school she had attended prided itself on its caring atmosphere rather than its academic achievement—and she knew she would never have the persistence to take a lowly position in a company and work her way up.

Her background made her turn naturally to voluntary work, community service. Confidence and an ability to get things done were all that seemed needed in that sector and she had those qualities in abundance. As her three children grew up she became steadily more influential. She chose high-profile projects with a satisfying element of social contact. In the organization of luncheons and celebrity appearances she became indispensable. The Grace Darling Project became her favourite charity. It brought her into contact with artists, musicians. She loved the bustle of the place, the strains of music, the younger people in leotards and tights gathering for the dance classes, the press attention. It made her feel important.

When the local councillor resigned she allowed herself, with some modesty, to be persuaded to stand as Conservative candidate for Martin's Dene, one of the few safe wards in Hallowgate. She impressed the voters with her style, flair, and commitment, and won with a much increased majority. It seemed that all her energy was devoted to public life.

Dennis, her husband, was content to allow his wife to take centre stage. He was busy making money. He supported her, of course, it did no harm for someone in his business to have connections on the council. As the recession developed in the south, the north-east became suddenly a more fashionable place to live. He bought up an old chandler's on the Hallowgate Fish Quay for next to nothing, converted it into flats which he sold at a profit. He saw the venture as a prototype, the first of many. But he was a grey, silent man, and he preferred to remain anonymous.

When Amelia left the Grace Darling Centre she was pleased with herself. Lynch was no fool. He had the sense to realize that his future lay, indefinitely, with the project. They would find it impossible to find another actor, with as high a profile, to be director. She drove down Anchor Street and along the edge of the Starling Farm council estate. A row of shops was boarded up and covered with graffiti and she felt a stab of personal annoyance that such vandalism could not be prevented. On a patch of wasteland a group of children were setting fire to the rubbish that had been dumped there. Their silhouettes against the flames had a demonic quality and she wondered automatically what their parents were thinking of to allow them out so late. Her children had been submissive, apathetic, and she had never had any difficulty in controlling them.

She drove past the concrete square of the sixth-form college towards the coast and the streets began to change. There were more trees and the gardens were bigger. She passed a tennis court and a church, a row of small shops, selling expensive dresses and French cheese. Martin's Dene had once been a village and still considered itself separate from the urban sprawl of Hallowgate which had grown up to the west of it. There was a prized open space—a hill where children flew kites on Sunday mornings and a scrubby valley beloved by dog walkers and the riders of mountain bikes.

The Woods' house was large, solid, rather unexciting. Dennis had bought it as an investment soon after they had married. He had recognized Martin's Dene as a place where property would keep its value. Amelia found it rather dull. When she invited the arty friends met through the Grace Darling to parties there, she felt she had to apologize for it. She found Dennis rather dull too.

He was sitting in front of the television with a cup and saucer on his knee. He had removed his jacket so that it would not crease. She knew that he would already have eaten. He was quite used by now to providing his own meals. The plates would be stacked in the dishwasher. All trace of mess would be cleared away. She knew his routine exactly. He would watch the evening news, make a general comment on the weather forecast, then retire to his office for an hour to catch up on paperwork.

'Had an exciting day?' she asked, sarcastically, hoping to provoke a fight, knowing there would be no response.

'So, so,' he said, not noticing the irony. He was grey haired, bespectacled. She wanted to scream.

She took off her coat and hung it up, then returned to him.

'What are you watching?' she asked, just to disturb him, because she knew perfectly well already.

'Only the local news.'

'Anything interesting?' she persisted.

'Yes,' he said. He turned his attention from the screen and looked at her directly. 'There's been a murder. In that Arts Centre where you're trustee. A young girl has been stabbed. They found her body in the boot of Lynch's car.'

When Prue Bennett returned to the house in Otterbridge where she had lived as a child she opened a bottle of wine. She and Anna sat at the kitchen table and drank it, quickly.

'I nearly brought out three glasses,' Anna said. 'I don't think I'll ever get used to the fact that she's not around.'

Everywhere in the kitchen there were reminders of Gabby's presence—her underwear strewn to dry on the radiator under the window, a jersey thrown over the back of a chair, a self-portrait stuck on the fridge, which had been a present to Prue on her last birthday. It occurred to Prue that Gabby must have made an impact wherever she went. Anna had lived in the house for most of her life yet there was little indication of her existence.

'Isn't it strange,' Prue said suddenly, 'that you were such good friends. You were really terribly different.'

'You mean that she was amusing, friendly, and attractive, and I'm dull,' Anna said sharply.

'No, of course not.' Prue was shocked by the bitterness.

'I'm sorry,' Anna said. 'I didn't mean it to sound like that. But sometimes it was hard not to be jealous. Not of the life she'd had. It must have been dreadful to lose her parents like that. But because she was always so popular.'

'Did she have a boyfriend, at the moment?' Prue asked. 'I suppose the police will want to know.'

'Oh,' Anna said. 'Gabby always had a boyfriend.' She paused. 'I don't know how serious it was,' she went on, 'but I thought she was rather keen on John.' She kept her voice even. 'I don't know if anything came of it. And she'd always had a crush on Gus, of course. If he hadn't been old enough to be her father she might have had a go at him.'

'She liked John Powell?' Prue's voice was tactfully calm. 'I didn't realize.'

'She never talked about it,' Anna said. 'She never talked about anything that was really important to her, if you think about it. She made everything out to be a great joke.'

'Didn't she even talk to you?' Prue said. 'I thought you two were so close. I could understand her not confiding in me. . .I thought perhaps I intimidated her. . .'

'Oh, Mum,' Anna said. 'Don't be so silly. She liked you. She really liked you.'

'Did she?' Prue looked up from her glass. 'As you say, with Gabby it was impossible to tell.'

When the bottle was empty Anna went to bed. She had to step over the slippers shaped like seal pups which Gabby had left at the bottom of the stairs and in the bathroom she stood for a moment, quite transfixed. The smell of Gabby's perfume still lingered there, so Anna felt that if she called out Gabby would answer her.

Prue stayed in the kitchen until past midnight. She opened another bottle of wine, which she began to drink more slowly. The cat jumped on to her lap and she stroked it absentmindedly, shivering slightly. She realized that the heating had gone off an hour ago, that she was very cold and a little drunk.

Joe Fenwick left the Grace Darling Centre at 11.30. The relief security man had been there for an hour but he had hung on, afraid of missing something, brewing tea for Ramsay and his men in the cupboard where he kept his things. There were no lights on in Hallowgate Square. Even the curious neighbours, who had heard of the murder on the telly and watched out for the police cars, had gone to bed. Usually, when he left work, Joe liked a quick drink in the Ship in Anchor Street. He liked the warmth, the conversation, even the piped Christmas music. He was well known in there. But tonight the doors were shut and the windows were dark. He walked on down the hill towards the river.

Joe Fenwick had lived in a basement flat at the bottom of Anchor Street for more than twenty years. During that time he had shared it on and off with Sal Grainger, the barmaid in the Anchor. She had been a big, impulsive woman who disappeared occasionally with other lovers, but they had got on well when she was there. They had shared a lot of laughs. Her death after a sudden illness had shaken him more than anyone realized. It had left him lost and lonely.

He was thinking of Sal when he was fiddling with the keys to his flat. He missed the anticipation of seeing her, sharing the news of the day, sitting in the stuffy little room in front of the gas fire, drinking tea or whisky. He was so lost in thought that the screeching brakes of the car turning from the square into Anchor Street shocked him. The car hurtled down the road, swerving from one side of the street to the other.

Bloody hooligans, Joe Fenwick thought, moving into the steps down to his flat, frightened that the car would mount the pavement and hit him.

The car sped past him. He saw that there were three people inside. The face of the driver was vaguely familiar, but disappeared so quickly that Joe could not place it. He swore again, under his breath, and opened the door to the cold and empty flat.

Chapter Five

The next morning Ramsay arrived at Hallowgate police station early. It was an impressive grey-stone building close to the quayside next to the Seamen's Mission. Along the street in the greasy café fishermen were eating breakfast and their laughter spilled out into the street. It was just getting light and very cold. Against the grey sky floated the white shapes of herring gulls, calling continuously. It was all very different from the inland county town of Otterbridge where he was usually based and he enjoyed the novelty of the surroundings, thought again that a new patch might rekindle his enthusiasm for the job.

Inside he was offered a bare, cold room on the first floor with a faulty radiator and no view but he accepted it gratefully. He would need somewhere away from the noise and hysteria of the Incident Room to collect his thoughts. Most of the morning was spent in meetings, organizing manpower, a press conference, negotiating overtime. Gabriella Paston was almost forgotten.

In the canteen Detective Inspector Evan Powell was giving Hunter a lecture about joy riding and ram raiders. There had been three more cases of TWOC in the night and a ram raid on the Co-op Hypermarket on the Coast Road, during which thousands of pounds' worth of small electrical goods, spirits, and cigarettes had been taken. Powell had had little sleep.

'It's all a symptom of the same lawlessness,' he said, his Welsh voice rising in passion as he spoke. 'There were villains on the patch in the past. Of course there were. But they came from the same families. We knew where to find them. We could control them. This is a different thing altogether. Far more widespread. On some of these estates there's a generation of kids who've been brought up without hope. . .'

Hunter, who had been hoping to enjoy a bacon sandwich in peace, muttered that Powell sounded like a bloody social worker. Powell, a Presbyterian, frowned in disapproval at the swearing, then continued:

'Their parents haven't got the wit or the interest to care about them, the schools can't control them, they live in a dump that the council tries to pretend doesn't exist. . . And then there's the boredom factor! They're not all dumb, you know, those kids. The Home Office like to think they're stupid. But they need a challenge like the rest of us. I know some of the joy-riding gangs go specially for the cars with the most elaborate security. Would you believe it? It gives them status, you see, in the eyes of their friends. And the ram raiders! Well, man, they're really at the top of the heap. Everyone on the estate knows who they are. They're heroes. You'd think every one of them was Robin Hood!'

He paused for breath. Hunter looked around him, searching for some means of escape. He was a policeman not a sociologist. All this talk made him uneasy. But Powell was going on.

'We let the situation get out of hand, of course,' he said. 'That's why we had those disturbances on the Starling Farm earlier in the month. The Chief decided we'd have to crack down on joy riding after that little girl was killed but by then it was too late. The kids had been getting away with it for years. We'd shown we weren't prepared to deal with it seriously. When we did go in hard they were ready for a fight. It was the boredom again. They liked the arson and the petrol bombs. It was like November fifth every night.'

Hunter saw that Ramsay had come into the room. Never before had he been pleased to see his superior. Powell, distracted at last, jumped to his feet to greet the Inspector.

'Stephen!' he said. 'I'd heard you were joining us. It's really good to have you on the team. I was just explaining to your sergeant here some of our special local difficulties.'

'They're hardly relevant to the Gabriella Paston case, though, are they?' Hunter said bluntly. 'No suspicion of auto-crime here.'

'All the same,' Powell said, a little offended, chiding. 'It never does any harm to understand your patch.' Pointedly he got up and walked away.

'He's a good policeman,' Ramsay said. 'You should listen to him.'

'I have been listening to him,' Hunter grumbled, 'for at least half an hour. He's a fanatic.'

Ramsay felt his usual irritation at Hunter's attitude returning. It would be hard enough in Hallowgate without offending their colleagues.

'Powell's a local man,' he said. 'He knows this patch inside out. We might need him.'

Hunter shrugged. If I ever need to ask for help from someone like that, he implied, it'll be time to give up.

'I'm on my way to the Starling Farm,' Ramsay said. 'I want to talk to Gabriella's grandmother and to the aunt again. At present she's the last person to have seen the girl alive. And there was something very odd about her attitude, didn't you think? No grief at all. It might just have been the shock, but all the same ...' If he had been talking to Powell he might have added that he wanted to be out, on the ground, listening, building an image of the girl he had lost during a morning of meetings. But Hunter would have considered the idea fanciful and he kept it to himself.

'What do you want me to do?' Hunter demanded. He too was bored with a morning of administration. He wanted some action.

'Go to Hallowgate Sixth-Form College,' Ramsay said. 'Talk to her teachers, her friends. Find out if she was there at all yesterday. Did she give any idea where she was going in the afternoon? Get a list of all her special friends, especially boyfriends—'

'All right,' Hunter interrupted. 'I get the picture.' He had never liked being told what to do and the thought of going to school made him nervous.

The Starling Farm was still not the worst estate of its kind in the area. It could not compete, for example, with the Meadow Well along the river, where the houses were almost derelict and the residents were bitter, embattled, or on tranquillizers. The Starling

Farm still had some streets where the gardens were tended, and the houses were all occupied. It was still safe for children to play in the streets during daylight, if they kept away from the broken glass. Women on their way to the only food shop which remained stopped to gossip and exchange jokes. But the place was shabby and dispirited. The disturbances had left it in a state of shock.

Alma and Ellen Paston lived in one of the older, more pleasant streets, in a crescent of semi-detached brick bungalows which had been built specially for the elderly at a time when the council could afford to care for you from the cradle to the grave. Some of the residents of Seaton Crescent had been children during the depression. Their dads had marched from Jarrow. They stood in the back gardens, with their rows of vegetables and home-made pigeon lofts, and discussed with puzzled voices the fact that nothing had changed. Starling Farm had been built with such hope just after the war and now it was just a slum, like the old slums of Jarrow and Shields. They blamed the young people, of course, for disturbing their peace with car chases, the loud unfamiliar music played from stolen ghetto-blasters in the streets, but they had grandchildren themselves. They understood the frustration. They wondered if they might be in some way to blame.

Ramsay followed a WRVS van delivering meals on wheels into Seaton Crescent. The spry white-haired woman who carried trays to the doors was herself of pensionable age. He wondered, uncomfortably, what he would find to do in retirement. No meals were delivered to the Pastons' house. Ellen, presumably, catered for her mother.

It was Ellen who came to the door. She must have recognized him but she did not ask him in.

'Yes?' she said cautiously.

'It's Inspector Ramsay,' he said. 'We met last night at the Grace Darling Centre. Perhaps I could come in.'

'I don't know,' she said. 'Mam's having her dinner. She doesn't like being disturbed.'

'Ellen!' said a deep, unctuous voice from inside. 'Who is it, hinnie?' And Alma Paston appeared behind her daughter. She was a huge woman, medically obese, with thick shapeless legs and blotched, flabby arms. Ramsay felt in his pocket for his warrant card, but he did not need to explain who he was. Alma Paston could smell a policeman from the other side of the Tyne.

'Eh, hinnie,' Alma said. 'What are we thinking of? Stand aside, pet, and let the officer in. We'll stick w' dinners in the microwave when he's gone.'

She led Ramsay into a front parlour. Ellen was left in the hall to shut the door. The room was very warm and dark. A fire burned in the tiled grate. There was a thick red carpet on the floor and red-and-gold patterned wallpaper. The table was covered with red-plush cloth. Alma waddled across the room, stood poised before a large armchair, then dropped into it. For a horrifying moment Ramsay glimpsed long grey knickers. Ellen stood, feet slightly apart, just inside the door.

'Now, hinnie,' Alma said. 'Sit down and tell me what all this is about.'

She peered at him, her small eyes almost hidden in folds of flesh. It was an affectation. She must know very well why he was there.

'It's about Gabriella,' he said.

'Of course,' Alma said. 'The poor bonny lass.' She sighed theatrically. Then: 'She wasn't living here, you know. You mustn't think that we can help you. She found herself lodgings with some folks in Otterbridge.'

As with Ellen, Ramsay was surprised by the lack of feeling. It was almost as if she had disowned the girl. Did they regard Gabby as her mother's daughter, hardly related to them at all?

'But you kept in touch? You must have seen her?' He was trying to get some angle on the relationship.

'Not for months,' Alma said quickly, then, realizing that she had been too abrupt, she added in explanation: 'I can't get out, you see, hinnie. I'd never make it to the end of the street. And she always said she was too busy to come to see her poor Gran. I had news of her, of course, through Ellen.'

'Why did she leave?' Ramsay asked. 'Was there a row?' It was hard to imagine a lively teenager in this house but something, surely must have provoked her into leaving. And if she had left amicably wouldn't she have made some effort to keep in touch with her grandmother?

'No,' Alma said. 'No row. Nothing like that. You know what bairns are like these days. They think they're so grown up.' But as she spoke she shot a warning glance at Ellen and Ramsay did not quite believe her.

'Did she take her stuff with her when she went?' he asked. 'Perhaps I could see her room.'

'She took everything,' Alma said. 'There'd be no point.'

There was a pause. Ramsay felt the questions were getting nowhere. He had come across unresponsive witnesses before but had known no one as impenetrable as the Pastons. Alma sat beaming at him, unruffled and in control. By the door Ellen stirred impatiently.

'Is that it, then?' she demanded. 'Can we have w' dinner now?'

Alma shook her head indulgently as if Ellen were a naughty child.

'You mustn't mind Ellen, Mr Ramsay,' she said. 'She's never liked the police. Not since her brother died. They were twins you know, as close as can be. She's never got over it.' And although Ellen was watching she tapped her head significantly to suggest mental derangement.

'I don't understand,' Ramsay said, 'how the police were to blame.' He realized later how cleverly Alma had changed the conversation and how defensive he had suddenly become.

'It was harassment,' Alma said. 'They covered it up at the inquest but everyone knew.'

'Everyone knew what?' It was an *Alice in Wonderland* conversation with a strange logic of its own.

'That Mr Powell wouldn't rest until he got our Robbie.'

'Evan Powell?' he said, shocked, giving away more than he had intended.

Alma Paston smiled, pleased by the response.

'He was still in uniform then,' she said. 'Based on the Starling Farm. We all thought he was such a nice man, didn't we, Ellen? At first. He went into the schools and talked to the bairns, visited the old folks. A community policeman, I suppose they'd call him now. It was a new idea then. He was supposed to solve all our problems.'

Ramsay said nothing. He could have defended Evan Powell but he waited, encouraging Alma Paston to continue. He suspected that a police operation twelve years before could have little relevance to the murder of Gabriella Paston, knew that in listening without comment he was condoning the spread of damaging and malicious rumour, but he needed all the information the spiteful woman could give.

'Our Robbie wasn't a saint, Mr Ramsay,' she said. 'No one could call him a saint. Not even Ellen. He worked hard but he drank too much, stood up for himself if there was any bother. He had a house on the other side of the estate with Isabella and Gabby. Isabella was Spanish, temperamental. Sometimes they had rows. She wasn't one for rowing quietly. It was all screams and throwing the furniture about. You'd think he was murdering her. Then the neighbours would call the police and our nice community policeman would come to sort it out.' She paused, still smiling. 'Mr Powell was a man of fixed ideas,' she said. 'He got it into his head that Robbie was a villain!' She paused again. 'He thought he was battering Isabella!'

'Well?' Ramsay said. 'Was he?'

'No more than she was battering him.'

'What else was Robbie up to, then?' Ramsay asked.

She moved her huge bulk in her chair and did not answer directly.

'It was 1980,' she said. 'Not an easy time on Tyneside, Inspector. Men losing their jobs. Worse even than it is today. Robbie had a family to support. And he was wild. I admit that. He needed the excitement.'

'So he stole cars,' Ramsay said. 'Is that it?'

She shrugged. 'There's no death penalty for stealing cars,' she said.

'You'd better tell me exactly what happened.'

'We don't know exactly what happened,' she said sharply. 'No one would tell us. There was a police operation, they said. Evan

Powell was driving the car following Robbie. They knew who he was. They could have picked him up at any time but they followed him so hard that he drove into the back of a lorry.' She squeezed tears from between the folds of flesh of her face. 'The bairn was six years old,' she said.

'You don't think this has anything to do with Gabby's death?' Ramsay said. 'Not after all these years.'

'I knew that he was there last night. At the Grace Darling,' Alma said sharply. 'Ellen saw him, didn't you pet?'

Ellen, still standing by the door nodded. 'He's in the choral society,' she said. 'He came into the cafeteria after for a cup of tea.'

'That's hardly a good enough reason to suspect him of murder,' Ramsay said lightly.

'I've reason enough,' Alma said. She lay back in her chair and slowly closed her eyes.

'If you've any information,' Ramsay said impatiently, 'you should tell me.' But Alma Paston gave no sign that she had heard him and remained with her eyes shut.

The door bell rang. Ellen stood uncertainly by the door and did not move. The bell rang again. Eventually Alma Paston opened her eyes.

'Go on, then, pet,' she said. 'Let's see who's there.'

Still Ellen hesitated and looked at her mother as if questioning her judgement. Alma nodded encouragingly and Ellen lumbered slowly to the front door.

'It's Gary Barrass,' she said cautiously.

'H'way in Gary, hinnie,' shouted Alma. 'Don't be shy.'

Ellen stood aside to let in a boy of indeterminate age. He was thin, with a grey unhealthy pallor. His hair was cropped short and Ramsay wondered if he had recently been released from some institution. Despite the cold he wore a short-sleeved cotton T-shirt. He shivered slightly and stared at Ramsay.

'This is our Gary,' Alma said to the Inspector. 'My friend's lad. He runs errands for us, don't you pet? Helps us out in the garden.'

The boy, obviously confused, simply nodded. He looked at his hands. LOVE had been written in black ink on the knuckles of one hand and HATE on the other. His nails were split and bitten.

'I don't think we need anything today, pet,' Alma Paston said. 'But perhaps you could come back later.' She winked at him.

'What time?' the boy said.

'Oh,' Alma said. 'Any time.' She laughed. 'I'm not going anywhere.'

The boy hovered. He shuffled from one foot to the other and seemed about to ask a question.

'Off you go now,' Alma said interrupting. 'This is Inspector Ramsay from Northumbria Police. You don't want to disturb him.'

And he disappeared before Ramsay could speak to him.

With his departure the atmosphere in the room changed. The women relaxed. Ramsay felt again that he had been outwitted in some way. The heat and Alma's superficially jovial words had worn him down. He thought he would get no more from them now. He stood up and sensed Alma's triumph.

'Are you off now, Inspector?' she said. 'You'll not mind if I don't get up. Ellen'll see you out.'

Ramsay stood in the doorway for a moment, enjoying the fresh air, reluctant still to go. He knew that the interview had been a failure. He wondered, as he always did at times like these, if Hunter could have done any better. But even Hunter would have found it hard to bully two ladies on their own. Perhaps he would have taken them at face value, commiserated with their loss, considered them characters in the great Tyneside tradition. What motive could they have for murdering the girl? The idea was ludicrous. But Ramsay was uncomfortable. As he hesitated on the step he heard a deep, uncontrollable chuckle from the depth of the house. Alma Paston was laughing. At a time of grief the noise was horrifying. Ramsay walked quickly to his car and drove away.

As he was approaching the main road which circled the estate Ramsay saw Gary Barrass, the boy who had come to the Pastons' house supposedly to run errands. The idea of Gary as an angel of mercy was improbable and Ramsay was interested. The boy was standing on a corner outside a big gloomy pub called the Keel Row, which had been famous once for its Saturday night fights, but which now attracted so few customers that it had lost even that distinction. Gary seemed to be waiting for someone. He was dancing up and down with the cold and seemed pathetically young. When Ramsay slowed the car and drew up beside him he approached at first as if this might be the person he was waiting for, then he recognized Ramsay and he started to run.

Ramsay jumped out of the car and chased after him, wondering as he did so why he was bothering. Gary crossed the pub car park and scrambled over a wall. Ramsay, already out of breath, stood and watched as the boy scuttled down an alley behind a row of almost derelict houses. He knew it would be pointless to follow him now. He would have friends or relatives all over the estate prepared to hide him. Besides, he would be easy enough to trace. Ramsay wished, though, that he had had a chance to tell the boy that he only wanted to help.

Chapter Six

When John Powell got up his father had already left the house. John had had very little sleep and would have been late for college if his mother had not woken him. She came into his room, still in her dressing gown, bringing a mug of tea for each of them, then sat on his bed and tried to make him talk about Gabby.

'I thought she was a special friend of yours,' she said. 'She was in your English group at college, wasn't she?' She lit a cigarette and inhaled it deeply. She had taken to smoking when his father was out of the house.

'She was just a friend,' he said. She had woken him in the middle of a dream, in which he was Smollett the highwayman being chased by a gang of soldiers. He felt the light-headed exhilaration which comes from too little sleep. His mind was racing. He was surprised by his mother's interest in the murder. His father had always protected her from the unpleasantness of his work.

'But you knew her quite well,' Jackie Powell persisted. 'I've seen you with her.'

John knew he would have to be careful. There was a rush of adrenalin and he found it almost impossible to lie still in bed. He breathed slowly, and reminded himself that if he was an actor this was just another performance.

'She was Abigail Keene in the play,' he said. 'We had to work closely together.'

'Did you see her yesterday?'

'Not at the Arts Centre,' he said, deliberately misunderstanding. 'You know that. She didn't turn up. She was dead.'

'But earlier?' His mother leaned forward and he could see the fine lines around her eyes and on her forehead. Without any make-up she looked old, desiccated. 'Did you talk to her earlier? At college?'

John considered carefully but could not decide what line to take.

'I can't remember,' he said flatly. 'She might have been there. Why do you want to know?'

Jackie Powell stood up.

'I don't want you involved in this,' she said quietly. 'The police will be asking questions everywhere. I don't want you involved.'

There was a trace of hysteria in her voice. He thought she was going to cry. He sat up, irritated by the unwelcome emotional demand.

'Look,' he said, trying unsuccessfully to control his impatience. 'What's the matter?' He had his own life to lead. What problems could *she* have? He viewed his parents almost as if they were a different species—respectable, untroubled, invulnerable.

'I'm sorry,' she said. She took a tissue from her dressing-gown pocket and blew her nose. 'I'm just upset. . .a young girl like that. It might have been you.'

He got out of bed and pulled a T-shirt over his head.

'No,' he said deliberately. 'You mustn't worry about that. I can look after myself. It wouldn't have been me.'

John walked to the sixth-form college from Barton Hill. The prosperous streets of the estate were empty. Most of the families who lived there had two cars. The children would be driven to school or to the childminder. The parents would already be at work. Most people needed two incomes to support a mortgage on Barton Hill. John wondered how his father managed it.

When he left the estate he avoided the main road, and chose instead the narrow red-brick terraced streets, sauntering, his hands in the pockets of the leather jacket which had been last year's Christmas present. He thought again about his portrayal of Smollett, a criminal, an outsider, trying to work out how he could give some depth to the character. He refused to see the play as a jolly jape, a pantomine. He wanted to be good. He ran over the lines in his head.

There had been a heavy frost and the cars still parked in the street were covered in ice. He watched irate motorists, already late for work, messing with kettles and de-icer spray. He saw how many of them left the keys in the ignition when they went back to their houses to replace the cloths and kettles and cans. Some of them even left the engine running. It would be child's play, John thought, to steal a car like that from right under the bastards' noses. Not that most of them were worth nicking. The majority were tiny Japanese hatchbacks or clapped-out family saloons.

He walked on, crossing Hallowgate Square to the grocer's shop on the corner to buy a Mars bar for his breakfast. The car park of the Grace Darling Centre was still roped off and policemen were searching the garden in the middle of the square and the bushes by the drive. He pretended to take no notice and continued down Anchor Street, past the shop and Joe Fenwick's flat, to the college. When he got there he felt fit and healthy and ready for anything.

His first lesson was history and everyone was talking about Gabby. They sat in a small group around the radiator, warming their hands as they waited for the teacher, speculating wildly about what might have happened to her. He was the centre of attention because he had been at the Grace Darling the night before.

'Come on!' they said. 'Didn't you notice anything?'

'No,' he said. He was beginning to enjoy the interest. He wished he had something to tell them.

'Weren't you there when they found the body?'

'No,' he said again, smiling, remembering. 'I left early. I didn't see a thing.'

The sense of excitement and wellbeing remained with him all morning.

Gordon Hunter arrived at Hallowgate Sixth-Form College at lunch time. He was met at the main door by a mute adolescent with greased black hair and acne and taken to the staff room. A maternal woman made him tea and introduced him to Ellie Smith, Gabriella Paston's personal tutor. Hunter looked around him and thought that teachers had never been like this when he was a lad. Ellie had long red hair and wore a very short skirt and black tights. She sat in a low chair with her legs stretched ahead of her, crossed at the ankle, and ate coleslaw from a plastic tub with a fork. Perhaps, Hunter thought, there was something in further education after all.

'Personal tutor?' he asked. 'I don't understand. What does that mean?'

'I monitored her general progress,' the teacher said, 'in all the subjects she was taking.' She pressed the lid on the coleslaw tub and bit into an apple. Hunter saw the stain of red lipstick on the apple's green skin. He was finding it hard to concentrate on the woman's words. Ellie munched and continued: 'In a college this size we felt it's important that there's a member of staff responsible for the pastoral care of the young people. We all supervise a small group of students. They're not necessarily the people we teach, although Gabby was in my English group.'

'And what was it like?' Hunter asked. 'Her general progress.'

Ellie shrugged. 'She wasn't a star academically,' she said, 'though I think with a lot of work she would have scraped through English and Art at 'A' level. Her real enthusiasm was drama and by all accounts she was outstanding at that. She was preparing to audition for RADA and the Central School. There was no guarantee, of course, that she'd be able to take up a place even if she was offered one. The grants for drama courses are discretionary. I tried to make her see that she might have to consider an alternative but she was so keen I don't think she really took it in.'

'How did she get on with the other kids?'

'Very well. She was lively, popular, always at the centre of the action.'

I bet she was, Hunter thought.

'She was very attractive,' he said. 'That didn't cause jealousy?'

'I don't think so,' Ellie said. 'Not in this case.'

'Did she ever talk about her family, her background?'

'Not willingly.' Ellie Smith became earnest. Hunter thought she would be competent, caring, too idealistic perhaps for her own good. 'When I first became her tutor I asked about her parents. I try to get to know the kids as individuals. She told me that they'd been killed in a car crash when she was young and she'd been brought up by relatives. I never met her guardian. For the past year she's been living with friends in Otterbridge.'

'Yes,' Hunter said. 'Did she tell you why she left home?'

'No. She was very quiet at about that time, rather withdrawn, but she never talked about problems with her family. I wasn't too worried about her. I'd met Prue Bennett several times through courses at the Grace Darling and she seemed a perfect substitute. Gabby was obviously happy there so I never pried.'

'You had no indication recently that Gabby had been worried about anything?'

'No. But I'd say that experience had made her very good at hiding her feelings. In all the time that I supervised her she never confided in me.' She paused. 'I had the feeling she was acting,' she said. 'All the time. None of us really knew her.'

'Wasn't there anyone she might have got close to? Boyfriend?'

Ellie laughed. 'She had lots of boyfriends,' she said. 'Half the Upper Sixth were infatuated with her. But I think she kept her feelings strictly under control. Unless. . .' She paused again, uncrossed her legs and leaned forward, her elbows on her knees. Hunter was momentarily distracted. He had never been out with a teacher.

'Yes?' he said.

'I think there might have been an understanding between her and one of the lads in the English group. There was nothing I could put my finger on. I never saw them walking arm in arm around the college. Nothing like that. But you get an instinct for these things. She always arranged to be sitting next to him at class and sometimes I'd see her hanging around waiting for him.'

'So you think she was interested in him and not the other way round?'

'There was nothing obvious,' she said. 'But yes, I'd say she was interested in John Powell and I'm not sure that he welcomed the attention. I got the impression he tried to keep his distance.'

'What's he like, this Powell?'

She hesitated, trying to find the right words. 'I don't know,' she said. 'Unusual, different. Bright enough if he puts the work in but you get the impression that he doesn't really care, that it's all beneath him. Arrogant, I suppose you'd call him.'

'A troublemaker?' Hunter asked.

'Not really. Not in the accepted sense. But I always find his presence in a class undermining. It's impossible to forget he's there. You don't feel you can treat him like all the other kids. He won't be taken for granted.'

'Friends?'

'No,' Ellie said. 'I don't think he's any close friends. Not here at least. Admirers perhaps. He's something of a cult figure. I'm not sure why.'

The staff room was starting to empty. There was a queue at the sink as the teachers rinsed their cups. Ellie looked at her watch.

'I'm sorry,' she said, 'I'll have to go soon. I'm teaching next period.'

'When did you last see Gabby?' Hunter asked.

'Yesterday morning. But not in a tutor group. There was an English lesson. From ten until eleven thirty.'

'And she was definitely there?'

'Oh yes. I remember quite clearly. We were doing *Hamlet*. She read Ophelia.' She paused, shocked. 'Quite prophetic,' she said, 'when you think of it.'

Hunter, who did not understand what she was talking about, kept quiet.

'Did you see where she went when she left the class?' he asked.

'No,' she said. 'She rushed off as soon as the bell went. As if she were in a hurry. It wasn't like her. She often stayed behind for a chat.'

A bell rang and Ellie Smith looked at her watch again. 'Look,' she said. 'I'm really sorry. I'll have to go. But if you want to come with me I can introduce you to some of Gabby's friends. I'm teaching the same group as I was yesterday morning.'

The classroom was in a different block and she led Hunter outside, across a yard where the frost still lay in the shadow. The building was 1960s glass and concrete with rusting window frames and noisy corridors. She opened a door and stood aside to let him in. The room was full of sunlight so Hunter blinked, then felt foolish, at a disadvantage. He saw twelve young people dressed in costumes which ranged from the bizarrely flamboyant to the threadbare. Ellie followed him into the room and sat on one of the desks. He stood, uncomfortably, intimated by their stares. He was not sure how to speak to these bright young people who spent all day reading Shakespeare. He felt he had more in common with the joy riders he pulled in on a Friday night.

'You'll all have heard by now,' Ellie Smith was saying, 'that the body of a young woman was found at the Grace Darling Arts Centre last night. The police have identified the victim as Gabby Paston.'

She paused. A girl had started to cry and turned to be comforted by a friend. Ellie went on.

'Of course it's an awful shock and terribly upsetting but the police obviously want to ask questions about Gabby and they especially want to trace her movements yesterday. This is Detective Sergeant Hunter. He'll ask you some questions now. If you have any other information about Gabby and there are details you'd prefer to remain confidential you can always arrange a private meeting with him through me.' She looked around. 'You do see,' she said, 'that this is a serious matter. Whatever views you might hold about the police generally, you must co-operate with them now.'

There was a silence and she turned to Hunter. He cleared his throat nervously.

'I understand that Gabriella attended the English class with you yesterday morning,' he said. 'According to Miss Smith she left in rather a hurry. Does anyone know where she was going?'

A skeletally thin girl with black spiked hair and huge eyes, blackened at the rims so she looked like an anorexic panda, raised her hand. She was wearing a long black dress which reached almost to the ground and the ubiquitous Dr Martens.

'Gabby had a date,' she said. 'Someone was taking her out to lunch.'

'Did she tell you who she was meeting?'

The girl shook her head.

'Does anyone know?'

Again there was silence.

'I know *where* she was going.' The girl who interjected was plump, quietly spoken, dressed in denims and a hand-knitted sweater. 'To the Holly Tree at Martin's Dene. She was teasing, you know, about the canteen food. How we'd have to put up with that while she was sitting down at the Holly Tree to something delicious.'

'When did she tell you that?'

'First thing in the morning. While we were all waiting for Miss Smith to come in.'

Hunter considered. The Holly Tree was expensive, well out of the range, he would have thought, of the average sixth former. It was unlikely that Gabriella's date had been with one of her schoolfriends. But if she had been there for a meal someone would have remembered her. At lunch time it would be full of business people who had driven out of Newcastle to do their entertaining. In her black leggings and boots Gabriella Paston would have stuck out like a sore thumb. Someone would haved noticed her companion too. Suddenly Hunter began to feel more hopeful. He resisted the temptation to leave immediately for the Holly Tree and went on, turning to the plump girl. 'Did she tell you anything about her plans for the rest of the day?'

'No. Nothing.'

'How did she seem to you?'

'Excited. Really high.'

'She didn't tell you why?'

Sadly the girl shook her head. Hunter considered the information. It was vague, subjective, but he would have put the girl down as a reliable witness.

'Yesterday morning Gabriella told her landlady that she had been invited to a friend's house after college. Was anyone here expecting Gabby to come home with them for a meal?'

There was no reply.

'Did anyone see her yesterday afternoon?'

Again there was silence.

'Is anyone here a member of the Youth Theatre at the Grace Darling Centre?'

The teenagers turned to face John Powell, who slowly raised his hand. Hunter looked at a tall boy with untidy hair and strong features, who stared back at him.

'And your name is?'

'John Powell.' The boy was slouched in his chair, his legs stretched in front of him. Without being overtly rude he managed to convey insolence. Hunter disliked him immediately. This then was the lad in which Gabby had shown a special interest. Hunter's antipathy towards the boy made him authoritative. He was no longer intimidated.

'I'd like to speak to Mr Powell on his own,' he said. He turned to the teacher. 'I take it you've no objections?' Ellie Smith shook her head helplessly. 'Then we won't take up any more of your time. Mr Powell!'

It was a summons and he waited while the boy uncoiled himself from his chair and followed him out into the corridor. Hunter had intended to find some empty classroom where they could talk but most of the rooms were occupied. Besides, the classrooms, with their books and maps and reminders of his ignorance, disturbed him. In the end he led the boy out into the open air and they talked as they walked past the playing fields where beefy young men ran in a line practising rugby passes, their breath coming in clouds in the cold air. A row of beeches threw shadows over the field and they walked alternately in bright sunlight and shade. As he followed the boy across the grass Hunter realized that something about the boy was familiar. He had not recognized it in class. It had more to do with the way Powell moved, the silhouette against the bright orange sun, than with his features.

'Aren't you related to Evan Powell?' he demanded abruptly, and the boy turned, more hostile than ever, and nodded.

It was a complication he could do without, Hunter thought. He would have to treat the boy carefully. He didn't want any more bloody lectures from Evan Powell. John regarded Hunter warily.

He felt suddenly very tired, drained of energy. The sleepless night was beginning to tell. He knew he would have to concentrate.

'Tell me about Gabriella Paston,' Hunter said. It was one of Ramsay's tricks, the open question which could not be answered with a monosyllable. Ramsay had his faults as a detective but Hunter was prepared to learn from him. Now they were walking side by side and Powell answered without breaking his stride.

'She was a bloody good actress,' he said reluctantly. 'Even Gus Lynch admitted that and he usually liked to think he was the only one with talent.' He stopped speaking suddenly, as if it were some sort of weakness that he had responded at all. If he weren't so tired, he thought, he'd be able to make a show of it, turn on the charm a bit. As it was all he could do was make sure he gave nothing away.

'Fancied her, did he?' Hunter said.

'What!'

'I'm asking you if Gus Lynch fancied Gabby.'

'No. . .at least I don't think so. She never said.'

'What were you doing yesterday afternoon?' Hunter asked conversationally.

'History,' Powell said. 'All afternoon.'

'You didn't take Gabriella to Martin's Dene, to lunch?'

'Are you joking? I couldn't afford that place. I was here. You can ask anyone.'

'And after college,' Hunter said. 'Where did you go then?'

'To the library to work.'

'The library here in college?'

'No. They close the library here at five. To Hallowgate library. It's just off the square. It's handy for the Grace Darling. I often work there on Mondays.'

'Were you with anyone?'

'No.'

On the rugby field the team was forming a scrum. Hunter, who had always been a football supporter, watched the swaying buttocks with distaste.

'What about Gabriella Paston?' he said. 'Didn't she come to the library to work with you before rehearsals?'

'Sometimes. She came sometimes. But not last night. I didn't see her after English in the morning.'

'But you expected her to be at the rehearsal? She hadn't told you that she wouldn't be there?'

'No. The last thing she said before she ran off at lunch time was "See you tonight!"'

They walked on in silence.

'Tell me about you and her,' Hunter said at last. 'Everyone says you were special friends. Tell me. How special was she?'

John Powell stopped and turned towards the policeman, irritated by all the questions, losing control for a moment.

'Look,' he said. 'If I told you, you wouldn't believe me.'

'Try me,' Hunter said.

'All right!' Powell said angrily. 'She fancied me. She really fancied me. Only I wasn't interested.'

'Why not?'

Powell shrugged. 'I suppose she wasn't my type.'

'What is your type?' Hunter demanded, goading. 'Got a girlfriend at the moment, have you? You'll have to introduce me so I can see what your type is.'

Powell swore under his breath and walked on, kicking up the beech leaves with his boots.

'Come on!' Hunter said. 'Don't be shy. Have you got a girlfriend?'

'No,' Powell shouted, losing his temper. 'I haven't got a girlfriend. Is that a crime? I'm busy. I'm studying for 'A' levels. I haven't got time for a girlfriend.'

Hunter did not believe him. Even brainy eighteen-year-olds had hormones. There weren't many lads who would turn away a girl like Gabriella Paston.

'Look,' he said, trying to sound friendly, approachable, to imply that after all they were much of the same generation. 'Is it your father? Did he disapprove of Gabriella? This conversation is confidential. I'm not going to say anything to him.'

'No,' John Powell said. 'It's not my father. You can say whatever you like to him. You don't understand anything at all.' He turned to face Hunter, blocking his path. 'I know my rights,' he said. 'I don't have to answer any of these questions. You haven't arrested or cautioned me. You've no business prying into my private life. So you can sod off and leave me alone.'

And he walked away, not back to college, to his English lesson and a discussion of *Hamlet* as a tragedy, but over the frosty playing fields towards the Starling Farm estate.

Chapter Seven

On his way from Hallowgate to Otterbridge Ramsay called in at his home. In Heppleburn, the village where he lived, the children were coming out of school and he was stopped by the fat lollipop lady in the shiny white coat which might have been fashionable in the sixties. His cottage was cold. The fire which had still been smouldering when he had left in the morning was out. He took the milk from the doorstep and picked up the mail. There was an early Christmas card from an aunt in Canada, who thought letters still took six weeks to cross the Atlantic. Ramsay, who never sent any to her, felt slightly guilty. The rest were circulars and went into the bucket by the grate. They would help start the fire when he finally got home that night. He washed in tepid water and put on the kettle for coffee.

He had thought of Prue Bennett many times since she disappeared to Cambridge. Occasionally he had dreamed of her. The memories had been gentle, romantic, idealized. He had sense enough to know that she would not live up to them, that disappointment would inevitably follow the new acquaintance. Diana had been something quite different. Diana had been a passion, an addiction, and he had married her knowing that it had little chance of succeeding but prepared for once in his life to take the risk. Even now, given the choice between Diana and Prue, he was not sure he would not take Diana. But this is ridiculous, he thought, the fantasies of a lonely middle-aged man. Prue's probably married, settled. Why would she be interested in you? And why do you think you have any choice?

She lived in the same house he had visited as a boy. It was called, for some reason, Minsmere, and the letters were painted in flaking gold on the semicircle of glass over the front door. He recognized them immediately. It had seemed very grand to him twenty years before to live in a house with a name and a number.

The house was red-brick and would have been rather ugly, but its outlines were softened by a Virginia creeper climbing up one corner and by large trees in the front garden. It was at the junction of two residential streets and was still shabbier, much less smart than the surrounding houses. At first it was quite unfamiliar to Ramsay and he almost walked past it, then realized that it only seemed different because he had never been there in the winter. He had only seen it when the trees were in leaf and his memory was so fixed that now, in the gloomy half light, it was almost unrecognizable. It was the letters over the front door which stopped him short and made him turn into the drive.

When Ramsay arrived at Minsmere it was nearly dark and the street lights were on. It was already very cold. Through the living-room window, where the curtains had not yet been drawn, he saw the shape of a grand piano and the stool where Mrs Bennett had perched to give music lessons. He knocked at the door and wondered why he had never bumped into Prue in a place as small and intimate as Otterbridge. He did not flatter himself that she had been avoiding him. He had not been as important to her as that. Perhaps he *had* seen her shopping in Front Street on a busy Saturday morning with her daughter and not known her. The thought distressed him.

She opened the door to him almost immediately then stood in the doorway staring out at him, waiting for him to take the initiative. She was still slim and straight and wore clothes she might have chosen as a girl—denim jeans and a long jersey.

'I'm sorry to disturb you,' he said, taking refuge in formality. 'I explained that I'd need to see you again.'

'Come in,' she said. 'We'll go through to the kitchen. It's still the only warm room in the house.'

She was wearing flat leather slippers which slapped against the red-tile floor as she walked ahead of him through the dusty hall to the back of the house.

He was disappointed that the room was different. It had been dimly lit, with old-fashioned painted cupboards. He had spent a lot of time there, drinking coffee, watching Prue cook, listening to the piano music, knowing that when it stopped they would be interrupted. Now there were new stained-wood units and the window seemed bigger. There were spotlights instead of the flickering neon, and pictures and posters and plants. On a cork pinboard he saw a photo of Anna and Gabby together, their arms around each other, grinning and waving madly towards the camera. Gabby was a small, slight figure, who only came up to Anna's shoulder. But the scrubbed wooden table, marked with the greasy rings of coffee cups and red wine bottles, was the same, and sitting on the boiler in the corner there was a black cat as there always had been.

He wondered what had happened to her parents and before he could phrase a tactful question she told him. They were both dead. Her mother had died suddenly when she was still at Cambridge. Prue had come back, eventually, to care for her father. He had died five years before and she and Anna had stayed on in the house.

'Was there nothing to keep you in the south?' he asked.

She shook her head. 'I was glad of the excuse to leave,' she said. 'There was never any prospect of settling down with Anna's father. We never married.'

'Where is Anna?' he asked. The girl was a reminder that he could make no assumptions about Prue, that things had changed.

'She went to school. I tried to persuade her to have a day at home but she thought she'd be better off with her friends.' She shrugged. 'It's hard sometimes to accept that she's reached an age when she can make decisions for herself.'

Ramsay did not know what to say. He stood by the boiler, feeling the warmth dull his brain, and stroked the cat until it started to purr.

'I was just going to make some tea,' she said. 'Will you have some?'

He nodded and sat at the end of the table, watching her fill the kettle and spoon tea into the pot. He tried to concentrate on the investigation, to form questions which he would normally put to a witness, but he was too interested in her.

'What happened after Cambridge?' he asked.

'I got caught by the theatre bug at university,' she said. 'Not acting. Producing. I'd never done anything so exciting. When I left Cambridge I got taken on as an assistant in a rather good provincial theatre in East Anglia. Then I blew it all by getting pregnant.' She paused. 'I tried to carry on working,' she said, 'but it wasn't so easy then. I couldn't find a reliable childminder and my friends all thought I was crazy to have the baby in the first place. In the end I gave up and became a full-time mother. It was a dreadful time, wretched. I was so bored and lonely. As I say I was quite glad of the excuse to come home and look after Dad.' She stopped again, then continued: 'I'm sorry. You don't want to hear all this. You'll want to ask some questions about Gabby.'

He could have said that in a murder investigation he was interested in any background information on the witnesses, but that would have implied that she was a suspect, and although it was true it would hardly be tactful to say so. It was impossible to pretend that they were strangers. Perhaps he should use her inside knowledge. Hunter would have no scruples about using a friend to further an investigation.

'Tell me about that place,' he said. 'What's the set-up there? How's it organized?'

'The Grace Darling?' She poured the tea into mugs and absentmindedly put a tin of biscuits on to the table. 'The building's administered by a charitable trust. It's supported by grants from the local authority and Gus and I are paid by the council but the trustees like to think they're independent.'

She hesitated and he picked up a trace of irritation.

'What is it?' he asked.

'I've just remembered that one of the trustees was there last night, talking to Gus. I was wondering what she wanted. She's a particularly active member of the trust. They're the ones that can make life difficult.'

'Ah yes,' he said. 'Mrs Wood. Do you remember if she was there when you found Gabriella's body?'

'She was with Gus when I went to ask him for the programme. That's why he gave me the car keys and asked me to fetch it for myself. But when I went back to the Centre to phone the police she'd gone.'

'Did you see her leave?'

'No, but Gus's car was at the far end, away from the door. I wouldn't have done.'

'Tell me about Amelia Wood,' Ramsay said.

'Oh,' Prue said. 'She's an active citizen. A magistrate. On the council. You know the sort.'

'Would it be usual for her to call into the Centre in the evenings?'

'I can't remember seeing her there in the evening before but it would be her style. She had a bee in her bonnet about us using the trust's resources efficiently. She might see it as a spot check. To make sure we were all on our toes. She was certainly giving Gus a hard time last night.'

'You don't like her,' he said. It was a statement not a question. She smiled—

'Amelia's all right,' she said. 'I suppose. She's one of those women with too much energy. Hyperactive. Interfering. Inclined to be bossy. Good at her job, though. Even I'll admit that. When the council was poll-tax capped we thought the Centre might have to close but somehow she found the grants to keep us going. She wangled some sponsorship deal with some local businesses too. I don't know the details ... But it is hard to like her. She thinks we should only use the Centre to house events which will attract a big audience and pay their way. She considers anything experimental as left-wing propaganda.'

She stopped, quite breathless, then smiled awkwardly. 'Look,' she said. 'That's only my opinion, my prejudice I suppose. I got carried away. I almost forgot you were here professionally. I wouldn't want you to take what I've said too seriously.'

'How does Gus Lynch get on with her?' he asked.

'He doesn't like her dictating artistic policy but there's never been any real confrontation. She knows that if he leaves they'll never get anyone else as famous to head up the Grace Darling Centre.'

'Did Gus mention yesterday that he had a meeting with her?'

'No. I had the impression that he was as surprised to see her as me.'

'Tell me about the famous Gus Lynch. How do you get on with him?' He tried to keep the question flat, his voice light, but was aware, despite himself, of an edge of mockery. Can I really be jealous, he thought, of a man because he works with the woman I made love to twenty years ago?

'It's hard to be objective about one's boss,' she said. 'Especially one with as high a public profile as Gus Lynch.' She smiled. 'Doesn't every assistant believe that they do all the work while their supervisor takes the credit?'

He smiled back. 'And you feel that about Lynch?'

'Let's just say that he's not very generous about acknowledging other people's contribution to his work.'

'But you've never thought of leaving? Of finding another job?'

'No,' she said. 'I love it. Especially the work with the kids. It's a real challenge. I learn something every day. I can handle having a boss who's so insecure about his own abilities that he has to put everyone else down.'

Is that how Hunter feels? Ramsay wondered suddenly. That he does all the work while I take the credit? That I'm so insecure that I'm always putting him down?

'Did Lynch have a special relationship with any of the girls in the group?'

'Gabby, you mean. No, I don't think so. He admired her talent, of course, but he kept his distance from all the kids.'

'How did she come to be living here?' he asked.

'She asked if we'd put her up,' Prue said simply. 'She said that things weren't working out at home and she wanted to move out.'

'Was there a row? A specific incident which led to her leaving?'

'She wouldn't say, but I think there must have been. Before that I had the impression that she was happy enough. The Pastons gave her more freedom than she was allowed here. There must have been some upset, I think, to make her decide to move so suddenly.'

'Why did you decide to take her on?' he asked. 'It was quite a responsibility to provide a home for a teenage girl.'

'I felt sorry for her, I suppose,' Prue said. 'It can't have been much fun living with two single women, one of them quite elderly. But it wasn't only that. She was good for Anna. Anna was always solitary and withdrawn, even as a small child. She found it hard to make friends. It was a worry. I didn't know how to handle it. I even thought of getting professional help but that seemed an over-reaction. I suggested that she came to the Youth Theatre when I started working there because I thought performing would give her confidence, but it was meeting Gabby that made the real difference. Gabby made her laugh. They became real friends. That's why I'm so worried about how Anna will cope with her death.'

'Gabby told one of her schoolfriends that she had been invited out to lunch yesterday, to the Holly Tree in Martin's Dene. You've no idea who might have made the invitation?'

'No,' Prue said. 'None. And she didn't mention it to me. Perhaps for some reason she thought I wouldn't approve.'

'Tell me about Gabby,' he said. 'What was she like?'

'She was an extrovert,' Prue said. 'Lively, fun, an instinctive actress.' She paused.

'Yes?' he prompted.

'I don't know,' she said. 'I suppose I've got a superstitious feeling that it's wrong to speak ill of the dead. Besides, I can't quite put it into words.'

'Try.'

'She had no sense of morality,' Prue said. 'I don't mean that she was wicked. On a personal level she could be immensely kind, generous. But she didn't have an intellectual'—she groped for the right word—'an *abstract* perception of right or wrong. She wouldn't hurt anyone deliberately but if she wanted something badly enough she would go for it without considering the consequences. She had no code of behaviour to live by.' She paused again. 'I'm not explaining very well. And perhaps most young people are like that.'

'Is that why she didn't bother with her family?' he said. 'Because she couldn't see the point? Because she had no idea of duty or responsibility?'

'Yes,' she said, pleased that he had understood. 'Yes, I think that's a good example of what I mean.'

She looked over his shoulder to the kitchen clock on the wall.

'Look,' she said. 'If you want to look at Gabby's things would you mind doing it now before Anna comes home? I really don't want her upset.'

'Yes,' he said. 'Of course.' He stood up, wondering if she was bored by his presence. Perhaps she just wanted to be rid of him.

Away from the kitchen the house was cold, and smelled a little damp. Ramsay supposed that the job in the Arts Centre paid peanuts. Prue led him up two flights of stairs to a room in the attic with a sloping roof and a small bay window. It was a big room, the width of the house. There was a sofa, a heavy old desk marked with ink stains, shelves full of teenage clutter. The single bed, in one corner, was almost hidden by cushions.

'It was Anna's playroom,' Prue said. 'Then as she got older I turned it into a sitting room for her. I thought it would be somewhere she could bring her friends, play her music without disturbing me, but until she met Gabby there were no friends to bring.'

'Anna didn't mind Gabby taking it over?' Ramsay asked carefully. Giving up the room was hardly a motive for murder and he did not want to offend Prue.

'Not at all. And Gabby didn't take it over. Anna was always welcome here. Lots of the things are hers.' She looked around at the clothes piled on a chair, the desk spread with tapes and magazines. 'I suppose I should sort it all out,' she said helplessly.

'Not yet,' he said more sharply than he had intended. 'If you don't mind. I'd prefer not to have anything touched until we've checked it.'

'Yes,' she said. She was shocked as if a guest had committed some rudeness. 'Of course. I expect you'd rather I left you to it. . .' And he heard her leather slippers flapping on the wooden stairs as she disappeared to the ground floor.

It was hard to know where to start. Every surface was covered and many of the objects could have belonged to Anna. There were the remnants of childhood—soft toys, a bookshelf full of Arthur Ransomes, coloured felt-tip pens which must long ago have dried up. But, Ramsay thought, Gabby Paston had been a private person. She had given nothing of herself away. Still no one knew what she had really thought or felt. A girl like that wouldn't have left anything personal around where Anna might read it.

He began with the desk. There were files with Gabby's name written on in a decorative script holding essays on a variety of subjects. The comments on the bottom were encouraging but the marks were hardly impressive. There was a pile of text books which looked as if they might once have belonged to Prue and had hardly been opened. There were birthday cards, post cards from friends, pop magazines. There was a typewritten script entitled *The Adventures of Abigail Keene* with the main character's words marked in orange highlighter. He looked at each item and set it aside on the bed. He piled the cassette tapes together and moved them on to the bed. Many had lost their plastic cases and the scribbled identifying labels meant nothing to him. He supposed that 'Bald Mice' was a group and it was while he glanced at the others, trying to find another, even more outrageous name, that he came across the Teach Yourself Spanish tape. Why, he wondered, did Gabby want to learn Spanish? Was it some romantic idea of recovering her roots?

By now the top of the desk was clear except for a swirling pattern of dust and Ramsay turned his attention to the desk drawers. He was afraid that the top one was locked but it was just stuck and when he lifted it and pulled at the same time it came out altogether. Ramsay set it beside him on the bed. It contained a diary, two sheets of paper, an envelope, and a building society passbook. This must be all that Gabby needed to keep from prying eyes.

The diary was small, of the size to fit in a handbag, and there were none of the teenage outpourings which Ramsay might have expected. In it Gabby noted her appointments, rehearsal times, the dates when essays were due to be handed in. The only inclusion of any interest was an E which appeared at approximately fortnightly intervals. Beside it was a time, usually different. Was E for Ellen, Gabby's aunt? Ramsay wondered. If so, why the secrecy. Unsatisfied, he moved to the other items in the drawer.

The first sheet of paper was a printed programme for *Romeo and Juliet*, a Youth Theatre production. Gabby had been playing Juliet. The programme had been autographed by each member of the cast and she had kept it, Ramsay supposed, for sentimental reasons. He noticed briefly that John Powell had played Romeo and wondered if that was Evan's boy. The second sheet was a lined piece of A4. He would have to check the handwriting but he presumed it was Gabby's and thought it was the draft of a letter. It was a love letter in which Gabby pleaded to be noticed, to be taken seriously. It was addressed to 'John' and Ramsay, whose memory of his own teenage pain was heightened by his meeting with Prue, thought that it had probably never been sent.

The building society account had been opened three months previously with £500 and payments had been made since then to bring the total to almost £800. Ramsay wondered where the money had come from. Her family? A holiday job? The timing of the opening of the account at the end of the summer would suggest that. He would have to check with Prue.

The envelope, which had been at the top of the pile in the drawer, contained no letter. It was cheap and white with Gabby's name and the Bennett's address printed in blue ink. It was post-marked the day before her death. Why had she kept it? Ramsay wondered. What had it contained that was so important? And where was the letter that had been inside? He straightened and returned to the warmth of the kitchen.

Anna was there, still in her outdoor jacket, already drinking tea, fending off her mother's concern about how she was feeling.

'I'm fine,' she said. 'Really. Please don't fuss.' But she looked tired and unhappy and had nothing in common with the girl who beamed out at him from the photo on the noticeboard.

'John Powell,' Ramsay said. 'Was he a boyfriend of Gabby's?'

'She liked him,' Anna said. 'I don't think they ever went out together.' She shivered slightly and dipped her head over her mug.

'She had a letter yesterday,' Ramsay said. 'Who was it from?'

'How would we know?' Prue said. She was quite angry. 'We never read her mail.'

'She might have told you,' he said, apologetically. Surely she understood that he was only doing his job. 'She did have a letter yesterday?'

Prue nodded, only slightly appeased. She stood behind her daughter with her arm round Anna's shoulder.

'Did she have a holiday job in the summer vacation?' he asked.

Anna answered. 'No,' she said. 'We both tried to find work but it was impossible.'

'She had a building society account with eight hundred pounds in,' he said. 'Do you know where she got the money?'

Prue shook her head. 'She was always pleading poverty. I kept her on her child benefit. She got a small allowance for pocket money from her family.'

'So you can't explain the money in the account?'

'I'm sorry,' Prue said firmly. 'I wish I could help.'

It was a dismissal and Ramsay left, excluded by the women's closeness, feeling that he had ruined any chance he might have had with Prue. He went back to Hallowgate police station to talk to Hunter, who had made up his mind already that John Powell was a murderer.

Chapter Eight

Amelia Wood spent the day on the bench at Hallowgate magistrates' court. She arrived early, feeling cheerful and optimistic but was soon worn down by the atmosphere of the place. She did not enjoy the practical business of being a magistrate. The prestige of being a JP, the training sessions with other professionals, the study of theoretical case histories, the social events, all these she found enjoyable and entertaining. But in the shabby and squalid court, with the smell of damp and urine seeping up from the police cells below she found little to entertain her. The defendants were wretched and inadequate. She did not despise their attempts to improve their financial situation. In their place she would have done the same. But she did despise their incompetence, their half-heartedness, the lack of imagination which prevented their seeing anything through.

The clerk of the court was a well-meaning, rather ineffective young man, who took seriously the Home Office circulars exalting magistrates to consider community based disposals instead of prison. He disliked working with Amelia Wood, whom he found unnecessarily punitive, irrationally arbitrary, but he found confrontation difficult. Stammering and blushing he would interpose at intervals to suggest an alternative sentence. The conflict between them made justice a slow and long-winded affair. There was a long list and the fat solicitors in crumpled suits who sat along the front bench sighed, looked at their watches, and knew that they would miss lunch.

In the afternoon there were two trials. The first concerned a driver with excess alcohol and was over quickly. The second dragged on despite its lack of substance and Amelia Wood found it hard to concentrate. The death of the girl might be an added complication but she did not expect it to make too much difference to her plans.

The defendant who sat in the dock opposite her was middle aged, over-weight, frightened. A few wisps of lank hair had been combed ridiculously across his bare head. He was sweating. He lived on the Starling Farm estate and had been charged with handling stolen property: car radios, which he had been caught selling in several of the Hallowgate pubs. He had remained uncooperative, the police said, throughout questioning. In court the man claimed he had bought the radios legitimately from a car breaker's yard in Wallsend but was unable to produce any witnesses to back up his story. The prosecutor brought evidence that the radios had been taken from cars stolen in the area. The defence solicitor cross-examined halfheartedly. Amelia listened, her attention wandering, and yawned. At last the trial was over and the magistrates retired to tepid coffee and to consider their decision.

Amelia was prepared to find the man not guilty. It was not that she believed him innocent but it would make things simpler. The case could be over immediately and they would not have to go into a prolonged discussion about sentence. She wanted to be home. Her two colleagues were shocked. They took their position as magistrates seriously. One, a retired bank manager with badly fitting false teeth and body odour, had even taken notes. The sentence of not guilty was out of the question. At a time like this, he said, of disturbance and riot, the courts should be seen to be supporting the police.

'You're right, of course,' said Amelia Wood, graciously. She knew better than to waste energy fighting lost causes. 'The only question then is what to do with him. I suggest a three-week remand for probation reports. That will give us the opportunity to consider all the options.'

Her colleagues agreed, relieved that they would not be forced into a decision about the man's future, glad to hand the responsibility to someone else.

Gus Lynch woke up late, at midday, disturbed by the men gathering outside the Seamen's Mission, waiting to be let in for lunch. He poured a Scotch for breakfast and carried on drinking all afternoon—not heavily but steadily enough to make him believe that his growing self-pity was justified. The police had closed down the Grace Darling until further notice. They had told him to stay at home and make himself available if required. He poured another drink and told himself that fate was against him. Fate and bloody Amelia Wood. The last thing he needed now was bad publicity.

He was tempted to phone Jackie. She would have come like a shot to comfort him. But he had already decided that she was in the way and he knew he would have to get rid of her. He ought to talk to her about this business with Gabriella Paston, make her see that there was nothing to be gained by coming forward, bringing the affair into the open. Would the forensic team find traces of her in his car? He had given her a lift occasionally. He thought that might be awkward but he took a sudden mischievous delight in the prospect of Evan Powell's wife being implicated in murder. The idea was so ridiculous that he laughed out loud, then stopped abruptly, realizing that he had nothing to laugh about.

He sat by the window, brooding. The affair had got out of hand, of course. Jackie had taken it so seriously and he had never taken her seriously at all. They had met at the party Evan Powell had given for the cast of the Youth Theatre's last production. He had gone along reluctantly, expecting suburban small talk, unappetizing bits of food on trays, sweet Spanish wine. He had gone because he would need people to think well of him. The young people, intimidated by Evan's profession, had been on their best behaviour, drinking moderately the beer and cider he had provided for them, leaving at the earliest opportunity. John had obviously hated every minute of it.

Jackie Powell had sat in a corner, drinking glass after glass of white wine, watching the proceedings with detachment, bored to distraction. When Evan Powell told a joke she smiled dutifully then returned to her drinking. Lynch found it impossible to believe that Powell did not realize she was unhappy. Was that how the affair had started, Gus wondered now, out of pity? He had always been attracted by pale and vulnerable women. But it was in an attempt to cause mischief that he had approached her, an attempt to shatter Evan Powell's complacency.

'How can you stand all this?' he had said to her in a low voice. No small talk. No politeness. He had seen that she had had enough of all that. 'Come on. Let's get out of here.'

Then in a louder voice he called to Evan. 'I'm going to steal your wife for an hour. She tells me she's never been to the Grace Darling. I'm going to show her round.'

And Evan had smiled foolishly, proud apparently that Lynch had taken an interest in his wife, too honest himself to suspect anything. Mesmerized, Jackie had followed him and allowed him to put a coat over her shoulders. He had given her a conducted tour of the theatre and they had made love on the stage, where the set was still up for *Romeo and Juliet*, with the curtains drawn. There had been a smell of dust and grease paint, of the real theatre. Joe Fenwick in reception had seen them go in but had never mentioned the incident to anyone.

So it had started as an impulse, because he had been bored one evening at a tedious party, because he wanted the admiration of a woman to whom he had brought a little excitement. He had expected never to see her again.

She had phoned him, a week later, obviously nervous. 'I can't stop thinking about you,' she said. 'I don't know what to do.'

He had been flattered. It had been a long time since he had had such an effect on a woman. When he was a household name, on the television every week, it had been easier. Still he did not know what he was letting himself in for. He had never thought she would get serious. A married woman whose kid's grown up, approaching middle age, wanting a bit of excitement on the side. That's what he'd thought. Something to push away the idea that the next great adventure in her life would be death.

'Why don't you come to my flat?' he had said. 'I'll cook you a meal. Dinner.' He was proud of his flat in Chandler's Court. He wanted to show it off to her.

'Are you sure?' she said, grateful as a child. 'Eh, I'd love to.'

And he imagined her going off, choosing what clothes to wear, making herself attractive just for him. It was a good feeling.

How did he let it get out of hand? he wondered. Laziness, he supposed. He just never bothered to contradict her. They would lie together in his bed, with the sound of the river outside, and she would talk of her dreams. He never thought of them as plans. They were fantasies. She couldn't bring herself to leave Evan, she would say. Not yet. Not with John still at school. Besides, he had a dreadful temper. He would kill her if he found out. No, they would wait until John had left school and Gus had got a job somewhere else, away from the district, where Evan couldn't find them. Then they would start a new life together.

Why had he never said anything? he wondered. Because he hadn't wanted to disillusion her, because he wanted to avoid the confrontation. And because, despite himself, he did not want to lose her. He had become addicted to her flattery. He loved the way she made him feel the most important man in the world. Then there were the practical things she did to make life easy for him—the row of ironed shirts in his wardrobe every morning, the washed dishes, the meals. He would have been a fool to give all that up. So he had gone along with her dreams, had even on occasion encouraged them.

But now he had other worries, he thought bitterly, watching the crew of a fishing boat on the quay working companionably to untangle a net. It was too much for him to cope with Jackie too. He stared out of the window as the afternoon wore on. The sun was covered by a grey mist which rolled in again from the sea so the river and the land beyond it became indistinguishable, luminous, broken by the silhouettes of the boats and the cormorants standing on the rocks uncovered by the tide.

At some point his agent phoned. Simon Jasper was thin, elegant, with the languid drawl of a pre-war English gentleman. Lynch could picture him in the untidy office in Covent Garden where he presided, pandered to by a gaggle of well-bred young women who considered employment with him as equivalent to a year in a Swiss finishing school. It only paid pocket money but provided culture and contacts.

'Gus!' Jasper said. The drawl was more pronounced than usual. Gus Lynch looked at his watch. It was half-past three. He guessed that Simon had been entertaining one of his more successful clients to lunch and was full of claret and brandy. 'Gus,' Jasper repeated. 'I'm sorry but I must have an answer by the end of the week. At the very latest.' He paused, expecting an answer, then went on more sharply: 'You know you won't get a better deal.'

'No,' Lynch said. 'I realize that.'

'I tried to phone you at the Centre,' Jasper said. 'Someone said it was closed for the day. No problems, I hope. I've told you the subsidized sector is very vulnerable at the moment. You should get out while you have the chance.'

'I want to get out,' Lynch said hurriedly. 'I explained that I'm ready for a move.' He hesitated and sensed that Jasper was becoming irritated, then continued quickly: 'It's just that I'm having problems persuading the trustees to release me from my contract at the Grace Darling.'

'What contract?' The affected drawl almost disappeared. 'I didn't know anything about a contract. I hope you didn't sign anything without consulting me.'

'No,' Lynch said. 'Of course not.' The whisky was getting in the way, preventing him from producing a coherent story. 'It's nothing formal. But I don't want to leave with any bad feeling. That sort of publicity would get in the way of the new job. You know that.'

'I suppose.' To express his disapproval Jasper withdrew his attention and shouted to someone in the room with him: 'Jemima, bring me some tea, there's a good girl.' There was a silence, then he relented and spoke to Gus again. 'You do realize,' he said, 'that if you're interested you'll have to sign by the end of the week, bad publicity or no.'

'All right, Simon,' Lynch said, losing patience. 'I understand. There's no need to spell it out. I'll sort it.'

'Good,' Jasper said. 'Right. Well, I'll expect to hear from you then.'

Lynch replaced the receiver before the agent could bully him further. He poured another drink and phoned Amelia Wood's home. He had her number, with a list of the other trustees, in his book. A cleaning lady answered primly like a servant in a television historical drama. Mrs Wood was not at home, she said. She thought she had expected to be in court all day, but she would be home soon. If he would like to leave a message she would make sure Mrs Wood received it.

'No,' Gus said. 'No message.'

He went out quickly, an impulse. There was a thick winter jacket at the back of a cupboard. He seldom wore it—he had never been one for outdoor pursuits—and scarcely recognized himself in the mirror in the hall. Before leaving the flat he drew the living-room curtains, then took the phone off the hook. If the police tried to contact him it would take them a while to realize that it was not simply engaged. With any luck they would assume the phone was out of order and leave him until the morning. Even if they sent someone to the flat that would take time and he did not expect to be away for very long.

The cold outside took his breath away. The light behind the mist had drained away and it was almost dark. He twisted a scarf around his neck and over his mouth and pulled up the hood of his jacket. In his pocket he found a pair of gloves and pulled them on.

The wholesale fish shops along the quay were beginning to close. Boards advertising the day's catch were lifted in and men stood with poles to pull down thick metal shutters over the windows. Lynch walked past anonymously, another man just finished work, on his way home or to the pub. One of the fishmongers even waved to him, certain that Gus belonged there. Lynch walked up the steep bank away from the river, past the red low light that guided boats into the quay. The exercise and the whisky made him light-headed and he had to stop half-way and gasp for breath.

In the middle of Hallowgate the shops were still open and busy. It was only half-past four. Gangs of teenagers on their way home from school walked aimlessly and gathered outside the Wimpy Bar to share a bag of chips. The jangle of inevitable Christmas carols came from the Price Savers Supermarket and from all the tatty clothes shops selling sequinned party frocks or threadbare denim. A pork butcher was scooping pease pudding from a huge tray into a plastic carton to sell to an old man who carefully counted pennies from a purse on to the counter and outside the greengrocer's next door two women were fighting over a pile of Christmas trees: both had chosen one that was less battered than the rest. Only the many charity shops seemed quiet and respectable. Genteel ladies in suede boots and tweed skirts stood awkwardly behind their counters, watching the clock tick on, knowing that the week's ordeal of charitable do gooding would soon be over. In the window of Barnardo's was a poster advertising *The Adventures of Abigail Keene*.

Gus Lynch took no notice of the shops or the passers-by, though walking through Hallowgate was a novelty for him. He did his shopping weekly in the big new Sainsbury's in Whitley Bay. He bought ready-cooked Indian meals, exotic cheese, and bottles of wine recommended by the *Sunday Times*, and spent more than most Hallowgate families would in a month. He hunched his shoulders, put his head down and looked at the pavement in front of him.

He knew where the Hallowgate magistrates' court was because he had been there once to pay a speeding fine. He walked past it slowly. The lights were on inside but everything seemed quiet. Now he was here he felt awkward. He was not sure what to do. A door marked *Staff Only* opened and two middle-aged men came out. They were pulling on identical raincoats and chatted about golf. They must have seen him but they took no notice. Who were they? Lynch wondered. Magistrates? Court officials? Plain-clothes policemen? He watched them walk together up the street, envying their easy conversation, their quiet consciences.

The door opened again and Amelia Wood came out. He stood with his back flat against the wall of the building but she went in the opposite direction and did not see him. She walked quickly. She wore a calf-length Burberry mackintosh and tied a silk scarf over her hair, worried that the damp in the air would affect her new perm. He heard the heels of her shoes tapping on the uneven pavement.

When Amelia Wood emerged from the court she was surprised to find that it was already dark. The court's business had taken longer than she had expected. It was over, at least, for another week. She had parked her car away from the court in one of the quieter, more salubrious streets close to Hallowgate Square. It was a precaution she had taken since a previous car had been vandalized by the friends of a defendant she had sentenced to youth custody. They had seen her arrive in it and while she dealt with other cases they had wreaked their vengeance with razor blades and spray paint. Besides, there was usually something therapeutic about the short walk in the fresh air after a day in court. It put a distance between her and the lives of the people on whom she passed judgement. As she walked briskly away she began to plan the dinner party she would hold at the weekend for some of the more prominent trustees of the Grace Darling Centre. Despite the tragedy of the girl's murder she would be able to promise them that the Centre had a secure future.

She took a shortcut through an alley up a steep and narrow flight of stone steps between blank brick walls known as Meggie's Cut. She always took the same path after court. Although it was poorly lit she had never been frightened. It never occurred to her that she might be vulnerable. A figure appeared out of the fog at the top of the steps: a plump young woman with a pushchair which she had tilted back at an alarming angle so the two back wheels jolted down, a step at a time. Amelia stood aside to let her pass. The child inside was quite awake but lay still and the eyes which were all that could be seen between quilt and anorak hood were wide and terrified. As Amelia continued she heard the thud of wheel against stone echoing away from her.

At the bottom of the steps Gus Lynch turned his back to the woman with the pushchair. He unwrapped his scarf and held it, one end in each hand, then began to run up the steps after Amelia Wood. She heard the footsteps but took no notice. She went through the guest list for the dinner party and wondered if they could run to smoked salmon for the first course. She felt she deserved a celebration.

The footsteps came closer and she turned, without curiosity, to see who was there. Through the gloom she saw a man, his hood pulled over his head, who seemed to stumble away from her. She decided he was a drunk.

'Mrs Wood!' She looked past the shadowy figure to an elderly man caught in the street light at the bottom of the steps. It was the court usher, a retired policeman whose name she could never remember. It was beneath her dignity to yell and as the usher was making no effort to join her she descended to talk to him. The drunk lurched past her and disappeared into the street above.

'Well,' she demanded. 'What is it?' She presumed it would be something trivial. Perhaps she had forgotten to sign an expenses form. 'Couldn't it wait?'

The man was wheezing painfully. He had run after her and the cold was bad for his chest.

'It's the police,' he said. 'They want to speak to you urgently. They've been trying to get in touch all day.'

'Well,' she said grandly. 'They know where to find me.'

'I wasn't sure you'd be going straight home,' the usher said sulkily. 'I thought it would be important.' He had expected gratitude. The least she could do was satisfy his curiosity about what it was all about.

'Oh yes,' she said. 'I'm going straight home. Thank you for coming after me, but really you needn't have bothered.'

When Gus Lynch got back to Chandler's Court Hunter was waiting outside the house in an unmarked car. Lynch recognized him and waited for the policeman to get out and join him on the pavement.

'I'm sorry I wasn't here when you arrived,' Lynch said hurriedly. 'I'd been in waiting for you all day. I really needed some fresh air. You know what it's like.'

Hunter nodded sympathetically. He had always enjoyed the television series which Lynch had starred in, had been one of the few people to stick with it to the end. Although he tried to keep his cool it was something of a thrill to be here, talking to the actor who had played Wor Billy. His mam would want to know all about it.

The flat lived up to all Hunter's expectations. It had a polished wood-block floor and deep rugs, a soft white leather sofa, and an expensive CD player. Without asking Lynch poured him a Scotch and Hunter felt it would be churlish to refuse. He was so taken with his surroundings that he did not notice Lynch replace the receiver on the telephone.

'How can I help you?' Lynch asked. He realized that he was shivering and bent to light a gas fire which was almost indistinguishable from the real thing. The flames leapt and were reflected on the shining floor. More composed, he stood and turned to face the policeman.

'Do you know when I'll get my car back? It's rather inconvenient, you know, without transport.'

'I should hire one,' Hunter said pessimistically. 'With forensic you're talking weeks. We'll need fingerprints from you and from anyone you've carried as a passenger recently. To eliminate from the prints we find.'

'Yes,' Lynch said absently. 'Of course.' He looked up from his drink. 'Do you know yet who it was, who killed Gabby?'

Hunter shrugged mysteriously to show that he could not pass on sensitive information but that he was optimistic. 'It'll soon be over,' he said. 'These things are often more simple than they first seem. Most murders are domestic, you know. It's usually the husband or the boyfriend.'

'I didn't realize Gabby had a boyfriend.' Lynch tried not to sound too interested.

Hunter realized that he had said too much. He set the glass on a polished oval table.

'Look,' he said. 'I'm only here to tell you that we've finished with the Grace Darling Centre. You can open again tomorrow if you want to.'

'Did you find anything?' Hunter was surprised by the anxiety in the man's voice but put it down to an honest man's natural awe of authority.

'No,' Hunter said. 'Nothing at all. They've been through it with a fine-tooth comb but they've found nothing, no murder weapon, no incriminating traces of blood . . .' He was playing on Lynch's discomfort and laughed to show he was teasing. The actor joined in uncomfortably.

'I'll have to go,' Hunter said. 'I've a meeting back at the station with the Inspector.' At the door he stopped. 'There is just one thing you could do for me,' he said awkwardly.

'Yes?' The tension returned to Lynch's voice.

'Your autograph. For my mam. She'd be thrilled to bits.'

Lynch seemed to relax then. He smiled. Perhaps after all he was beyond suspicion. He found a publicity photo in a drawer and signed it with a flourish. Hunter took it gratefully. The man had aged a canny few years since the photo was taken but his mam would never know the difference.

When he had seen the policeman out Lynch stood by the window and watched until Hunter's car had driven away. He picked up the telephone receiver and dialled. There was someone he had to speak to.

Chapter Nine

Evan Powell was not a member of the team working on the Gabriella Paston case. He had been too close to it because of his attendance at the Grace Darling Centre on the night of the murder. There was also the fact, unmentioned, that he had been involved in the death of her parents. Instead he continued to lead the auto-crime group and spent the day talking to witnesses of the ram raid on the Coast Road the night before. They were little help. The security guard had recorded all the details of the car which had smashed through the plate-glass window of the Coop Hypermarket, but it had been stolen from a pub car park in Tynemouth on the same night and dumped immediately afterwards. People living in nearby houses had heard the sound of breaking glass, the screech of tyres, but had been too frightened to go out on to the street to see what it was all about.

'What about the men?' Powell demanded of the security guard. The window had already been boarded up and the business of the shop continued around them. An instore disc jockey was extolling the virtues of Co-op frozen turkeys and suggesting that its customers should already be fully prepared for the Christmas festivities. 'Good God, man, the car came through the window and landed within feet of your office. You must have some description of the gang.'

'There were three of them, all in overalls,' the guard said resentfully. 'Navy overalls. Like a mechanic would wear. And hoods. I couldn't see a thing.'

'You must have heard them speak!'

'They didn't say a word,' the guard said. 'Man, it all happened so fast. They were in and out in minutes. The organization was magnificent. I've never seen anything like it. They must have known I'd press the panic button, but the break-in would have triggered the alarm anyway so they didn't bother to stop me. They left me alone. They were cool, I'll say that for them. You'd almost say professional.'

Evan, irritated by the note of admiration in the man's voice, turned away. He was outraged that the general public regarded these ram raiders as almost heroic, modern day Robin Hoods, and he was beginning to see his battle against them as a personal crusade. It was a question of morality. The car thieves seemed to taunt him. He had been through it all before with Robbie Paston. . .

The news that Tommy Shiels from the Starling Farm estate had been found guilty in Hallowgate magistrates' court of handling stolen goods was welcome but it reminded Evan too that he had only been capable of tracing the insignificant people involved in car thefts. He had interrogated Tommy Shiels himself but had been unable to persuade him to give any information at all. The man had claimed to have no knowledge about who was organizing the robberies and by the end of the interviews Powell had almost believed him.

Jackie Powell saw her husband and son out of the house and spent the morning waiting for the phone to ring. She knew that her infatuation for Gus Lynch was a madness. It was making her ill and was in danger of wrecking her marriage. But she could think of nothing else. In her saner moments she compared Lynch unfavourably with her husband. Evan was a good man, she told herself, kind, upright, decent. But boring! she cried then. Was it so wrong of her to want some excitement and passion before she grew too old to enjoy it? And she pushed the guilt away, knowing that if she allowed it to it would destroy her.

She had a shower to clear her head but left the bathroom door open, worried that she would not hear the phone. She dressed in black velvet ski pants and a long red jumper, then changed because the red made her face seem paler than ever and she wanted to look her best in case there was a summons from Gus.

She knew there was no logic to her affair with Lynch. Her mood changed daily. She wanted some commitment from him, some public sign that they had a future together, yet she was terrified that her husband would discover her infidelity. She no longer knew what she wanted. She was confused and exhausted and thought that she would only make sense of it if she could have more time with Gus.

She spent the morning in restless housework, ripping sheets and duvet covers from the beds, polishing the sink and bath to a dangerous shine, ironing everything in the linen basket, even towels and underwear. She had not eaten breakfast and stopped at midday only to drink a mug of black coffee and smoke a cigarette. By the end of the afternoon she could stand the waiting no longer. With trembling hands she dialled Lynch's number but the line was engaged and, frustrated, she replaced the receiver.

John Powell had spent the afternoon on the Starling Farm estate. He was in no mood to return to college. He had taken to spending more time on the estate, attracted despite himself by the danger, the tension, the possibility of violence. A group of teenagers sat on a wall outside the Keel Row and stared at him with undisguised hostility as he walked past. He ignored them and walked on to find Connor. He had known Connor since infants' school. He was one of the friends from the old street of whom Evan Powell so disapproved. John was almost certain that he knew where to find him. He would be in the Neighbourhood Advice and Community Centre, a square fortified building at the heart of the estate. Technically unemployed, Connor often worked more than a full week at the Centre, making tea for the old people, organizing activities for the kids, holding the whole thing together. Although only a year older than John he was an expert on welfare rights and dished out advice and mediated with the authorities with an immense confidence. He was a short, intense young man with a bony forehead and a prominent nose, obsessed with politics. As recreation he would sell the Militant newspaper in Newcastle outside the Monument metro station. He spent every Saturday there, shouting slogans, trying to convert passers-by to his point of view.

When John arrived at the Community Centre Connor was playing pool with a group of young teenagers in a windowless games room. He was bent over the table, concentrating on the shot and did not see John, lounging just inside the door, until he straightened.

'What are you doing here?'

John shrugged. 'I wanted to talk to you.'

'What is it?' All his attention was still on the game.

John looked at the boys. 'Not here,' he said.

For the first time Connor looked directly at him, frowning.

'I'll be in the office,' he said to the boys, 'if you need me.'

The office was a tip. There were boxes full of information booklets, rolled-up posters, a row of dirty coffee cups, and half a bottle of sour milk. Against one wall was a table with a heavy manual typewriter and a phone. Connor cleared a pile of paper from the only chair and motioned John to sit on it. He squatted on the floor.

'What's bugging you?' he said.

'The police have been to the school,' John said.

'Who?'

'A detective sergeant called Hunter. I don't think he's local. He was asking questions about Gabby Paston.'

'That's all right then. Just tell him what he wants to know. Within reason.'

'I don't know,' John said. 'It's not that easy.'

'Of course it's easy. But you must keep your nerve. Use your head. Did anyone see you come here?'

'No,' John said. 'I don't think so.'

'Go and have a game of pool with the lads just in case. It'll explain you being here if anyone asks.'

'Why should anyone ask?' There was a trace of panic in his voice.

'Don't worry. They won't. But just in case. Now piss off. I've work to do.'

John played two games of pool with the boys in the games room, then wandered back to say goodbye to Connor, who was still in the office. He was talking animatedly on the phone, replacing the receiver as John came into the room.

'That was Tommy Shiel's wife,' he said. 'Tommy was found guilty this afternoon of handling.'

John said nothing.

'That bitch Amelia Wood was chair of the bench,' Connor said. 'He'd not stand a chance with her. She'd bring back flogging given the chance.'

'Look,' John said awkwardly. 'I'll be off.' But when he got outside he saw it was still only five o'clock and he decided not to take the direct route home.

He must have arrived back at Barton Hill just after his mother because her car was parked on the drive and she sat still in the driver's seat as if she was exhausted. When she saw him she got out and began to pull carrier bags of groceries from the boot. She'd just been to the supermarket, she said, for the late-night shopping. She'd meant to go earlier but she hadn't been able to face it. What would Evan say? She hadn't even thought about what they'd eat tonight.

They stood together in the white security light, surrounded by carrier bags while she fiddled with her key to let them into the house. He could feel her unhappiness.

'What's the matter?' he said. 'You look awful. What is it?'

She pulled away from him. 'Come on,' she said. 'Let's get this shopping inside. There's a pile of stuff for the freezer and it'll all be melting.'

When Evan Powell arrived home at eight o'clock the frustrations of the day were compounded by the fact that the table wasn't set and there was no meal ready for him. He was lucky to get the overtime. He only worked it for Jackie and the boy. It would have been nice to have been appreciated. But he restrained his feelings. Jackie looked so tired and ill, was so apologetic about the lack of a cooked meal.

'I could do an omelette,' she said nervously. 'That wouldn't take long.'

Evan felt suddenly very protective. He put his arm around her and sat her on his knee. She sat where he had placed her and he could feel her bony frame shaking slightly with anxiety. He was overcome by tenderness and guilt.

'Come on,' he said gently. 'What sort of monster do you think I am? I know I take you for granted but I'm not going to throw a tantrum because supper's not ready. Look, I tell you what. Why don't we go out for dinner? The three of us. It's not too late to book a table at the Holly Tree. We haven't celebrated my promotion yet. Let's give ourselves a treat.'

'I don't know,' she said. 'I don't think so. I'm really tired. And I'll need to change.'

But she turned to him, trapped by his kindness like a moth by a light.

'Go on,' he said. 'Go upstairs and make yourself beautiful. I'll phone the restaurant. It's mid-week. They'll fit us in.'

He thought she was going to argue again but she did not move. 'Yes,' she said at last. She had always been incapable of standing up to him. 'Yes.'

The Holly Tree was a double-fronted Georgian house on the edge of St Martin's Hill. It was part of an elegant crescent and had a long back garden with a famous herb bed and a terrace where diners could take their drinks in the summer. Access was from the road at the front and from a small gate at the back used by Martin's Dene residents who walked to the restaurant over the hill.

In the Holly Tree Evan Powell was determinedly cheerful. He praised the table they were given near a long window overlooking the garden, the atmosphere, the menu.

'Now!' he said. 'What about a drink?' He never drank himself but he prided himself on being broadminded. He wanted them all to be happy. He had a sudden recollection of a family outing to the beach when John was a toddler, of splodging in rock pools and fish and chips eaten in the car on the way home. It seemed to him now that when he was with them he spent all his energy trying to recreate the same closeness. It was the first time the three of them had been out for months yet they seemed to have nothing to say to each other.

Jackie ordered a gin and tonic which she drank very quickly. She was thinking inevitably of Lynch, of what a mess it all was. She wished she could tell him how much she had sacrificed, make him understand what she was going through, but she knew the man well enough to realize that if she put him under pressure he would just lash out and destroy her. Evan had begun to talk about his day at work, the robbery on the Coast Road, and she tried to concentrate on what he was saying.

John drank lager and thought about Connor and Sam Smollett and of how much the two had in common.

How Connor would sneer, he thought, if he could see him now.

'Gabby Paston was here yesterday,' he said suddenly. From Sam Smollett he had gone on to think of Abigail Keene and he spoke the words without thinking. He regretted them immediately.

'What do you mean?' Evan Powell looked up from his meal.

'She was here yesterday. She had an appointment for lunch. She told someone in class.'

'Do the police know about this?'

'Yes,' John said evenly. 'Someone was in college today asking questions. A detective sergeant called Hunter.'

Evan grunted to show what he thought of Gordon Hunter.

'What else did she say?' Jackie asked. 'That poor girl. I haven't been able to get her out of my mind all day. Do they know yet what happened to her? What did he tell you?'

'Nothing,' John said. 'He didn't tell me anything.'

Ramsay called into the Holly Tree on his way home from the police station. Hunter, thinking of the overtime, would have been glad to go, but Ramsay knew he could be more discreet, that he would find it easier to persuade people to talk. The owner, a dynamic woman with a county voice called Felicity Beal, was an old acquaintance. She had been at school with Diana, his ex-wife, and during his brief marriage he had been a regular at the restaurant. Diana always claimed that Felicity fed them for nothing, simply as a token of friendship, but he suspected that Diana had paid the bills secretly. He could never have afforded to take her there.

He was greeted at reception by the restaurant manager, a young man with Mediterranean good looks who shared Felicity's bed, and according to Diana, took all the profits. His English was perfect, his accent cultivated.

'Mr Ramsay,' he said. 'Sir. We are just about to finish serving but if you come to a table now I'm sure we can accommodate you.'

'Not tonight, thank you,' Ramsay said. He had forgotten the man's name and felt awkward about it. 'Is Miss Beal working today?'

'Of course,' the man said smoothly. 'She works every night. Sometimes I think she doesn't trust me. I'll tell her that you're here.'

'No,' Ramsay said. 'Please don't bother. I'm sure I can find my own way.'

He walked past the restaurant door to get to the kitchen and saw the Powells, their meal over, standing up to leave. Jackie was in profile, her face tense, staring out of the window and Evan touched her shoulder to gain her attention. Ramsay felt awkward about being there. He didn't want to explain his presence in front of the other diners and he hurried on before they saw him.

Felicity was sitting by a stainless-steel table with a large glass of red wine. In a corner a young girl was stacking plates into a machine.

'Stephen Ramsay!' Felicity shouted in a voice which had been honed during her hunting days. 'Come in and pour yourself a drink. I can't get up. I'm bloody knackered. I did most of the cooking myself tonight. The chef claims to have flu. How's that bitch Diana?'

'I don't know.' Ramsay said mildly. 'You've probably seen her more recently than me.'

'What are you doing here then? If you're fed up with the police canteen you've had it, old son. I'm not cooking another thing tonight.'

'No,' Ramsay said. 'It's work. I need your help.'

'And how can I help Ramsay the great detective?' She took another swig from her glass.

'You may have heard that a girl was found murdered yesterday evening in the Grace Darling Centre in Hallowgate Square. We've traced her movements for the morning but no one seems to have seen her after midday. She claimed to have had a lunch appointment here. I was wondering if she came.' He took a photograph from his pocket and set it on the table. 'Her name's Gabriella Paston,' he said. 'She was wearing black leggings, a navy jumper, and heavy boots.'

'She'd stick out like a sore thumb then, wouldn't she?' Felicity said. 'I spent all lunch time in the bloody kitchen so I didn't see her, but if she was here someone will recognize her. They should all be finishing soon. Sit down and have a drink until we've got rid of the punters. I don't want you wandering round the restaurant in your big boots. I might get a reputation.'

He sat beside her on a tall stool and accepted a glass of wine.

'Of course I'd like a description of the person she was with,' Ramsay said. 'That's most important. And some idea of the time they left.'

'Don't worry,' she said. 'Leave it to old Felicity. It wasn't desperately busy here yesterday lunch time, and the same staff are on, so I'm sure we'll be able to sort it out for you.' She looked at him through narrowed eyes. 'Diana always said that the stress would kill you,' she said. 'Relax and leave it to me.'

But when the waiters and waitresses came into the kitchen, complaining that their feet were killing them, grumbling at each other with the familiarity of family members, no one was able to identify Gabriella Paston. They tried. They passed the photo round between them, tried to remember similar customers served in the past.

'When was she supposed to be here? Yesterday? No. No one like this was here yesterday.'

'If she had smartened herself up?' Ramsay said. 'Put on make-up? Tied up her hair?'

No, they said. The day before had been fairly quiet. There had been a big party of executives from a Newcastle insurance company. All men. The only woman in the place was at least sixty.

He gave up and let them go away to their homes.

'I'm sorry,' Felicity said. 'She can't have been here. They're a good crowd. If she had been they would have noticed.'

'You take reservations for the tables in the restaurant, don't you?' Ramsay said.

'Of course. Most regulars know they won't get in without booking.'

'Would you have a record of the reservations made for yesterday? And a note if any of them failed to turn up?'

'Yes,' she said. 'I get Carlo to make a note. It's a bloody nuisance if you've turned away custom because someone's booked and then the table's empty.'

'Perhaps we could look,' Ramsay suggested gently.

'Of course.' She did not move but screamed through the kitchen door. 'Bring the reservations diary, Carlo, there's a dear.'

The young man came immediately. 'What is it?' he said with theatrical resignation. 'What have I done now?'

'Nothing, my sweet. You're perfect. You know that. The inspector wants to see if someone made a reservation for yesterday lunch time and didn't keep it.'

'Yes,' Carlo said. 'There was one. I remember. I wrote it down on the black list.' He turned to the back of the diary. 'Here we are: Miss Abigail Keene.'

'Oh Carlo,' Felicity said. 'You donkey. Didn't you realize? Someone was having you on. That's no good to the inspector.'

'I don't know,' Ramsay said. 'It might be important. The murdered girl was playing Abigail Keene in a Youth Theatre production.' He turned to Carlo. 'Did you take the phone call?'

'Yes, sure. I take all the phone calls. Felicity thinks she can manage without me but I do all the work in this place.'

'Who made the reservation? A woman?'

'Yes. A woman.'

'A young woman?'

'Hey! I don't know about that,' Carlo said, smiling so widely that Ramsay could see the gold crowns on his molars. 'All English people sound the same to me!'

Across St Martin's Hill Dennis Wood arrived home to a quiet and cold house. He had worked late, then met a friend for a drink in one of the smart new hotels on Newcastle's quayside. The friend was a developer who had had a part in the building of the hotel and was inordinately proud of it. Dennis Wood hoped to interest him in a similar development at Hallowgate, and plied him with drink, hoping that he would mellow to the idea at least to the extent of agreeing to visit Chandler's Court; Dennis had drunk too much himself to keep the friend company, and he could remember nothing of the drive home. He was glad that Amelia was out. She would only have scolded him about driving when he had been drinking, nagged about the scandal there would be if he were caught and made to appear in court. There had been similar conversations on other occasions.

He put himself to bed, folding his clothes meticulously but forgetting to remove his socks. He fell immediately and deeply to sleep.

Chapter Ten

Amelia Wood's body was found by a jogger at eight in the morning while Dennis Wood was still sleeping off the excess of the night before. The jogger, a PE teacher at St Martin's High School, took the same route every day: through the village, across the hill, and down the footpath through the dene. When he crossed the hill it was still dark and the ground was hard. There was no pleasure in the running and he wondered what crazy obsession prompted him to maintain the daily ritual. In the solid houses which backed on to the hill the lights in the bedroom windows reminded him that he could be still at home, drinking tea, reading the paper. The sky was clear and by the time he reached the path into the dene it was light enough to see where he was going. A high wall marked the boundary of the gardens and gave some shelter from the frost.

Amelia Wood lay only yards from the open hill. The teacher thought at first she was a pile of summer rubbish blown into the undergrowth and left to rot. He even began to develop in his mind a lecture on the subject of litter to be delivered at the morning's assembly. But as he approached he saw that it was a woman's shape. She was lying on her side, dressed in a dark velour track suit, her buttocks curved towards him. She was quite close to the path and little attempt had been made to hide her.

He ran back on to the hill looking for someone to help, someone with whom to share the responsibility of the discovery. There was no one in sight. He could have returned to the village, used the phone in Front Street, but that would have taken time and the situation seemed urgent. He chose instead to go through a gate in the high wall which bounded the common, into one of the gardens, and up to the house beyond. He had time to think, even in his panic, that he was in the wrong job and he wished he could afford a place like this. At first he could find no way into the house. There was no light and when he banged on the back door there was no response. He ran round the house over a lawn scattered with leaves, past bare fruit trees. On a semicircle of gravel a BMW was parked. Presumably then, someone was at home. As he ran to the front door he was joined by a Labrador which appeared from nowhere. He leaned on the door bell with all his weight until he heard movement upstairs, then stood, suddenly breathless and shaky waiting for someone to answer it.

Dennis Wood was wakened by the shrieking of the door bell below him and by the barking of the dog. He groaned and turned over, hoping that Amelia would be up and would answer it. But it continued, making his head pound, and eventually he padded downstairs, still wearing the socks of the night before, pulling on a dressing-gown and tying it around his paunch. When he opened the door he saw a madman in a track suit and running shoes who yelled incoherently about an emergency, about needing to use the phone. As a good citizen he let the man in, but showed no interest. He thought the incident had nothing to do with him.

Ramsay was sitting at his desk at Hallowgate police station when he received the news of Amelia Wood's death. He had been there since seven, reading through the statements taken the day before from people who had been at the Grace Darling Centre on Monday evening, realizing with increasing frustration that no one had seen anything unusual. His first reaction to the discovery of the body was anger, directed not at the murderer but at Hunter. He had told the sergeant that someone should interview Mrs Wood. What had happened? It was the sort of incompetence that irritated because it was unnecessary. Hunter disliked the routine of statement taking and avoided it. He claimed it was boring, usually a waste of time, but Ramsay thought it was the listening which he found so irksome. He could not bear to give someone else his full attention. He had assumed apparently that like all the other witnesses Amelia Wood had no useful information to give. Her murder contradicted the assumption.

Ramsay drove to Martin's Dene alone, leaving instructions that Hunter was to follow him when he got in. He drove down the wide avenue of Martin's Close looking at the smart houses without envy. The Woods' home was at the end of a cul-de-sac, 1930s mock-Tudor, large, separated from the street by a row of trees. A police car was blocking the drive so Ramsay parked in the street and walked in. The front door was open. He shouted and stepped into a wide hall, then went through to the kitchen where he could hear voices.

The kitchen was sleek and expensive and gave no sign that food was ever prepared there. Dennis Wood was perched ridiculously on a stool by a breakfast bar—there was nowhere else to sit. He was dressed in a grey suit and striped shirt, but the shirt was unbuttoned at the collar and he wore no tie. After letting the jogger into the house he had gone on to prepare for work. The policeman called first to the scene had recognized the woman as Amelia Wood—he had seen her in court—and broke the news to him.

'Didn't you notice,' the policeman had asked, polite but incredulous, 'that she'd been missing all night?'

'No,' Wood had said, still fuddled by the hangover, by the shock. 'She was a busy woman. I'd assumed that she was still out when I got in last night. There was no sign of her car, you see. She must have put it away in the garage as soon as she got home. Then this morning I thought that she'd left early.' Seeing the young policeman's disbelief he added: 'She wasn't the sort of woman, you know, that you worried about.'

The PE teacher was obviously still in shock. He was standing by the window, staring out into the garden. Ramsay introduced himself but the man hardly seemed to register his presence.

'I've never seen a dead person before,' he said, almost to himself. A policeman handed him a mug of tea and he took it absently, turned to him, and repeated the phrase like a chant.

'I want someone on the front door,' Ramsay said. 'No unauthorized access. We'll need back up. Immediately. I want to get to the scene of crime as quickly as possible. If my sergeant arrives send him on down to me. Tell him no interviews at this stage. I'll talk to Mr Wood myself later.'

The last thing he needed after the cock-up of failing to see Mrs Wood the night before was Hunter bullying the witnesses.

'Which is the quickest way?' he asked.

'Through the garden. There's a gate in the wall with access straight on to the hill. You won't miss it from there.'

Ramsay thought that the Woods must have paid for help with the garden. Apart from a few beech leaves on the lawn it was immaculate. The vegetable plot had been dug over for the winter, the paths were clear, the trees and shrubs regularly pruned. He could not imagine Dennis Wood getting his hands dirty and even with her ferocious energy Amelia would hardly have had the time. Besides, from what he had learned of her, horticulture would have been too tame an interest. The door through the wall was arched. It could be bolted from the inside but had been left ajar. Ramsay went through it and stood for a moment to take his bearings.

The hill was a piece of windswept common surrounded on three sides by houses and bordered on the fourth side by the dene. There was a view over roofs to Tynemouth and the sea. Ramsay stood now at the corner where the dene and the houses met. There was access to the hill from a number of points but a well-trodden footpath led from Martin's Dene village opposite him to the corner, where a cinder track had been created through the trees down the steep side of the valley. At the village end of the footpath was the Holly Tree restaurant.

There was already a considerable police presence by the body and he was impressed by the efficiency of at least some members of the Hallowgate force. A Land-Rover had been driven over the hill and a policeman in a navy anorak was marking the area with blue and white tape. As he walked towards it Ramsay caught the jolly Scottish voice of the pathologist unnaturally loud in the still, clear air. It was still cold and the grass and each branch and twig were covered with hoar. At the bottom of the dene a pool of mist lay over the burn. He stepped over the tape and joined the group of people looking down at the body. Among them he recognized Hallowgate's chief superintendent, a quiet, studious man, nearing retirement. He was considered soft by some of his subordinates, too liberal by far, but Ramsay liked and respected him.

'Ah, Ramsay,' the superintendent said. 'Thank you for getting here so quickly. Any connection, do you think, with the Paston murder?'

'Almost certainly,' Ramsay said. 'Mrs Wood was at the Grace Darling Centre on Monday evening, when Gabriella Paston's body was discovered.'

'You think she witnessed something?' Ramsay was aware of a sharp intelligence.

'It's possible,' he said. 'Unfortunately she'd left the Centre before the girl was found and we couldn't get hold of her yesterday to take a statement.'

'Yes,' the superintendent said quietly. 'I see. That was unfortunate.' He said nothing else. He was not the sort of man to be critical in front of outsiders.

'Have you discovered any other connection between Mrs Wood and the Paston girl?'

'None at all at this stage.'

'But it seems sensible to you to consider both murders as part of the same investigation?'

'Definitely. Unless we come across any evidence to the contrary.'

'Well then,' the man said, briskly indicating, as he intended, his confidence in Ramsay. 'I'll leave you in charge. Report back to me later today. We'll need details at some stage for a press conference.'

'Of course,' Ramsay said, wishing that his boss in Otterbridge was half as sensitive. He watched as the superintendent, slightly stooped, more like a scholar than a policeman, walked back towards the Woods' house.

'What have you got for me, then?' he asked the pathologist.

'Hey, man. Give me a chance. What do you want? Miracles?'

'Cause of death would do for a start.'

'She was strangled,' the pathologist said. 'Not with a rope or wire. Something thicker. A scarf maybe.'

'Time of death?'

'Hard to tell at this stage. Got to allow for the cold. It's bloody freezing. Yesterday evening probably.'

'Can't you be more specific?'

'Not yet.' He stood up and grinned. 'Find out when she last ate and I might be able to help you later today.'

On his way back to the Woods' house, at the garden gate, Ramsay met Hunter. The sergeant was defensive.

'I tried to get hold of her,' he said. 'I found out she was at court all day, but when I phoned there she'd already left. The usher chased after her and gave her the message to get in touch. I phoned him back to check that he'd got hold of her and he said she was going straight home. She hadn't contacted the station when I left so I called here on the way to Otterbridge. There was no reply. I can't see that I could have done any more.'

'No,' Ramsay said. There *was* nothing more that Hunter could have done. 'What time were you here?'

'About nine, I suppose. We left together, didn't we?'

'You didn't see anything unusual?'

'No. There was a light on at the back of the house but I thought it might be a normal security measure to leave a light on when the family was out.'

'Yes,' Ramsay said. 'I see.'

'What do you want me to do now?' Hunter asked.

'Keep people off the hill and out of the dene until we've done a search. I suppose you can organize that.'

He walked back to the house thinking he had been unfair to Hunter, too abrupt. In the kitchen he found the jogger, still staring out of the window, still clutching a mug of tea which was obviously cold. When he saw Ramsay he turned with a start.

'Can I go now?' he said. 'I've classes to take this morning. It won't be easy for them to cover for me.'

'Just a few questions,' Ramsay said. 'What made you come to this house? Did you recognize her?'

'No. I didn't even stop to look at her closely. When I touched her hand it was freezing. She was obviously dead. This was the closest place.'

'You came in through the back gate?'

The man nodded.

'Was it open?'

'Yes. Slightly open. I was surprised. You expect people in houses like this to worry about security.'

'Was there a light on in the kitchen?'

'No, the house was quite dark.'

When Ramsay had begun talking to the teacher, Wood had made his excuses and left the kitchen. Ramsay found him in a cold living room, slumped in a chair, his eyes shut, his face grey.

'I'm sorry to disturb you,' Ramsay said. 'But I do have to ask some questions.'

Wood sat up and hunched forward, his elbows on his knees.

'Yes,' he said, 'of course.'

'What time did you get home last night?'

'I'm not sure exactly. About midnight.' He looked apologetically at Ramsay. 'I'm afraid I'd had a skinful.'

'But you must have noticed that Mrs Wood wasn't here.'

'Oh, yes. Of course I'd *noticed*. But it wasn't unusual. We lived very independent lives. I thought she was out at some council function or charity do.'

'Yes,' Ramsay said. 'I see.' Evan Powell would never have understood that sort of marriage but it made sense to him. He had never known where Diana was.

'She had been home,' he said, 'after finishing at court?'

'Was she at court yesterday?' Wood was faintly curious, unsurprised. 'Yes, she had been home. I realize that now. Her car's in the garage.'

'Were there any lights on in the house when you got home?'

Wood hunched further forward, concentrating.

'Yes,' he said. 'The kitchen light. I turned it off before I went to bed. I suppose it should have struck me as odd, but I was in no state to think clearly about anything.'

'You can't remember what plans your wife might have had for the evening?'

'No,' Wood said. 'I'm afraid not.'

'Was there any reason for her leaving the house on foot?'

Wood sat up and shook his head slowly as if he had been a fool. 'Yes,' he said. 'Of course. The dog.'

'I'm sorry,' Ramsay said.

'Whichever of us was first home in the evening let the dog out for a run on the hill. Amelia was more thorough about it than me. She actually took him for a walk. I'm afraid I just let him out on to the common and called him back five minutes later. After that we'd lock the back gate for the night. The dog was still outside this morning. He must have found his own way home.'

'I see. Would your wife take the dog out as soon as she got home from court?'

'No. She'd shower first. She always said the courtroom stank. Change into something more comfortable, a cup of tea, then take the dog for a run.'

'So how long would all that take?'

'I don't know. Three-quarters of an hour, perhaps.'

'Thank you,' Ramsay said. 'We should be able to estimate the time of death very precisely with that information.'

'So you think she was killed then? When she took the dog out on to the hill?'

'Probably,' Ramsay said. He was lost in thought. 'I think so. Yes.'

They sat in silence.

'Was he some sort of madman, then?' Wood demanded at last. 'First that girl at the Grace Darling Centre, then Amelia. What would they call him in America? A serial killer. Was he one of those?'

Ramsay gave the proposition serious consideration. 'No,' he said eventually. 'Really, I don't think so. The murders weren't random. It can hardly be a coincidence that Mrs Wood was at a meeting at the Grace Darling on the night that Gabriella's body was found there.'

'So you think she might have seen something. She was killed to keep her quiet.'

'It's a possibility, though there are obvious problems with the theory. If she'd seen something obviously suspicious why didn't she get in touch with us immediately? She was a magistrate, concerned, responsible.'

There was a pause and then Wood answered slowly. 'She was all those things, Inspector. But she was also a woman who enjoyed power. If she had come across information which she could put to her advantage she wouldn't hesitate to use it.'

Ramsay was surprised by his honesty and detachment. Bereavement usually made people sentimental. Wood sensed the surprise.

'We had a successful marriage, Inspector. We understood each other's needs. There was respect and admiration. But not what you could call romantic love and that's what clouds one's judgement.'

'Did you discuss the Gabriella Paston murder yesterday evening?' Ramsay asked.

'Only briefly. Amelia didn't know about it when she came in. I'd seen a short report on the local news and passed on the details. I knew she'd be interested because of her connection with the Centre.'

'Had she ever met the girl?'

'I don't think so. She would have told me last night if she'd known her personally.'

'Do you know what she was doing at the Arts Centre yesterday?'

'I'm sorry, Inspector. I haven't a clue. As I've explained, we led very separate lives.'

'She'd arranged a meeting with a Mr Lynch, the director,' Ramsay persisted. 'She didn't mention it? The name doesn't mean anything to you?'

'Oh, yes, I recognize the name. I've had business dealings with Lynch but Amelia wasn't connected in any way.'

'Could you tell me what sort of business dealings?'

'He bought a flat from me.' Wood stood up and stretched. The colour had returned to his face. The shock and the hangover were beginning to wear off. 'In Chandler's Court just off Hallowgate Fish Quay. I'm an architect and my firm bought the building and converted it. It was rather a successful venture for us and we hope to do more of it in the future.'

'Was there anything unusual about your negotiations with Mr Lynch?'

'Not really. At first he haggled about the price. He tried to bring Amelia into it, said that he'd taken a massive drop in salary to come to work at the Grace Darling and he thought I should make a gesture by reducing the asking price.'

'What did you say?'

'That his dealing with Amelia was quite separate from his business with me and that if he didn't want the flat there were lots of people who did.'

'And he managed to find the asking price?'

Wood shrugged. 'Of course.'

'When did he move into Chandler's Court?'

'Two and a half years ago.'

'Where was he living before that?'

'I don't think I ever knew. He'd been renting somewhere since he moved up from London but I sent all the correspondence about the sale to the Arts Centre.' The architect returned to his chair.

They sat for a moment in silence. Outside there was the sound of cars pulling up in the street, doors banging, voices, as the team who would search the hill were directed through the garden to the back gate.

'Have you ever been to the Holly Tree restaurant?' Ramsay asked.

Wood was surprised by the question but answered easily. 'Yes. It's a convenient place to entertain. I often take business clients there and Amelia and I went quite regularly, perhaps once a month, for dinner or Sunday lunch.'

'Is it possible, do you think, that Mrs Wood booked a table there on Monday lunch time?'

It seemed unlikely, Ramsay thought, though the question had to be asked. Why would Amelia want to buy Gabriella Paston an expensive lunch? And why not use her own name? As a regular customer it would guarantee her a better table. It could not be because she wanted to keep the trip to the restaurant a secret—she would be recognized as soon as she arrived.

'Quite possible,' Wood said. 'She went there sometimes with her friends.'

'She didn't mention it to you?'

'No. But she wouldn't have done. She would have written it in her appointments diary though. Everything went in there. I'll find it for you.'

He stood up and left the room, glad it seemed of the excuse for movement. As Ramsay waited for his return a minibus pulled up in the street, and a pile of men in navy anoraks trampled over the gravel and across the grass to the back of the house. Wood came back almost immediately with a thick desk diary which Ramsay opened at November 30th. A string of appointments was listed in small neat handwriting. Amelia's day had started with a Cancer Research coffee morning, there was a meeting of the planning subcommittee at 2.00, tea with D.Y at four and a meeting of the governors of Hallowgate Sixth-Form College at 6.30.

'D.Y?' Ramsay asked.

'Deidre Yeoman. Another Tory councillor. They met occasionally for moral support and to discuss strategy.'

Ramsay considered the appointments. They would check of course if Amelia had kept them all. She must have gone straight to the Grace Darling after the governor's meeting. It was just possible that she could have fitted in an early lunch at the Holly Tree and still be at the council meeting at two but unlikely surely that she would have made the arrangement. The mysterious Abigail Keene who had booked the table must be someone altogether different.

His thoughts were interrupted by Hunter, who tapped on the door and stood just inside the room, scarcely able to suppress his excitement.

'Sorry to disturb you, sir,' he said, obviously not sorry at all. 'If I could have a word.'

Ramsay followed him into the hall and shut the door.

'We've found something,' Hunter said. 'Something really interesting.' He paused for dramatic effect and then continued. 'A sports bag. The sort all the kids use to carry their gear in, full of books and files. It belonged to Gabriella Paston.'

'So,' Ramsay said. 'She did come to Martin's Dene on the day of her death. Where exactly did you find it?'

Hunter paused again, like a child wanting to savour a moment of triumph. 'Well,' he said. 'That's the most interesting thing of all. We found it here. In this garden. In the middle of the shrubbery next to the wall. Quite a coincidence, don't you think?'

Chapter Eleven

At midday Ramsay left St Martin's Close and drove back to Hallowgate to report to the chief superintendent. The Close was filled with police vehicles and he made a mental note that when the case was over he should write to all the residents to thank them for their forbearance.

In his office the superintendent listened carefully to what Ramsay had to tell him. On the wall above his head was a watercolour of St Mary's Island which he had painted himself. From the window was a view of the mouth of the river.

'Not a coincidence then,' he said, 'if the girl's things were found in the Woods' garden.'

'Definitely not a coincidence,' Ramsay said, 'but nothing to connect the women yet either, except the Grace Darling Centre.'

'You think Gabriella Paston was murdered in Martin's Dene too?'

'That seems the most obvious explanation. She'd told her friends she was going there. Her bag was found at the end of the garden. It could have been thrown over the wall from the common.' Ramsay paused. 'I think the focus of the investigation will have to shift to Martin's Dene,' he said. 'We'll need to make that point clearly at the press conference. Presumably Gabby Paston got there by public transport. Someone must have seen her. And she was quite a striking figure. We'll need a house-to-house in the village. I'm having photos printed now. 'Then we'll need everyone who was out on the hill yesterday evening to come forward.'

'Any other lines of enquiry?'

'Someone was paying regularly into the girl's building society account. It could have been her family of course. I'll check that. If not it would be interesting to know who was giving her the money.'

'You think it could have been payment for services rendered?'

Ramsay shrugged. 'It's possible. She was an attractive girl. And she seems not to have sustained any lasting relationships with lads of her own age. She'd not be the first drama student to sleep her way through college.'

'Where does Mrs Wood come into it?'

'At this stage,' Ramsay said, 'I haven't a clue.'

'You don't see Dennis Wood as Miss Paston's mysterious benefactor?'

'It's a neat explanation,' Ramsay said. 'But no. I don't think Dennis Wood's a murderer.'

There was a moment's silence while the superintendent leaned forward, his arms on his desk.

'I'd be grateful to get this cleared up quickly,' he said, awkwardly.

'Of course.' Ramsay was surprised. He had not expected to be put under pressure.

'There should be no difference in our response to a teenage lad stabbed to death in a pub brawl on the Starling Farm estate as to a magistrate strangled in Martin's Dene.' The superintendent was speaking almost to himself but looked up to check that Ramsay understood what he was saying. 'Morally there's no difference at all. But practically. . .' He smiled wryly. 'Practically there's all the difference in the world. The respectable citizens of Martin's Dene will be affronted by an outrage on their doorstep. They'll take it personally. When you spend that much on a house you expect to be insulated from the nasty realities of the outside world. I get enough flak about dog mess on the pavement. They'll write to their MPs, to the members of the police committee, to me. They'll make my life hell.' He smiled again, more gently. 'I was hoping for a peaceful year before I retire. As I said, I'd be grateful.'

'I'll have a try,' Ramsay said, but his voice gave little room for hope.

From his cold, depressing office in Hallowgate police station

Ramsay phoned the Grace Darling Arts Centre. The call was answered by Joe Fenwick on the reception desk. It was a small piece of luck but made Ramsay feel optimistic for the first time that day.

'Ellen Paston,' he asked. 'Is she working today?'

'Aye. She got in half an hour ago.'

'That's fine then. You'll not tell anyone I was asking.'

'Me!' Joe Fenwick laughed. 'Man, I'll not tell a soul.'

Ramsay sent a car to bring Ellen Paston to the police station. It was a gamble, of course. She might just refuse to come. He had been tempted to go to the Grace Darling to talk to her there, tempted too by the prospect of seeing Prue Bennett again. But in the end he had decided to bring her into the police station. Away from her own home ground, her mother and her work, she might be more prepared to talk. And he thought that she *would* come. Curiosity would bring her along.

He had hoped to find somewhere more pleasant to interview her, thinking she might be persuaded to relax her guard in less formal surroundings, but no other room was available and he saw her in his office. He phoned for a WPC to bring them tea, hoping to make Ellen Paston feel important, special. She spent her life waiting on others, dominated by her mother, patronized by the customers at the Grace Darling. He felt she would be susceptible to flattery.

'I believe you'll be able to help me,' he said. 'I'd like you to tell me about your meetings with Gabriella.'

She looked up at him but said nothing. A policewoman knocked at the door, then came in with a tea tray which she set on the table. She took a chair to the corner of the room where she sat, apparently lost in thoughts of her own throughout the interview. Ramsay poured tea, offered biscuits.

'You *did* meet Gabriella quite regularly,' he said gently. 'She kept a record of your appointments in her diary.' He held his breath, hoping that he was right and that the E of the diary was Ellen Paston.

'Yes,' she said at last. 'We met. She'd never come to the house but she wanted to keep in touch.' She spoke bitterly. 'We weren't much but we were all she had.'

'Why didn't she come to the house?'

Ellen shook her head as if it was beyond her understanding. Ramsay tried to control his impatience.

'Was it because she knew she wouldn't be welcome?'

'No,' she said. 'She'd have been welcome enough. We'd have had her back to live if she'd wanted to come. She didn't want to go there. That's all.'

'Did your mother know that you were meeting Gabriella?'

'She knows I saw Gabby at the Grace Darling,' Ellen said, 'but not that I saw her away from work.'

'Why didn't you tell her?' Ramsay asked.

Ellen shrugged. Perhaps she had so little privacy that any secret, however harmless, was important to her. Perhaps there had been so much animosity between Alma and Gabriella that her mother had forbidden her to see the girl. Whatever the reason she refused to say.

'Where did you meet?' he asked.

'Usually in the coffee shop in Martin's Dene,' Ellen said. Had they chosen Martin's Dene, Ramsay wondered, because they were unlikely to meet any of their acquaintances from the Starling Farm there? Ellen leaned forward greedily and took another biscuit. 'We had tea, cream cakes. It was a treat, something to look forward to.'

'Who paid?' he asked.

'We took it in turns,' she said resentfully, 'if it's any business of yours.'

'Did you ever give her money?' he asked.

'Yes.' She obviously saw it as an admission of weakness. 'I know it was all her own fault storming out of the house like that, but it didn't seem right that she should live off a stranger. Not completely. I wanted her to have some cash of her own.'

'How much did you give her?'

'Ten pounds, twenty pounds, whatever I could afford.'

That would be a lot, Ramsay thought, for Ellen Paston. Probably a day's pay. But it didn't explain the eight hundred pounds in the building society.

'Did you ever give her more than that?' he asked. 'Perhaps for her to start a savings account?'

Ellen shook her head. 'Where would I get more than that?' she demanded. 'There's only Mam's pension and what I get from the Grace Darling.'

'Yes, of course,' he said, surprised by her aggression. 'Is that why Gabby came to meet you?' he asked, suddenly brutal. 'For the money?'

Ellen's mood changed quickly, like a child's. She forgot her anger and smiled.

'Nah,' she said. 'She'd have got that anyway. She knew I'd not see her go short. I told you. She wanted to keep in touch.'

'What did you talk about?'

'Everything,' she said. 'Bit of news from the estate. She'd lost contact with most of her friends there. What was going on in the Grace Darling. Gossip, I suppose you'd call it. A bit of a crack.'

Ramsay saw that it was quite plausible. Gabby Paston had lived on the Starling Farm for sixteen years. Despite Prue's kindness it must have been a strain to be uprooted into a middle-class household. The rules of engagement would be different. The talk would be of books, the theatre, politics. He remembered his own introduction to the Bennetts. It had been an exhilarating experience but he had been frightened always of betraying his ignorance and it had been a relief at times to escape home, to soap operas on the TV and his mother's chat. So Gabby had sneaked away every couple of weeks to eat cream cakes with her aunt. With Ellen she could relax for an hour and use the dialect words and expressions which the Bennetts would hardly understand. And she could listen to gossip, to the trivial, salacious, and amusing bits of news which would be despised in her new life, but which would make her feel part of the estate again. Then why had she left in the first place, he wondered, if it was such a wrench? He did not put the question immediately to Ellen Paston. He thought she would refuse to answer it and he had other things to ask while she was being co-operative.

'Did you talk about Amelia Wood?' he asked. 'She was a trustee at the Grace Darling and there must have been stories to tell about a woman like that.'

'Maybe,' she conceded, 'but we didn't see enough of her at the Centre to find out.'

'Had you heard that she'd been murdered?' he asked quietly.

She shook her head and for a brief moment he thought he saw her mouth turn up in a strange lopsided grin. Was it shock? Embarrassment? Or the pleasure in having information which he needed and which she was not prepared to share?

'She was strangled,' he said more sharply. 'Like Gabriella.'

'When?' The question surprised him. He had expected some expression of regret.

'Yesterday evening,' he said. 'At some time after six.' He paused then asked deliberately. 'What were you doing then?'

She seemed pleased to have gained accurate information from him and answered almost absentmindedly.

'I was at home with Mam. There was no work. The Centre was closed for the day.'

'You didn't leave the house all evening?'

She shook her head and looked up at him, a challenge. 'Ask Mam,' she said. 'She'll tell you.'

Oh, yes, he thought. I bet she will.

'Tell me,' he said. 'Why did Gabriella leave home?'

She looked straight at him, not caring whether or not he believed her.

'I've told you,' she said. 'It was her age. She just got fed up with us.'

'She fell out with your mother,' he said.

'Aye. It was something like that.'

'What was the row about?'

She smiled maliciously. 'You'll have to ask Mam,' she said. 'Won't you?'

Ramsay did not answer. They both knew that Alma Paston would give little away.

'Look,' Ellen said. 'I should get back. I've work to do.'

'Don't worry,' he said. 'I'll clear it with Mr Lynch. And I'll take you back myself. There's just one more question. . .' He looked directly at the hunched, ungainly figure sitting on the chair on the other side of the desk. 'Gabriella had eight hundred pounds in a building society account. Do you know where she got the money?'

Ellen gave a hard laugh and he could have sworn that her astonishment was genuine.

'The mean little madam,' she said. 'And she still took money off me!'

The resentment was directed not at the fact that Gabriella had money, but that Ellen had known nothing about the account.

Joe Fenwick heard the news of Amelia Wood's death on the transistor radio he kept behind the reception desk to liven up the duller moments of the day. The afternoon was always quiet. There were a few old ladies in the small lounge for a reminiscence session, sharing stories of their childhood in the twenties, but Joe thought that most of them were so deaf that they would not be disturbed by the strains of Radio Newcastle coming from the lobby. There was an extended report of the murder during the two o'clock news and Joe thought the information was too interesting to keep to himself.

He found Prue Bennett and Gus Lynch in the theatre. They were arguing in an irritable, petulant way about the following week's rehearsal of *Abigail Keene*. Prue thought the whole production should be cancelled or at least postponed. How could they go on with the rehearsals, she said, pretending that nothing had happened? The information, given by Joe, that Amelia Wood had died only strengthened her argument. They must cancel now, she said. They couldn't go ahead when both a member of the Youth Theatre and a trustee had been killed. Besides the question of taste it was a practical matter. They couldn't encourage young girls to come out after dark. Not at a time like this. The parents wouldn't stand for it.

'If the parents don't like it,' Gus Lynch said crossly, 'they can arrange to bring the kids to the square and pick them up after the rehearsal. It's not beyond the wit of man to organize some sort of rota.'

His reaction to Amelia Wood's death surprised Prue. She was shocked and frightened—it seemed to her that everyone connected with the Grace Darling was a potential target—but Gus seemed overtaken by a terrible excitement. He talked about the murders all the time and became feverish and restless, insisting even more strongly that the production should go ahead. 'The publicity won't do us any harm,' he said. 'It'll ensure a full house at least. And the press will certainly be there.'

'No,' she said. 'It's terrible. We don't want that sort of publicity.'

'There are lots of parallels with the play when you come to look at it. Sam Smollett was accused of murder. He just never got caught.'

'But who'll play Abigail?' Prue cried, hoping that a discussion of the practical details would make him calmer, give her a chance to make him see sense.

'Anna, of course,' he said, as if Prue were a fool. 'She'll make a perfectly adequate understudy.'

'Look,' Prue said. 'I'm not sure she's up to it. Not after all this strain.'

'Don't be ridiculous,' he said impatiently. 'Of course she's up to it. It's a group piece. She won't be on her own. Besides, shouldn't you ask her, before making up her mind for her?'

'Yes,' Prue said. 'I suppose I should.'

But Gus had walked away without waiting for an answer and she was left in the theatre alone. She shivered with a sudden panic and was tempted for a moment to phone Stephen Ramsay. But what would she tell him? That she was concerned by her boss's reaction to the news of Amelia Wood's murder, that he seemed under some psychological strain? The call might give her fears more weight than they deserved. It might even give the impression that she saw Gus Lynch as a murderer.

She was still in the theatre when Ramsay arrived at the Grace Darling. He left Ellen Paston in the lobby and went to look for Prue, wanting to get the most awkward interview over first. She heard the door bang and watched him walk across the polished wood floor to join her. In the unnatural light of the theatre she saw him as a stranger and wondered even if she would have recognized him that first evening if he had not given his name.

'I'm sorry for the intrusion,' Ramsay said. 'You'll have heard about Mrs Wood?'

She nodded. She was wearing the jeans and sweater of the night before and her face was tense and strained. He wanted to comfort her and to make her smile.

'I'm afraid I have to ask you some questions about your movements yesterday evening,' he said.

She did not answer.

'What did you do after I left?'

'I went to see a friend,' she said. 'Anna wasn't very good company and I needed someone to talk to.'

'I'll need the name of the friend,' Ramsay said apologetically. 'You do realize we'll have to check.'

'Yes,' she said. 'Of course. Her name's Judy, Judy Delaney. She's a solicitor. She lives in a flat just round the corner from me.'

'You won't mind if someone goes to speak to her?'

'Not at all. She'll love the drama. She's quite a character, great fun.' She paused. 'I needed fun,' she said. 'Last night.'

'Was Anna left in the house on her own?' Ramsay asked.

'Of course. She's not a child. I tried to persuade her to come with me to Judy's but she said she wanted to be on her own. In fact she practically begged me to go out. She had a bath and went to bed early. When I got back she was already asleep.'

'Did you take your car to visit your friend?'

'No. I've told you. It was just around the corner. Otterbridge isn't New York.'

'Does Anna drive?'

She looked at him, horrified. 'What are you saying?' she demanded. 'That Anna drove my car to Martin's Dene and strangled Amelia Wood? You must be mad!'

'I have to ask,' he said uncomfortably. 'I don't like it any more than you do.'

'She hasn't passed her test,' Prue said angrily.

'But she has taken lessons? It would be possible for her to drive your car?'

'Yes,' she said reluctantly. 'She only failed her test last time because of nerves. But it's impossible. She wouldn't do it. What motive could she have?'

'None,' he said. 'Probably none. But you do understand that it's my job to ask?'

'I suppose so,' she said. 'But it's a shitty sort of job.'

They stood in silence, staring at each other. The hostility made her feel closer to him than she had in all their previous polite exchanges. There was an emotional charge between them. She wondered again whether she should pass on her anxieties about Gus Lynch but before she could make up her mind to speak Ramsay had apologized again for taking up her time and walked away.

When Ramsay knocked at Lynch's office door the man was on the telephone. He shouted for the policeman to come in then, with his hand over the receiver said: 'Sit down, Inspector. This'll not take a minute.'

'Look, I'm sorry.' Lynch spoke in a brisk, business like way into the phone, but his eyes flickered wildly about the room. 'I'm busy now. I'll call you later.' He replaced the hand set and focused his gaze on the policeman. 'I suppose this is about Mrs Wood?'

Ramsay nodded.

'How can I help you, Inspector? I can't give you much time. I'm very busy today.'

'When did you last see Mrs Wood?'

'On Monday evening. Just before Gabriella's body was found.' He spoke as if Ramsay was a fool.

'She hadn't been in touch since then?'

'No. Why should she?'

'I'll need an account of your movements yesterday evening,' Ramsay said.

'Good God, man!' Lynch said with an unpleasant laugh. 'You know where I was. Your sergeant came to see me.'

'Hunter arrived at your house at five o'clock and left at about half past,' Ramsay said calmly. 'I'd like some details of your movements after that please.'

'There were no movements,' Lynch said. 'How could there be? You've still got my car.'

'But I understand from my sergeant that you had gone out earlier by foot.'

'Oh that!' Lynch said. 'That was just to get some fresh air. I was only gone ten minutes. I didn't go out again.'

'Can anyone corroborate that?' Ramsay asked quietly.

'Of course not. I was in the flat on my own.'

'Did you receive any phone calls, for example?'

'No,' Lynch said. 'No.'

He got to his feet as if he expected the interview to be over, but Ramsay remained seated and he returned awkwardly to his chair.

'I'd like you to tell me about your business dealings with Mr Wood.' Ramsay said.

'I have no business dealings with him.'

'I understood that you'd bought your flat from his company.'

'Oh. Yes, of course. But that was a very straightforward transaction.'

'You never met him since then?'

'I don't think I even met him at the time,' Lynch said. 'One of his staff showed me around the property and all the negotiations were done through our solicitors or by post.'

'They were lengthy negotiations? You questioned the asking price?'

'Of course. Doesn't everyone when they're buying property? Look, Inspector, I don't mean to be rude but I don't understand what this has to do with Mrs Wood's murder.'

No, Ramsay thought. Nor do I. But he knew Lynch was anxious about something and wished he knew what lay behind the fear.

'Just routine enquiries,' he said. Blundering around in the dark, he thought.

John Powell left Hallowgate Central Library and walked through the empty streets towards the square. At the Grace Darling he stopped and went into the lobby to use the pay phone there. Joe Fenwick looked up from his desk and stared at him.

'It is all right to use the phone?'

'Oh, aye,' the man said. 'That's all right.' But still he was staring and John turned his back to him and spoke softly so he wouldn't be overheard. He dialled the Starling Farm Community Centre and asked to speak to Connor.

'Are you on for tonight?' he asked.

'No.' Connor's voice was guarded. 'Not tonight.'

'Why? Is there a problem?'

'You could say that,' Connor said. 'Haven't you heard the news?'

'What news?'

'It's our friend Mrs Amelia Wood. She was found dead this morning on St Martin's Hill. She'd been strangled.'

'I don't see,' John said, 'what that's got to do with us.'

'No?' Connor said shortly. 'Think about it.'

Chapter Twelve

Prue Bennett left work early, irritated by Gus Lynch and anxious about Anna. She knew that in Otterbridge her daughter should be safe but she could not relax while she thought of her in the house on her own. When she arrived home she saw that Anna was already there. Her coat was hanging over the bannister in the hall and music came from her room.

'It's me!' Prue shouted up the stairs. 'I'm just making some tea if you want some.' It was what she always said when she came in from work and the repeated words reassured her.

Anna was still wearing her school uniform. She looked very young and Prue thought again how absurd it was that Gus could consider her a suitable Abigail Keene. Abigail had to be sexy, sophisticated, confident of her ability to attract.

'Amelia Wood's dead,' Anna said. 'I've just heard it on the radio.'

Prue looked at her daughter for signs that she was upset but Anna's words were calm, matter of fact.

'I know,' Prue said. 'The police were at the Centre today.'

'That Stephen Ramsay? Your old flame?'

Was she sneering? Prue wondered, but again it was impossible to tell. What's wrong with us? she thought. Why can't we communicate? Then she thought she was getting paranoid: they'd muddled along well enough in the past.

'Yes,' she said. 'Stephen was there.'

'Does he know who killed Mrs Wood?'

Prue shook her head. 'I don't think so. Not yet.'

'Will it make any difference to the production?'

Prue shrugged. 'I wanted to cancel but Gus thinks we should go ahead.'

'So do I,' Anna said firmly. 'It can't make any difference to Gabby and Mrs Wood now.'

Prue was surprised by the strength of her words.

'Gus thinks you should play Abigail Keene,' she said.

'Does he?' There was no clue in the girl's voice to what she thought of the idea. 'Does he think I can do it?'

'Apparently.'

'And you?' Anna asked quietly. 'What do you think?' Then before Prue could answer she cried: 'You don't think I'll be anywhere near as good as Gabby. I've never lived up to your expectations, have I? You don't want me to try in case I make a fool of you.'

'No,' Prue said, distressed, wondering if that *was* what she thought. 'I didn't mean that.'

As they stared at each other angrily, shocked by the unusual tension between them, the telephone rang.

After speaking to Connor, John Powell hung round the lobby of the Grace Darling, reading posters on the noticeboard advertising the Contemporary Dance Festival in town and Shakespeare at the Theatre Royal. He was putting off a decision about what to do next. The evening stretched ahead of him as a prospect of unendurable boredom. Sod Connor, he thought. This was no time to lose his nerve.

He was just about to leave the building when Joe Fenwick called him back.

'Hey!' he said. 'You. Young Powell. I want a word with you.'

'What is it?' John stood at the door.

'Come here, bonny lad. I don't want the whole world to hear. And nor will you.'

'What is it?' John said again, sauntering towards the desk, refusing to be rattled.

'What were you doing playing silly buggers in Anchor Street a couple of nights ago?' Joe said.

'I don't know what you mean.' He was superior, haughty. It was a faultless performance.

'Don't come the innocent with me. I saw you and your mates driving like lunatics. What had you been up to, eh? It wasn't your car you were driving. Don't you think the police would be interested?'

'No,' John said calmly. 'I don't think they would. They've more important things to worry about than a few lads mucking about. Besides I'd deny it.'

'Deny what you like, bonny lad. But if I see you at it again I'll be on to your father as quick as you like. Or to that Inspector Ramsay.'

'I shouldn't do that,' John said. 'That would be a mistake.'

He was more worried by the exchange than he let on but he refused to run away. He wasn't going to be intimidated by an old man like Joe Fenwick. He told himself it was the lack of information which was frightening. If he knew which way the police investigation was moving he'd have more to work on. He'd know what line to take. He thought then that Anna Bennett might be a source of inside information. Her mother was close to the inspector leading the investigation. It was an outside chance but he'd always been willing to gamble. Ignoring Joe Fenwick's disapproval he walked defiantly back to the pay phone.

'Hi!' he said when Anna answered. 'I think we should meet.' He thought it was beneath him to identify himself. He took it for granted she would recognize his voice. He knew she liked him. 'We'll need to talk about the play if you're taking over from Gabby. You *are* going to take on Abigail Keene?'

'Yes,' she said, then consciously echoing her mother: 'Apparently.'

'I'll borrow my mum's car and pick you up,' he said and replaced the receiver before she had a chance to refuse.

Anna walked slowly back to the kitchen. She was flushed with excitement.

'That was John,' she said. 'He's asked me out.'

'Tonight? Will you go?'

'Yes,' Anna said, then added sarcastically, 'if it's all right with you.'

What can I say? Prue thought. She's eighteen. An adult. At her age I was making love to Stephen Ramsay in the dunes at Duridge Bay.

'Yes,' she said. 'Of course it's all right. I hope you enjoy yourself.'

'Oh, Mum,' Anna said impulsively. 'You don't know how much this means to me.'

Prue did not know what to say.

John arrived at the house later than they had expected and the waiting only increased the tension between them. When the door bell rang Anna rushed off to answer it. Prue wished that she was not so eager. She would be so easily hurt. Through the open kitchen door she heard John say, without apology, that he was late because he'd had problems arranging transport. Then the front door slammed and Anna went off without saying goodbye.

John knew from the beginning that the evening was a crazy idea. Why Anna Bennett, for Christ's sake? It had started logically enough with a desire to find out more about the police investigation but as soon as he got hold of the car he knew he wouldn't be satisfied with a quiet drink and a chat. He needed danger like a drug. Her affection for him was a challenge, as Gabby's had been. He wanted to shock her out of it.

'Where are we going?' she asked. She had changed from her school uniform into a long black skirt and boots. He could tell she had made an effort for him. She sat primly with her hands on her lap. What had she expected? he wondered. The pictures? A meal in a wine bar in Otterbridge? Did she think he fancied her when he could have had Gabby Paston? Her passivity made him want to hit her.

'You'll see,' he said roughly. 'It's a surprise.'

He drove fast out of Otterbridge and joined the main road south. He realized it wasn't too late to save the evening, to stop him making a fool of himself. He could buy her a pizza, a few glasses of wine, make her feel good and deliver her safely home to her mother. But he had never played safe and he recognized the self-destructive excitement, the lack of control, which made him drive too fast and spend his time with Connor and which was his only antidote to boredom.

'I thought we were going to talk about the play,' she said. He overtook a lorry and just missed an oncoming vehicle. She clasped her hands in her lap more tightly.

'Not talk,' he said. 'Talk's not enough. We'll never understand Abigail and Sam just by talking. They took risks. They lived on the edge.'

'So,' she said more loudly, too proud to let him see how frightened she was by the speed. 'Where are we going?'

'We're going to the races,' he said and braked sharply as they approached a roundabout. She thought she must have misheard and did not like to ask what he meant. She felt out of her depth. As they waited for the traffic to pass he said: 'What do the police say then about these murders? Your mam must know. They were at the Grace Darling today. And didn't you say she was a special friend of Inspector Ramsay's?'

'My mother was at school with him,' Anna said, 'but they've not seen each other for years. I don't think he'd confide in her.' She paused. 'Wouldn't your father be able to tell you more?'

'Oh, him!' John said. 'He'll give nothing away. Not to me.'

'I never knew my father,' she said. 'It made me different right from the start not having a dad. I hated being different.'

It was a difficult admission for her to make but he seemed not to hear.

'Who do you think killed Gabby Paston?' he asked suddenly.

'How would I know?' she said. She shivered. She never wanted to think of Gabriella Paston again. The traffic cleared and John drove on, down Anchor Street to Hallowgate Fish Quay and over the cobbles past the new flats at Chandler's Court. The fog had returned to the river with dusk.

'I'm hungry,' John said. He looked at his watch. It was nine o'clock. 'There's an hour to wait yet. Do you fancy fish and chips?'

She nodded and he pulled in under a street lamp close to the Seamen's mission. They crossed the road together and she wondered if he would put his arm around her, give her some sign of affection.

She longed to touch him but he seemed wrapped up in thoughts of his own and oblivious to her presence. A queue snaked around the inside of the chip shop and they joined it, standing one behind the other as if they were strangers. Inside the shop it was beautifully warm and the windows were misted with condensation. The talk in the queue was comfortingly domestic: of family rows and minor illnesses. No one mentioned the murders. Anna turned to John hoping to establish some contact with him but at the same time a customer opened the door to leave the shop and John's attention seemed caught by a movement outside.

'What is it?' she asked.

'Nothing,' he said. 'I thought I saw someone I recognized in the street. But it couldn't have been.'

Because he thought he had glimpsed his mother running across the road towards Chandler's Court, her raincoat blown open, and he knew that was impossible. His mother would be at home in their dull grey sitting room waiting for his father to return and provide a brief vicarious excitement with news of his work.

John would not let Anna eat the fish and chips in the car. It was his mother's, he said. She would object to the smell and not let him borrow it again. They sat, huddled in their coats against the cold on a bench looking out over the river and still there was no physical contact between them.

He jumped up impatiently before she had finished, making a ball of the chip papers and throwing it into a rubbish bin.

'Come on,' he said. 'We'll have to go now if we're going to get any sort of view.'

She followed him, caught up by his mood of expectation and his restlessness. Suddenly it seemed the most exciting thing in the world to be out with him with no idea how the evening would end.

This is it, she thought. This is how Abigail Keene felt when she left her stuffy family and went out into the world looking for adventure.

He drove up the hill away from the river past an old industrial estate. Most of the factories were empty and grass grew in cracks through the concrete. The few units still in production were protected by grilles and covered by spray painted graffiti. John turned into a wide street which Anna recognized immediately.

'This is the Starling Farm estate,' she said. She had never been anywhere near the place but she had seen it on the television. There was a small row of shops—a launderette, a bookmaker's, a general store—which had been pelted with rocks and petrol bombs. Further up the street she saw the boarded-up houses, from which even the roof tiles had been looted. Because she had seen it on television she thought the estate was glamorous. It was like seeing a famous film star walking down the street.

'Where are we going?' she asked.

'I told you,' he said. 'To the races.' He reached into the glove compartment and took out a cassette. The car was filled with music and she had no chance to ask what he meant.

The roads were quite empty and almost dark. Some of the street lamps had been shattered in the previous weeks' disturbances. Anna thought it must have been like this in the blitz. She found it hard to believe that behind the blacked-out boarded-up windows families were living normal lives. The association with war-time Britain made the place seem exotic, different from anything she had ever known. It conjured up the nostalgia of an age—big-band music, Land Girls, stolen love affairs before men went away to fight.

John pulled off the road on to a piece of grass, a school playing field. Once it had been separated from the street by a high wire-mesh fence but the fence had been flattened and lay in a tangled heap to one side. In the headlights she saw white football goals, a climbing frame. There were dozens of other cars parked in an orderly line, facing the road. John found a space, switched off the music and the engine. In each of the cars were passengers staring at the darkness. Somewhere in the distance a clock struck ten.

'We were just in time,' John said. His hands were still clenched tight on the steering-wheel. 'Now you'll see.'

But still the street was quiet and she sat, waiting for something to happen.

She heard the engines first, revving up somewhere to the right of them, shattering the silence. Then there was the sound of a horn, loud as a starting gun, and the race had started. Two cars sped past them, bumpers almost touching so close to the audience that Anna could feel the vibration, smell the burnt rubber as they braked to turn the corner. John leaned forward, tense with concentration. It was as if he were competing himself.

'This is the finishing line,' he said. 'They'll do two complete circuits of the estate and end up here.'

'Isn't it dangerous?' she asked.

'Of course it's dangerous!' he said, not taking his eyes from the road. 'That's the point.'

'How can they afford that sort of car,' she asked, 'living here?' They had passed so quickly that she had not been able to identify the make but could tell they were big, powerful, expensive.

'Don't be dumb!' he said. 'They're all stolen. It's hotting. Haven't you heard of it?'

Where do you think I got this one? he wanted to say. I chose it specially because it looks respectable, but it's stolen just the same. I'm an expert. When I put it back tonight they won't even have missed it. But he said nothing. Perhaps some faint instinct of self-preservation remained.

Before she could answer him the cars flashed past again. This time there was a gap between them and he said, almost to himself: 'That's Baz in front. I knew he could do it.' Then, under his breath: 'Hang on, man.'

'You know these people?'

For the first time he looked at her cautiously. 'Some of them,' he said. 'I went to school with some of them.' Then more aggressively: 'It doesn't make them different, you know, living in a place like this.'

'No,' she said. 'Of course not. I didn't mean that.' But as she watched the tail-lights disappear into the darkness she thought that they *were* different. Her conventional upbringing re-asserted itself. 'They're breaking the law,' she said. 'They're criminals.'

'Abigail Keene and Sam Smollett broke the law,' he said savagely. 'We think of them as heroes. It's all a question of perspective.'

As the race reached its climax she expected the audience to leave their cars, to gather together at the roadside to cheer and shout but they remained where they were, insulated from each other by the vehicles. Still she could sense their tension and excitement. John wound down the window to listen for engine noise.

'They'll be changing gear at the Community Centre,' he said, almost to himself. 'Up the hill to the Keel Row. . . Here they come.'

Suddenly the place emptied into noise and light with the blaring of horns and the flashing of headlights to make the end of the race.

'Who was it?' she demanded. 'Was it your friend?'

He looked at her. 'Do you care?'

'Of course I care.'

'Yes,' he said. 'It was Baz.'

'What does he win?' she asked.

'Win? Nothing. He does it for the honour and the glory.'

She stared at him but found it impossible to tell if he was being serious.

'Will you go and congratulate him?'

'No,' he said. 'Not today. I just wanted to be here to see him do it.'

'Is that it?' she said. 'Will there be another race tonight?'

'It depends,' he said, 'if they get the chance.'

'What do you mean?'

'That,' he said suddenly. 'That's what I mean.'

In the distance there was the wailing of a police siren and beyond the houses she saw a flashing blue light.

'Come on,' he said. 'We'll have to get you out of here.'

'But we've done nothing wrong,' she said. 'It can't be illegal to watch them?'

'Do you think that makes any difference to them?'

All around them the cars were scattering, some driving over the grass towards the school. John switched on the ignition and pushed the gear into place. He drove forward with a jerk, swerving to avoid the battered mesh fence, and down the street away from the flashing blue light. He felt drained and exhausted. Was it worth it? he wondered. For a few minutes of excitement.

'Look,' he said. 'I'd better take you home.'

'I won't say anything,' she said. 'About tonight. I won't tell anyone where we've been.'

He shrugged. 'It's up to you,' he said. 'As you say it's not illegal to watch.'

'I'd like to come again,' she said. 'If you're going.'

He looked at her in surprise and realized that he was disappointed. He had been hoping to scare her and she had been excited. She had treated it all as a game.

'All right,' he said. 'But next time I go I'll be racing.'

From the kitchen Prue could not hear the traffic at the front of the house and she went every so often to the front bedroom to peer down the street to watch for her daughter's return. She found it hard to account for her unease. It was not that she believed John could be involved with the murders but she was unsettled. She told herself that there was nothing wrong with him. He was bright, from a respectable family. Most mothers would be glad to entrust their daughters to a boy like that. But it did no good and she could not relax. Absentmindedly she cooked and ate an omelette.

She told herself she should be pleased by Anna's new confidence. Hadn't she spent the past ten years wishing she would be more assertive? Yet as the evening wore on her anxiety increased and she remained in the front bedroom despite the cold, with the curtains slightly open so she could look down into the street below and watch for headlights coming up the hill.

Because of that she saw the car quite clearly, registered that it was new, a bright red Polo. She was surprised when it slowed down and stopped outside the house. Policemen could not be so badly paid, she thought, if they could afford to let their offspring run around in a thing like that, but she felt no real envy. She was just ridiculously relieved to have her daughter safely home. She shut the curtains quickly before Anna could say she'd been prying. Would she invite him in for coffee? Would they kiss? It was not, she supposed, any of her business. When Anna came into the kitchen immediately afterwards she found her mother apparently engrossed in a book.

'Did you have a good time?' Prue asked, stretching as if she had been in the chair for hours.

'Very good, thank you,' Anna replied politely and before Prue could express any further interest in her evening she said she was very tired and would go straight to bed.

Chapter Thirteen

Hunter sat in Ramsay's cottage in Heppleburn, looked at his watch, and thought that by the time he got back to Otterbridge the pubs would be closed. He would have liked half an hour in his local to unwind, a couple of pints, a flirt with the barmaid, a quick game of darts.

'What do you make of it all, then?' Ramsay asked.

It was one of those open questions again, Hunter thought, which were designed to catch you out or make you look foolish. It was bad enough sitting here after a long day's work, drinking the boss's Scotch and pretending they were great chums. What was the man playing at?

Ramsay might have said that he was playing at man management, building a team—he had been sent on all the right courses and knew the jargon—but it was more simple than that. The day had been frantic and he needed time to think, to share his ideas, to test them. Hunter's scepticism, even his prejudice, made him a useful sounding board. Ramsay could sense his sergeant's suspicion but could think of no way of putting him at his ease without appearing patronizing, so he repeated: 'Well, what do you make of it?'

'I don't know, sir. Too many bloody complications.'

'Like what?'

'Like Gabriella's bag being found in Amelia Wood's garden. Like the reservation at the Holly Tree being made in the name of the character Gabby Paston was acting. It's as if someone's playing games. I'd like to know what it all means.'

'I suppose it means,' Ramsay said, 'that a certain amount of calculation has gone into the affair. Someone's trying to cover their tracks. Or send us in the wrong direction. Perhaps there was an attempt to implicate Amelia Wood in the Paston murder by planting Gabby's bag in her garden.'

'Why kill her then? She's not much use as a decoy suspect dead.'

'No,' Ramsay said. 'Quite.' He stood up and prodded the fire with a poker, letting air under the coal, watching the flame with satisfaction. He had lit the fire when they got in and it was only just starting to release some warmth. The curtains at the back of the house were still open and they could see a thin, hazy moon. A tawny owl called very close to the window and made Hunter start. He was glad he didn't have to live out here in the sticks.

Ramsay returned to his seat. 'I know it's unlikely,' he said, 'but I suppose it's just possible that Amelia Wood killed the girl.'

'Then why the second murder?' Hunter thought it was all in the realms of fantasy. Ramsay was taking the idea of considering all the options to extremes.

'I don't know,' Ramsay said. 'Revenge?'

'Hardly. No one cared enough about the girl to bother.'

'Her family?'

'Those two old biddies. You must be joking.'

'I suppose so.' But the thought of Alma and Ellen disturbed him. He could believe Alma Paston capable of anything. 'I'd still like to know why Gabriella first left home,' he said. 'Perhaps we could make some enquiries on the estate.'

'We could try.' Hunter was dubious. 'But that place is like a tinderbox. It'd only need someone to take offence and you'd have a full-scale riot. They're not known for their co-operation with the police.'

'Gabriella was one of them,' Ramsay said. 'They'd surely want her killer found.'

'Was she one of them? She left, didn't she? They wouldn't like that.'

Hunter tried to shuffle his chair closer to the fire.

'I've still not found out who gave her the money to start the savings account,' Ramsay said. 'All the payments were made in cash so the building society can't help. Ellen claims to know nothing about it.'

'Perhaps it was a present from some other relative,' Hunter said. 'Someone on her mother's side. And she didn't tell her gran in case she expected a cut.'

'Yes, perhaps.' But it was unlikely, Ramsay thought, that her mother's family would get in touch after all this time. They would have to be traced just the same. Through the Spanish police.

Hunter emptied his glass and set it on the window sill, hoping that Ramsay would offer a refill but the inspector seemed lost in his own thoughts and did not notice.

'I still think the boy's hiding something,' the sergeant said at last.

'John Powell?'

He nodded.

'I hope he's not involved,' Ramsay said, 'for Evan's sake. It would be very difficult, very unpleasant. He was there of course last night in Martin's Dene at the Holly Tree but he was with his family all the time. I checked with Evan today. And the timing's all wrong. They didn't arrive at the restaurant until nine. Amelia Wood left court before five and told the usher she was going straight home. Allowing for the drive, a shower, tea, she would have been out on the hill by six thirty at the latest. We haven't had a time of death from the pathologist yet but I'd be surprised if it was much later than that.'

'He could have killed her beforehand then,' Hunter said stubbornly. 'According to his statement he arrived home at seven. He left me at the school in the early afternoon. He'd have had plenty of time to get to Martin's Dene.'

'But not to get home after committing the murder,' Ramsay said. 'He doesn't have a car and it would be pushing it on foot or using public transport. Besides, what motive could he have?'

Hunter shrugged. 'As I see it,' he said. 'None of them have got a motive.' He looked wistfully at his empty glass. This time Ramsay took the hint and poured him a drink.

'I was with Lynch between five thirty and six,' Hunter said. 'His car's still with forensic so he'd hardly be able to make it to Martin's Dene in time to kill Mrs Wood. Unless he had an accomplice who drove him and that's not very likely.'

'No,' Ramsay said. 'Perhaps not. But I don't think we can rule anyone out at this stage.'

He stood up and moved restlessly to the window. The cold penetrated the glass and he shivered.

'You're quite right,' he said, 'about our lacking a motive. I'm certain that the killings weren't random or opportunistic. As you said it's all too complicated and well planned for that. We need a motive that connects the two women. The only link we have at the moment is the Grace Darling Centre so we should start there.' He paused. 'I was interested in something Dennis Wood said. About Lynch. Apparently Wood developed the flats at Chandler's Court. He told me that when Lynch was first interested in buying a flat he had difficulty getting together the finance. Then, miraculously, he found the money. I'd like to know where it came from. He won't be making much as director of the Arts Centre. The local authority's not known for its generosity.'

'He must have had savings,' Hunter said, 'after all that time on the telly.' He thought Ramsay was clutching at straws.

'Perhaps,' Ramsay said. 'All the same it might be worth looking into. Check tomorrow with one of those credit agencies. See if he had any debts.'

'What else?' Hunter asked. He preferred to be out, knocking on doors, making things happen.

'It occurred to me that Mrs Wood must have made enemies during her time on the bench. She was notorious for her controversial judgements. There's a record that her car was vandalized after one unpopular decision. Look into all the cases she'd dealt with in the last few months. See if there's anything that connects with Gabriella Paston.'

'All right.' Hunter was unenthusiastic. It was the sort of work he hated, sitting in an office with a pile of paperwork and a telephone. 'What will you be doing?'

'Me?' Ramsay said. 'I'll be tracing a lad called Gary Barrass.'

It did not take Ramsay long the next morning to find out about Barrass, the boy he'd met at the Pastons' on the day after Gabriella's death. The lad already had a string of convictions which ranged from shoplifting to carrying an offensive weapon. He was described in reports as 'easily led'. His most recent charge for burglary had resulted in a six-month sentence at Castington Young Offenders' Institution. At first Ramsay thought that Barrass might provide the link he was looking for between Amelia Wood and the Pastons, but with all his criminal experience he was still a juvenile and Mrs Wood had never sat on the juvenile bench.

The police file gave Gary's address as 53 Windward Avenue, the Starling Farm estate. The whole country had seen Windward Avenue on their television screens in the previous weeks. At one end was the small row of shops which had been the target for looting. It had formed the front line between angry teenagers and the police who had tried to stop their joy riding. Later, politicians, churchmen, and reporters had stood on the pavement to hold forth on the causes of the disturbances.

When Ramsay stood on the same pavement he saw that there had been no improvement to the street since the riots had headed the news. He had parked outside the launderette and wondered, without anxiety, if the car would still be there on his return. Two houses at the end of the avenue still had blackened paintwork and crumbling walls. Bright yellow signs nailed to the wall warned that the buildings were unsafe but otherwise it seemed that no steps had been taken to begin repairs. Ramsay saw that it would not be easy to find number fifty-three. The boards used to cover the doors on the empty houses had been used before and were scrawled all over by painted numbers. Many occupied houses had no numbers at all. Was it a deliberate ploy, Ramsay wondered, to confuse the police? There was no one to ask for directions, no sign of life at all except a pit-bull terrier which barked as he walked past, chained to a rusting car.

Then he came to number thirty-seven, which must have been bought by the tenants when the council's right to buy scheme was first introduced. The house had mock-mullioned windows and a stone-clad exterior. There was a Georgian-style door and a lightly polished brass number plate. The effect was ridiculous but Ramsay could not help but admire the determination which sent someone out every day to polish the brass.

From there he could count the houses until he reached fifty-three. He stood on the pavement for a moment to check that he'd found the right place. It was hard to believe at first that the house was lived in. There were no curtains at the window and in the garden there was a pile of rubbish—a rabbit hutch with a wire-mesh door, an ancient mattress, and a rotting roll of carpet. But as he walked up to the door he saw through the window a Christmas tree made of silver tinsel, hung with baubles and paper chains, and heard a Metro Radio disc jockey announcing the next record then a woman's voice, singing along with it. He knocked at the door.

The woman who opened it was wearing a threadbare pink dressing-gown, so thin in places that it was almost transparent. She clutched it around her with nicotine-stained fingers. As she opened the door the noise of the radio was suddenly louder and she had to shout over it. She was still swaying to the rhythm of the music.

'Yes,' she said. 'What is it?'

'Is Mr Barrass at home?' he asked.

'Him!' she said. 'He left five years ago. I've not seen him since.'

'It doesn't matter,' he said. 'It's Gary I wanted to see. I'm from Northumbria Police.'

'Just a minute,' she shouted. 'I'll turn that off.' And she shimmied reluctantly down the hall to the kitchen, her hips swaying, enjoying the music while she could. There was a sudden silence.

'What's he been up to now?' she said, resigned.

'Nothing,' he said. 'Not so far as I know. It's information I'm after. I think he can help me. That's all.'

'He's still in his bed,' she said. 'Bairns today, they've nothing to get up for, have they? Stay there and I'll rouse him.' She left Ramsay standing in the hall and disappeared up the stairs. He could see through to a kitchen where a box of breakfast cereal and a pile of dirty bowls stood on a table. Presumably there were younger children who had already taken themselves off to school.

The boy came down on his own, stretching and only half awake. He wore black Wrangler jeans and Reebok trainers. His mother hadn't bought *them*, Ramsay thought, from her Income Support. The boy led him through into the room with the Christmas tree and motioned uneasily for him to sit down. There was a leatherette suite and a television set and video recorder. In a corner a budgerigar in a cage on a stand scratched at a piece of millet. The walls were covered with orange gloss paint. Gary Barrass perched on the window ledge and stared out at the street.

I should have sent Hunter to talk to him, Ramsay thought suddenly. He would have shouted and bullied and got what he wanted immediately. He felt his own pity for the boy getting in the way.

'I need to talk to you, Gary,' he said. 'It's important.'

'It's no good asking me,' the boy said. 'I wasn't there.'

'Perhaps you should explain,' Ramsay said evenly.

'I wasn't at the races last night. I can't help you.'

There had been reports of joy riders tearing round the estate, Ramsay knew, and complaints from respectable residents because the police could do nothing to stop it. But the joy riding was a regular event. Gary had seen him with the Pastons and must have connected him with Gabriella's murder. They'd be talking about little else on the estate. Was he too stupid or too sly to admit the connection?

'I'm not here about the racing,' Ramsay said. 'It's more serious than that. I'm investigating Gabriella Paston's murder. Did you know her?'

The boy turned to face him. The corner of an eye twitched with tension.

'Aye,' he said. 'We were at school together. She was two years older than me.'

He was sixteen. From his appearance Ramsay would have guessed he was three years younger.

'You heard what happened to her?'

Gary nodded and Ramsay saw that he was dumb through terror not insolence. Yet he must have been interviewed by the police dozens of times. What was different on this occasion to make him so frightened?

'When did you last see her?' Ramsay asked.

'I don't know,' Gary muttered. 'Not for ages. Not since before I got sent down. She'd left the Starling Farm before I went to Castington.'

'Do you know why she left?'

'No!' the boy cried. 'What are you asking me for? I don't know anything.'

'Yet you seemed very friendly with the Pastons,' Ramsay said quietly. 'With Alma and Ellen. I understood you were a regular visitor. Didn't they say anything about it? Didn't you ever talk about Gabby?'

'No!' he said, looking about him wildly. 'They wouldn't talk to me.' He was like a backward child facing accusations he did not quite understand. He began desperately to bite the fingernails of his left hand.

'What's wrong with you?' Ramsay said. He had allowed his impatience to turn to anger, thinking that it might be a reaction the boy would understand. 'I'm not playing games. We're talking about murder.' Then, when Gary continued to stare dumbly into the street he added sharply: 'Let's get your mam in here. Perhaps she'll help you see sense.' He raised his voice still further. 'Mrs Barrass. Could you come here, please? We need your help.'

She had changed into a pink track suit which was a size too small and stretched across her stomach and breast. Her hands were soapy with washing-up liquid. She stood just inside the door, eager, optimistic, hoping this time it was true Gary had done nothing wrong. She had tried to keep her son out of trouble, always tried to think the best of him, but the pressures of the estate had been too much for her.

'I'm trying to explain to Gary that he should tell me all he knows,' Ramsay said.

She wanted to help him, he was sure of that. He thought she was a good woman, law abiding, honest.

'H' way man Gary, tell the man what he wants to know,' she said. 'Those friends of yours'd do nothing to save you.'

'I'm interested in the Paston household,' Ramsay said. 'Do you know what Gary was doing there?'

Her reaction changed abruptly and he saw a panic which mirrored the expression he had seen on the face of her son.

'No,' she said. 'I don't know anything about what goes on in that place.'

'You're not friendly with the Pastons, then?'

She turned away as if the question were not worth answering. 'Look,' she said. 'I'll keep him in. Make sure he stays away from them.'

'Why?' he said. 'What's wrong with them?'

'I don't know,' she said firmly. 'I keep myself to myself.' She was jolly, good natured. He did not believe her. She'd look forward to a night out with the girls, a few drinks, a bit of a chat.

'Look,' he said, more persuasively. 'I don't need evidence, facts. Not now. There must be talk on the estate about Gabby Paston, about why she left, about her murder. You must have heard rumours about Alma and Ellen Paston.'

'No,' she said, as stubborn as her son. 'I know nothing.'

'But you do *know* them.' But she would tell him nothing more. She stood her ground with a nervous dignity that he could only admire. It was her house, she said, and if he didn't mind they had things to do, her and Gary. She would like him to go.

'I want to help,' he said, as he stood at the door, preparing to leave. 'I'm not here to cause trouble.'

'Maybe not,' she said more sadly. 'But there's no bugger can help us.'

Then she smiled at him hoping there were no hard feelings between them.

In Hallowgate police station Ramsay sought out Evan Powell.

'You know the Starling Farm,' he said. 'What's your opinion of the Paston women?'

'They're mad as hatters,' Powell said. 'The pair of them.'

'In what way?'

'When Robbie Paston died they took it personally. Thought it was my fault. Thought for some reason that I'd meant to do it. Ellen threw a fit at the inquest and accused me of murder. They started sending hate mail. It came here first. Then they must have found out where I lived because it arrived at my home. Nothing subtle, mind. Always the same writing on the same sort of envelopes and in the end I threw the letters away without opening them.'

'You were sure the letters came from them?'

'Of course. Who else would it be?'

'You didn't prosecute?'

'What would have been the point? It would only have made things worse. Feeling was running pretty high on the estate as it was. Imagine how it would have been if we'd took the bereaved relatives to court. If you remember it was the time of the Toxteth riots. We had instructions from above to treat with kid gloves. Much like now. I didn't mind. The Pastons didn't bother me. I thought they'd get used to the idea of Robbie's death, that they'd learn to forgive and forget.'

'Did they?'

'I'm not sure about that but they stopped sending malicious mail. I had a bit of a shock when I joined the choral society. I walked into the Grace Darling cafeteria and saw Ellen behind the bar. She seemed to haunt me for a while after that. Wherever I'd go I'd see her. She never approached me, just stood and watched as if she wanted me to know she was there. But even that stopped when we moved to Barton Hill. Perhaps she's mellowing with age, got better things to do with her time.'

'Yes,' Ramsay said. 'Perhaps.' He paused. 'Do they have a big following on the estate?'

Powell shrugged. 'There was sympathy of course when Robbie died, but that was a long time ago. I wouldn't have thought they'd have much influence now.'

'You don't think they could be stirring up the disturbances on the Starling Farm? As a way of getting back at the authorities?'

Powell laughed. 'I wouldn't put anything past them,' he said. 'But it's a bit far fetched, isn't it, after all this time? Why would anyone take any notice of them? What power could they have?'

'I'm not sure,' Ramsay said. He stood up and seemed about to leave Powell to his work, then returned to the desk.

'Did John know that you were involved in the death of Gabby's father?' he asked. 'Had you warned him to keep his distance?'

Powell shook his head. 'I never talked about it at all,' he said. 'I thought if the Pastons wanted to spread the dirt that was up to them and I'd explain if it arose. And I've never interfered in any of his friendships. I'd have welcomed it if he'd started going out with Gabby. She seemed a pleasant girl and I'd have been glad of a better relationship with the family.'

'He never brought her home?'

'Once,' Powell said. 'We threw a sort of party after the first night of one of the Youth Theatre productions and all the cast came along. Otherwise I've only seen her at the Grace Darling.' He stood up to face Ramsay. 'John isn't involved in all this,' he said. 'He has too much to lose.'

'Yes,' Ramsay said. 'I'm sure you're right.' But he did not meet Powell's eyes and his attention seemed to be elsewhere.

Chapter Fourteen

In the Incident Room at Hallowgate police station Hunter was bored and frustrated. Any junior officer could have undertaken the routine chore of checking Gus Lynch's finances and it was turning out to be more time consuming than he had expected. He wanted to be out on the street, feeling he was getting somewhere. Besides, he was convinced it was all a waste of time. Gus Lynch was a television star. If anyone could afford a spanking new flat down on the Fish Quay it would be him.

When Ramsay came into the Incident Room Hunter was defensive. He wished he had more information to pass on.

'Look,' he said. 'I've nothing for you yet. I'm waiting for some people to call me back.'

'That's all right.' Ramsay was surprisingly calm. All around him was the noise and bustle of people who wanted to prove to a superior that they were busy but he took no notice. 'I'll find someone else to do that. I want you to organize a surveillance team. On the Pastons. I want to know who comes to the house. That's all.'

'Why?' Hunter demanded. 'What have they been up to?'

'I'm not sure,' Ramsay said. 'But people on the estate are frightened of them. I want to know why.'

'Is that all?' What have you got? Hunter thought. You lucky bastard. You're on to something. I can tell.

'Yes.' Ramsay shrugged. Humour me, he implied. 'It's a hunch, I suppose,' he said. 'It's worth a try for a day.'

'Of course,' Hunter said. Anything was better than hours in the office.

'You'll need to be discreet,' Ramsay said. 'It's a quiet street. Any unusual vehicle would be noticed. Don't park directly outside the house. It's a culde-sac, so you'll see anyone approaching from a distance. Any ideas?'

'I'll get hold of a council van,' Hunter said. 'After the disturbances the council sent dozens of officers to assess the damage. No sign of any work being done yet, but you see those red vans parked on every street corner.'

'Fine,' Ramsay said absently. 'Choose your own team.'

'I'll be off then,' Hunter said. He felt a wonderful sense of freedom. This was how villains must feel when they were given bail.

Ramsay took over the investigation of Lynch's finances. The task, methodical and detailed, relaxed him. It was easier at least than being out on the streets confronting people like Gary Barrass and his mother. And as he worked throughout the afternoon he became convinced that he was on to something, and that the information he gathered in tidy piles on his desk was significant.

He went off as often as he could to the top and his politeness and respect combined with his air of authority usually persuaded the people he spoke to that they should help him. From the Director of Finance of Hallowgate Borough Council he learned that Lynch had been in arrears with his community charge two years previously. A summons had been sent and there had been one court appearance. Almost immediately afterwards the debt had been paid in full. The records of the North-East Electricity Board and Northern Gas showed a similar pattern—Lynch had ignored final demands and threats of disconnection and then on the same date had paid up. At around the same time he had miraculously found enough money to put a deposit on the flat at Chandler's Court.

Ramsay thought at first that Lynch's failure to pay his bills might be the result of carelessness, absentmindedness. He was an actor, an artist. Would he consider the settlement of such routine debt as unimportant? But the coincidence was too strong and he began to wonder about the source of the dramatic and timely windfall.

He phoned Prue Bennett at the Grace Darling Centre and made discreet enquiries about the pattern of Lynch's work. She had been his assistant for three years. During that time had he undertaken any outside work? A television part perhaps or an advertisement?

She was bewildered and slightly hostile but answered as accurately as she could.

'No,' she said. 'I don't think so. He's appeared on television during that time of course but as a representative of the Grace Darling, talking about forthcoming productions or as a contributor to a discussion show on the arts.'

'And neither of those would have been particularly lucrative?'

'I shouldn't have thought so. I suppose there would be an appearance fee and expenses but we're only talking about local television, not the *South Bank Show*. What is all this about?'

'Oh,' Ramsay said vaguely, 'it's probably not important. Just routine. You know.'

'No,' she replied tartly. 'I don't.'

'Well,' he said, 'when all this is over perhaps you'd let me explain. . .'

There was a discouraging silence at the end of the telephone. At last she relented. 'I have some news about Gus which might interest you,' she said. 'A news release has gone to the press today so you'll hear about it soon anyway. He's leaving the Grace Darling in the new year. He's going to be artistic director of a theatre in the West Country. It's quite a step up for him actually, after running a community project like this. He's horribly pleased with himself.'

So, Ramsay thought, there was another interesting coincidence: Lynch had decided to leave the Grace Darling immediately after the deputy chairwoman of trustees had been murdered. But could it have any real significance? The move must have been planned months before. It could hardly have been triggered by Amelia Wood's death. Then it occurred to him that Lynch's resignation might have been the subject of his conversation with Amelia Wood on the night that Gabriella Paston's body was found. If so, why had he been so secretive about it in the interview? He could surely have trusted the police not to release the news of his resignation until he was ready to make the move public. Ramsay made a cup of strong black coffee and sat in the gloomy office to drink it, allowing different ideas to connect in his mind until he had come up with a theory.

He phoned the Woods' home in Martin's Dene but there was no reply so he dialled Dennis Wood's business number. A breathy young receptionist said: 'How may I help you?' and 'Please hold,' then a computer played a tuneless jingle in his ear as he waited. The synthesized music irritated him so intensely that he was about to replace the receiver when Wood's voice came on quite suddenly.

'Inspector,' he said. 'What can I do for you?'

'I'm interested in any records Mrs Wood might have kept on the Grace Darling Centre. Presumably she had minutes of trustees' meetings, copies of accounts, that sort of thing. Where would I find them?'

'In her office at home. She had a filing system which would put any business to shame. Look, I'm not expecting to be home until later but you've still got a key. Why don't you help yourself?'

So in the late afternoon Ramsay drove to Martin's Dene. He slowed down in the village past the Georgian terrace inhabited mostly now by university lecturers from Newcastle and past the Holly Tree restaurant where two businessmen were emerging from a late lunch. St Martin's Close was quiet. The big houses were set well back from the trees. He thought it was not surprising that none of the residents had seen a strange car in the street on the evening of Amelia's death.

He let himself into the house and switched off the alarm. The dog, apparently shut up in the kitchen, began to bark but again the houses were too far apart for any neighbours to hear and worry about intruders. Eventually the animal lapsed into an exhausted silence. The study was a pleasant square room at the side of the house. Along one wall was a set of filing cabinets and it seemed that, as Wood had said, Amelia's record keeping had been meticulous. A three-drawer cabinet was given over entirely to the affairs of the Grace Darling Centre and Ramsay began at the top and worked his way carefully through the envelope files contained there.

Copies of the minutes of trustees' meetings went back to the opening of the Centre. Amelia, apparently, had been on the steering committee which lobbied for its formation and began the unending business of fund-raising. In none of the meetings, however, had there been any discussion about Lynch in relation to financial matters. If Amelia had any suspicions about his integrity she had kept them to herself. Next came a bundle of copy letters sent out to local businesses asking for sponsorship of the Arts Centre. It seemed that Amelia had experimented with the format of the letter and had made a note of the different levels of response to each one. Ramsay wondered how many other local charities would be equally efficient and if Lynch had been aware of the degree of detailed interest that Amelia had taken in the finances of the scheme.

About three years previously the borough council had cut its grant to the Centre. The council had been threatened with poll-tax capping and the Community Arts fund had been chopped in half. Amelia had been put in charge of a special fund-raising exercise for the Grace Darling, an attempt to replace the missing grant. She had kept a list of the sponsorship she had achieved during that time. The sums were substantial and had totalled more than fifty thousand pounds. Amelia had been a persuasive woman.

Pinned to the back of the word-processed list of sponsors was a bank statement covering the period of fund-raising. Amelia had ticked off each entry as it appeared on the statement but it seemed that one of the sponsors had failed to meet its commitment to the Centre, or at least that its cheque had not been paid into the bank. A company called Northumbria Computing had pledged ten thousand pounds over two years but there was no record of the amount on the bank statement. Amelia had obviously seen the omission because beside the company's name on the list was a large question mark.

Ramsay allowed himself a moment's self-congratulation. He must be right. The theory devised in his office was almost proved. He was convinced that a fraud had taken place.

Then he began to wonder how it had been done. Surely Northumbria Computing would have made its cheque payable to the Grace Darling Centre, not to Gus Lynch personally. How then had he managed to get his hands on the money? And if Amelia

Wood had realized that he had stolen from the trust, why hadn't she taken steps to bring the matter to light? If she had taken her suspicions to an auditor he would discover immediately what had happened to the money. Ramsay could understand that a charity like the Grace Darling would want to avoid damaging publicity but there were ways to deal with the thing discreetly. He had seen it done before.

When Prue Bennett left her office at six o'clock she came across Ramsay in the lobby, leaning on Joe Fenwick's desk, chatting to the porter as if they were old friends. It was clear that he was waiting for her, and she did not know what to make of it. She had persuaded herself that she rather despised him. There was something grubby and unpleasant about his prying into other people's business. Yet now she found his presence reassuring.

'I'm glad to have bumped into you,' he said, as if the meeting had been quite by chance. 'There are one or two questions I need to clear up.'

'I can't stop now,' Prue said. 'Anna will be expecting me. We've hardly seen each other in the last few days.'

'Perhaps I could come back with you,' he said, 'if it wouldn't be too much of an intrusion.'

She would have liked to assert her authority, to tell him to get lost, but she couldn't quite manage it. She was curious and it was hard to see him now as the sleazy detective she had long imagined. Most of her friends were younger, people she'd met through the theatre. They were enthusiastic, passionate, changing their philosophies to suit the latest trend. They were fun. Ramsay's solidness and constancy was different and attractive.

'No,' she said. 'It wouldn't be an intrusion.'

She wondered if she should invite him for a meal then thought that might cause him embarrassment. Perhaps there was some rule preventing policemen eating with the murder suspects. There should be.

He followed her up the dual-carriageway to Otterbridge in his own car. She saw his headlights in her mirror and though she usually drove home far too fast she maintained the regulation 60 m.p.h. Is this what it would be like? she thought. Living with a policeman? Having to keep all the rules. Could I stand it?

In the house the lights were on and as usual she called up the stairs to Anna. Ramsay followed her through to the kitchen where she automatically switched on the kettle then took a tin from the fridge to feed the cat. Anna wandered in ten minutes later, poured herself a mug of tea and went away without a word.

'I'm sorry,' Ramsay said. 'You wanted some time together.'

'That's all right,' Prue said. 'She's not communicating much anyway. I think she's in love.'

'Who's the subject of her affection?'

'John Powell. He took her out last night.' She smiled, making a joke of her unease. 'You policemen can't be badly paid,' she said. 'He brought her home in a very smart new Polo. His mother's apparently. My car's fifteen years old and held together with string.'

'It's about money that I want to talk to you,' he said.

He had intended to stick to a story that his enquiries into the Grace Darling finances were a matter of routine police work, but she was too intelligent to believe that. Even after all these years she knew him too well. He saw that the only way to obtain her co-operation was to tell her the truth.

'I think Gus Lynch might have been stealing from the Arts Centre,' he said. 'Had you ever suspected anything like that?'

She shook her head. 'But I'd have no way of knowing,' she said.

'Amelia Wood had a bank statement which seems to show that any payment to the Grace Darling—grants from the local authority and money from sponsors—was put on deposit and transferred into the current account when it was needed.'

'Yes,' she said. 'That's right. I was joint signatory to both accounts.'

'Presumably each year the trustees would appoint an auditor to go through the books and make sure that any cheque from either account had a legitimate purpose. You had to keep receipts?'

She nodded. 'Of course.'

'I want to know if there was another account,' he said quietly.

'A secret account that the trustees didn't know about and the auditors never got to see.'

She blushed. 'There was nothing dishonest in that,' she said defensively. 'Gus started it soon after I arrived. There'd been a fuss about the expenses he claimed after a Youth Theatre production which we took to the Berwick Festival. He'd hired a minibus. The trustees said he should have charged the parents for the transport cost and that in future he should consult them before making a similar gesture. He was furious and said he wasn't going to them every time he needed five pounds from the petty cash. They should trust him. He'd given up enough to come and work for them.'

'So he opened a new account in the Grace Darling's name?'

She nodded. 'With the Wallsend and Hallowgate Building Society. We paid in money that didn't go through the books—small cash donations given by the public, money raised by the kids in informal fund-raising events, that sort of thing. It was used on projects which the trustees might not have approved of. For instance last summer we hired a mime artist to run a workshop and paid him from the account. I suppose it wasn't strictly honest but there was nothing illegal going on.'

'You were joint signatory on that account too?'

'Yes. The banks and building societies insist on two signatures for charitable accounts.'

'Did you always watch Mr Lynch write the cheque before signing it?'

'No,' she said. 'Of course not. You know what it's like. It's always a mad house there, always busy. He rushes into my office waving the cheque book. "Sign a couple of cheques for me pet. I'm just on my way into town." So I sign them.'

'Without asking what they're for?'

'Sometimes,' she admitted, 'if it's really hectic. Usually he tells me what they're for—costume hire or transport or to take some supporters for a meal.'

'You never check?'

'No,' she said. 'Of course not.'

'The building society must send you a statement every six months.'

She shrugged. 'I suppose so. I've never seen it.'

'Who opens your mail? A secretary?'

'Oh,' she said, 'the trustees don't believe in paying proper secretaries. We've had a series of YTS trainees who leave us just as they're getting competent.' She paused. 'You think Gus was making out the cheques I'd signed to himself?'

'More probably for cash. That would be less easy to trace.'

'How much did he get away with then?' she asked cheerfully. 'Fifty quid? A hundred? There could never have been much more than that in the account.'

'Oh, considerably more than that,' he said. 'I believe that Mr Lynch paid some sponsorship money into the account. A firm called Northumbria Computing donated ten thousand pounds to the Grace Darling about three years ago.'

'And you believe he took all that?' She was astounded.

'Not all at once,' Ramsay said. 'I think he withdrew it in cash. Over a period.'

'And I signed the bloody cheques,' she said. 'What a bastard!'

There was a silence. In her room Anna was playing lyrical and sentimental music. Prue took a knife and a board from a drawer and began violently to chop an onion.

'It isn't the theft itself which is of most concern at the moment,' Ramsay said. 'It provides a motive, you see, for Mrs Wood's murder.'

'You think she found out about it?' Prue stood, poised for a moment with the knife in her hand. 'Do you think that's why he decided to look for another job?'

'I think it's almost certain that she suspected he'd been stealing,' Ramsay said, almost to himself. 'She'd have heard from her husband that he wanted to buy the flat in Chandler's Court. She might even have been on the bench when Lynch was charged with non-payment of the community charge. So she went through the bank statement herself to check. But it all happened years ago. If she'd wanted to get rid of him she'd have done it before now.'

'But she wouldn't have wanted to get rid of him!' Prue was suddenly excited, caught up in the investigation despite herself. 'Don't you see, he was the best thing that had ever happened to the Grace Darling. He was a famous actor. Even better, a local famous actor. It meant that we got all the publicity we could handle. It meant that the Grace Darling was successful when other similar projects were closing down. It would be worth ten grand to her to keep him.'

'So you're saying that she used the information that he'd been stealing to put pressure on him to stay? A sort of blackmail?'

She nodded.

'It's certainly very significant that he only decided to announce his resignation on the day after she died,' Ramsay said.

'Does that mean,' Prue said incredulously, 'that you think he killed her?'

'There's no evidence,' he said slowly. 'We need more than motive.' He knew this was all a mistake. He had no right to discuss the case with Prue. He had never been so unprofessional, but he was certain he could trust her discretion. She had information he needed, and he continued: 'Besides, there's Gabriella Paston. Where could she fit into all this? Is there any way, do you think, that she could have discovered the fraud?'

'I don't know,' Prue said. 'I think Gus gave her a contribution towards her RADA audition expenses from the building society account but she'd surely have no way of knowing where it came from. Unless. . .' she hesitated.

'Yes?'

'Unless Ellen told her. Ellen Paston. She's a dreadful snoop. I've even caught her going through the mail on my desk. It would be hard to keep anything in that place secret from her.'

'And we know that Gabby met Ellen regularly. It's marked in her diary.' It's all coming together, he thought. At last. Gabby and Ellen met for a gossip. Of course Ellen would pass on her suspicions. There was no more juicy gossip than dishonesty of a famous man. And then Gabby must have acted on it. Surely the contribution towards audition expenses wasn't all she received from Lynch. There was the five hundred pounds which started her savings account. It couldn't be coincidence that both murder victims had blackmailed the director.

'All the same,' Prue said. 'I can't believe it of Gus Lynch. He wouldn't have the guts.'

She stood up and rinsed mushrooms under the tap, then returned to the board to slice them.

'You do understand,' he said awkwardly, 'that this is all confidential. I'm sorry. I've put you in an unfair position. You have to work with the man. But I must ask you to keep it secret.'

'Oh,' she said lightly. 'I've always been good at secrets. Are you going home? To your cottage in Heppleburn? I should like to see it some time.'

'No,' he said. 'Back to the police station. There's still work to do. It won't be long, I hope, now.' He touched her shoulder clumsily, but there was no invitation to his cottage and she thought she had made a fool of herself. He was only interested in her as a means of clearing up his case.

Back at Hallowgate police station Ramsay wondered why he had not asked Prue to come to Heppleburn. He would like to have shown her the cottage. He was busy but he could have made some vague, friendly gesture. He decided that a sort of superstition had prevented him. He did not have a good record in protecting the women he came close to in murder cases. He wanted to keep her safe and when the investigation was over he would make his move.

The telephone rang. It was Hunter reporting on the surveillance operation outside the Pastons' house. He had called it off now, he said. The van would cause suspicion if it were parked there after dark. Especially if it was there in the morning with all the wheels still on.

'How did it go?' Ramsay asked. He thought his interest now was academic. Gus Lynch must be his most likely suspect.

'It was like St James's Park on Derby match day, kids in and out all afternoon. And one of the visitors might interest you.'

'Who was it?' He tried to sound excited to humour Hunter.

'John Powell. Now what do you make of that?'

Chapter Fifteen

By the next morning the weather had changed. The wind had gone westerly and was mild and damp, carrying squalls of rain. In Hallowgate police station Ramsay and Hunter had a meeting with the superintendent. From his office at the front of the building they saw the bright splash of colour of the yellow oilskins worn by the men driving fork-lift trucks on the Fish Quay against the grey of the river. Ramsay stared out at the scene below him and found it hard to concentrate.

'So,' the superintendent said, 'what are we going to do about Gus Lynch?'

'I'm not sure.' Ramsay knew he must appear indecisive and tried to gather his thoughts. 'I'm tempted to bring him in for questioning on suspicion of fraud but technically that's awkward because the Grace Darling trustees have never reported a crime. The matter's complicated of course by his high profile.'

'You've not got enough to charge him with murder?'

Ramsay shook his head. 'There's nothing to put him in Martin's Dene on the evening of Amelia Wood's death. We had his car and so far no one's come forward to say that they gave him a lift. Of course someone might be protecting him. But until we have something more substantial than motive to link him to the murders it would be too risky to bring him in.'

They all knew the problem: once the PACE clock started ticking there was only a limited time before a decision had to be made whether to charge or release a suspect. And if Lynch was released after questioning Ramsay would have shown his hand and given the actor the opportunity to cover his tracks. That's why he hadn't asked to see the slush account records.

'Of course we do have substantial evidence to implicate Lynch in the Paston murder,' the superintendent said. 'Her body was found in the boot of his car.'

'Yes.' But Ramsay's voice was uncertain. Paradoxically it was only the body in the car which made him question their case against Lynch. An intelligent man would have found somewhere to dump it. But perhaps it was all an elaborate counterbluff. Or the result of the sort of panic which leads to inaction.

'There's nothing we can do without more evidence,' he said, taking a decision at last. 'We can't even talk to him informally about the missing funds without giving too much away. We need proof that he was in Martin's Dene on Monday lunch time and Tuesday evening. Either a witness or forensic evidence. He's well known. You'd think he'd be recognized. We've taken the clothes he was wearing on Tuesday for testing but there's no result yet.'

'I presume you've checked his alibi that he was in the pub in Anchor Street on Monday lunch time?' The superintendent spoke apologetically, implying he was sure they had checked, but they must realize that he had to ask.

'Yes,' Hunter said. 'He was definitely there. But the barmaid thought it was early, about twelve, and we know from Ellen Paston that Gabby was still in Hallowgate then. She was seen running through the market.'

'She might have been killed somewhere in Hallowgate, of course,' Ramsay said almost to himself. 'We know she never reached the Holly Tree. It's only supposition that she got to Martin's Dene. We've had no response from the press campaign asking for witnesses and you'd think someone would have noticed her if she were waiting outside the restaurant. It's a busy road. . .'

'So we're agreed then,' the superintendent said, 'that we make no move to question Lynch, at least over the weekend. We can re-assess the situation on Monday. We should have something back from forensic by then.' He looked up at them. 'What about this other business on the Starling Farm?' he asked. 'Is that relevant to the murder enquiry or is it just something you've turned up in the course of the investigation?'

'It's hard to say at this stage, sir,' Hunter said. 'But I'd like to get a search warrant to find out what is happening in the Pastons' bungalow. There's something going on in that place. There were kids running in and out all day. If you ask me it's a right Fagin's den.'

The superintendent raised his eyebrows.

'You have evidence for that?'

'Look,' Hunter leaned forward earnestly. 'I've been asking around the station, talking to officers who know the patch. They've suspected for ages that someone was organizing these car thefts, getting rid of the stuff stolen for them from the kids who nick it. Twelve lads went to that house during the course of our surveillance yesterday. Some were carrying boxes and bags. And they weren't all collecting for bob a job.'

'But two single ladies. They wouldn't know how to go about it.' Ramsay was sceptical.

'Why not?' Hunter demanded. 'Robbie must have carried out a similar business from the same premises.'

Ramsay was silent. He thought Hunter's Fagin analogy was a good one. There was something Dickensian and grotesque about Alma Paston. 'I suppose it would be an excellent cover,' he said. 'Who would suspect them?'

'You do realize how sensitive this could be?' the superintendent said. 'It's not only that the estate's so tense at the moment, and any heavy-handed police operation could provoke worse violence. It's the Pastons. Memories on the Starling Farm go back a long way. They all remember Robbie Paston. They thought he was a bastard when he was alive but his death turned him into a folk hero. If news gets out that we've been harassing Robbie Paston's defenceless mother and sister the whole place'll go up. We'll have to tolerate a bit of unlawful receiving until the mood there improves. There's no way I can authorize a search.'

'But there could be more to it than unlawful receiving!' Hunter said. 'We've been looking all along for a link between Gabriella

Paston and Amelia Wood, something more than their involvement with the Grace Darling. Perhaps this is it. If the Pastons were dealing in stolen goods Gabby must have known. Perhaps that's why she left home. She didn't want to be involved any more. She knew she had too much to lose. And on the day of her death Amelia Wood convicted Tommy Shiels, a bloke from the estate who was selling nicked car radios. He wouldn't tell Evan Powell who was organizing the racket but perhaps he said something in court which gave Mrs Wood an idea what was going on.'

'I don't know,' Ramsay said. 'That's not very likely. What would Amelia Wood know about it?'

'All right,' Hunter said, unabashed. 'Perhaps not. But there's the John Powell connection. That must be significant.'

'Powell?' The superintendent looked up sharply. 'Evan's boy?'

Ramsay nodded. 'He was one of the teenagers who visited the place yesterday.'

'This would explain why John Powell kept Gabby Paston at arm's length,' Hunter said. 'Everyone said she fancied him but he pretended not to be interested. He wouldn't want her tagging along, talking to his mates. If she knew what was going on at the bungalow she could soon put two and two together.'

'And if she did,' Ramsay said slowly, 'we've got another motive for murder.'

'We have to get into that bungalow,' Hunter said excitedly. 'See what's going on there.'

'No,' the superintendent said sharply. 'And certainly not today at the start of the weekend when all the wild boys on the Starling Farm will be tanked up and ready for trouble. I'll not take the risk. You can continue making discreet enquiries. We'll see how the mood is on the estate at the beginning of next week. I'll reconsider my decision then.'

Hunter opened his mouth to argue but the superintendent interrupted him. 'I'm sorry. It isn't up for discussion. Besides anything else there's the weekend overtime to consider. We're already over budget!' He smiled but it was only half a joke. 'Have a break,' he said. 'You could both do with a rest. You'll come back to it fresh on Monday.'

They stood to leave and Hunter was already out of the room when he called Ramsay back. 'Stephen,' he said. 'I'd like a few words. On our own.'

Ramsay shut the door and returned to his seat.

'I'm worried about young Powell's part in all this,' the superintendent said. 'You must see that it has wider implications. If he's on the fringe of some teenage gang stealing cars that's one thing. Of course we prosecute. Charge him with all the others. It'll be embarrassing for Evan but there's no alternative. It's happened before. . .'

He paused.

'What are the wider implications?' Ramsay asked, to help him out.

'The possibility that Evan Powell is in some way involved. That's the nightmare. Either personally or by covering up for the lad.'

'Why should he be involved personally?'

'I don't know. He took a lot of stick from the Paston family and the community after Robbie's death. At the time I thought he handled it well but perhaps it affected him more than we realized. Then there's the possibility that all the facts of Robbie Paston's accident didn't come out at the enquiry. If he's been hiding something for all this time he could be dangerous.'

'Yes,' Ramsay said. 'I see. What do you want me to do about it?'

'Talk to him. Talk to the boy. Try to get a picture of what's going on there.'

'And if I find out that Evan or his son is involved?'

'We deal with it. Out in the open. There's no other course to take.'

It was still raining when Ramsay went to the Powells' house at six o'clock. He had found out that Evan had finished work at five. He hoped to catch the whole family in, to get at least an impression of the relationships between them. He thought that the superintendent was expecting too much of him and there would be little else he could achieve. Evan opened the door to him.

'Come in, man,' Evan said. 'Have some tea. You'll drown out there.'

'I was hoping to speak to John,' Ramsay said. It was almost true.

'He's not here yet. He'll be in the library revising. He's got 'A' levels this year and he's dead keen. But now you're here you'll come in all the same.'

'Well,' Ramsay said, 'if Mrs Powell won't mind.'

Inside the house he stopped, awkwardly, hesitating at the expanse of grey carpet in the living room. He wondered if he should take off his shoes but in the end dried them carefully on the door mat and followed Evan through to the kitchen.

'We've got a visitor,' Evan said cheerfully. 'I don't think you've met my wife, Stephen. Jackie, this is Stephen Ramsay, a colleague. Put the kettle on, love, and make some tea.'

She stood up and Ramsay saw a thin woman with high cheekbones and intense grey eyes. She said nothing and he was surprised. He would have expected Evan's wife to be more conventional, more restful.

'I'm sorry to disturb you,' he said. 'I was hoping to talk to your son.'

'Why?' she demanded. 'What do you think he's done?'

'Nothing,' Evan intervened reassuringly. 'What would he have done? It's all a matter of routine. That's right, isn't it?'

Ramsay said nothing.

'You won't mind if I get on,' Evan said. He was in the middle of preparing a meal. On the table was a chopping board laid out with green chillies, peppers, an aubergine, root ginger. There were jars of spices and Madhur Jaffrey's *Indian Cookery* was propped open against the garam masala. 'I always do a curry on Friday night if I'm not working, don't I, love?'

'Oh, yes,' she said. Ramsay recognized the irony in her voice but Evan seemed not to notice. 'It's always curry on Friday.'

'Why don't you stop and have a meal with us,' he said. 'It can't be much fun having to fend for yourself. John'll be back soon. You can talk to him then.'

'No, thank you,' Ramsay said. 'It's very kind, but I don't think so.'

'Can we help you, then?' Evan said.

'Yes,' Ramsay said. 'Perhaps you can. Does John have any friends who live on the Starling Farm estate?'

'I expect so,' Evan said. 'Kids from there go to the sixth form college. We don't encourage it but you can't choose their friends for them.'

'Was he on the Starling Farm yesterday afternoon?'

'He might have been. After school. He wouldn't tell us. He'd know we'd disapprove.'

'He used to hang around with Connor,' Jackie said. 'He works at the Community Centre. John might have gone there to see him.'

'Connor?' Ramsay asked.

'I'm sorry,' she said. 'I don't know his second name. They were at first school together.'

'No,' Ramsay said. 'I don't think John went to the Community Centre. He was seen coming out of the Pastons' house.'

'Don't be daft!' Evan said. 'What would he have been doing there? Someone's trying to wind you up. To get back at me.'

Ramsay did not answer. Something had been troubling him since he had come to the house at Barton Hill, an inconsistency which had been niggling at his subconscious throughout the exchange with Evan Powell.

'Is that your car on the drive, Mrs Powell?' he asked abruptly.

'The Renault? Yes. Evan keeps his car in the garage. Why?'

'Did you loan your car to your son on the evening before last?'

'No. He might have taken it, though. He knows he can use it whenever he likes. That's not a crime.' But she was uneasy.

'*You* didn't use it then?'

'I might have done,' she said. 'I can't remember. Was that the night I was babysitting?'

She turned to her husband but he shook his head. 'I don't know,

I was at work on Wednesday.' Even as he spoke he watched Ramsay, trying to judge where the questions were leading.

The inspector ignored Evan's stare and continued with his questions to Jackie.

'You don't own a red Volkswagen Polo?'

'Of course not!' She was losing patience. 'What would I want with two cars?'

'I think,' Evan said, 'you'd better explain what this is about.'

'On Wednesday night John was driving a red Volkswagen Polo,' Ramsay said. 'He claimed it was yours, Mrs Powell.'

'What business is it of yours what John was driving on Wednesday?' Evan said. Concern had made him angry. 'And how do you know he was on the Starling Farm yesterday? Are you following him? What gave you the right to do that?'

His hands were shaking and he could hardly control his temper. 'I didn't think you used that sort of tactic, Stephen. I didn't think that was your style of policing. Harassing young kids.'

'There's no question of harassment,' Ramsay said. He was hating this confrontation. He was tempted to apologize and leave, to take the superintendent's advice and give himself a break. 'The information came up on the course of routine enquiries.' He paused. As in the conversation with Mrs Barrass he knew it would be impossible to convince Evan that he wanted to help. He would have to let the facts speak for themselves.

'We suspect the Pastons of trading in stolen goods,' he said. 'John was one of a number of young people seen going to the house during a surveillance operation. There must be some suspicion that the car he was driving on Wednesday was stolen.'

'No!' Evan shouted. 'You must be mad? Why would he do something like that?'

Ramsay ignored the outburst and continued calmly: 'If your son is on the fringe of illegal activity on the Starling Farm estate it wouldn't be so terrible. He'd be prosecuted, of course. You'd not want any special treatment for him. But we're most concerned with the murder. He's a first offender. He'd get probation, community service, specially if he gave himself up. It wouldn't need to interrupt his education. But don't you see? If he doesn't explain his part in it now, there's a danger that he could get mixed in the murder investigation. None of us want that.'

'No,' Evan bellowed again. 'I'll not accept it.' He sat at the table with his head in his hands then began again, more reasonably: 'Have you any evidence that the Polo was stolen?'

Ramsay shook his head. 'The significance didn't occur to me until I saw your wife's car on the drive.'

'Then he could have borrowed it from a friend, anything. The least you could do is check that a similar vehicle had been reported missing before you come here making accusations. Without that you've nothing to go on.'

'Of course I'll check,' Ramsay said. He stood up. 'But you will talk to John,' he said. 'If he's involved in any way he should tell us. You can call me at home over the weekend if you don't want to take him in to the station.'

'I'll talk to him,' Evan said. 'But don't expect to hear from me. You've made some mistakes in your career, Ramsay, but none as big as this.'

And with the hint of that threat between them Ramsay left.

Outside it was still raining. Ramsay ran from the house to the car, but put his foot in the gutter and still managed to get wet. In the doorway Evan stood and watched until he drove off. Ramsay was in his own car and switched on the radio and tuned to *The Archers*, hoping that the rural fantasy would distract him, at least for a while, from his sense of failure. But he could not concentrate and in the end he drove in silence back to the police station.

He thought he had achieved none of the objectives the superintendent had set him. He had alienated Evan Powell without coming to any conclusion about John's role in the car thefts. He still did not know the extent of Evan's knowledge—was he protecting his son? It had been foolish and ill thought-out to ask about Mrs Powell's car. If course he should have found out first if a Polo had been stolen. If he had gained anything positive from the interview it was a firm belief that Evan was innocent of any part in the murders. His hostility had been on his son's behalf. He had no personal fear, no idea even that his integrity was being questioned.

The police station was quiet. There was a smell of damp which reminded Ramsay as he entered of an empty school changing-room. The walls ran with condensation and everywhere was too hot. The people who remained in the Incident Room were tense and expectant. Friday night was busy in the town—all the recent disturbances had taken place at the weekend. Everyone who could be spared was out on the street. For a moment Ramsay wished that he was one of them, sharing the camaraderie of the relief, with no responsibility except to do as he was told.

Hunter was still in the Incident Room. His desire to get a search warrant for the Pastons' house was stronger than his dislike of paperwork. He was going through the details of young people convicted of auto-crime, matching the descriptions with the visitors he had seen going to the house on the previous day. Besides, he wanted to be around if something exciting happened. Something like arson or riot. Hunter had a very low boredom threshold and he was prepared to sacrifice a night out with the lads for a chance like that.

'Can you do something for me?' Ramsay said. 'Find out if a Volkswagen Polo was reported stolen in the last few days. Red. J Reg. I haven't got the number.'

'Is it relevant to the murders?'

'Probably not.'

He went to his office, watched the rain on the window and brooded. Hunter knocked on the door.

'No,' he said. 'No car of that description's been reported stolen.'

So, Ramsay thought. Evan was right. He had no evidence against John. That did not mean of course that the car had *not* been stolen. It could have been replaced in the street without the owner realizing it had gone. The record of the theft could be lost, the owner away on holiday. But it meant they could take no further action. At least until after the weekend. It meant that he could go home and get quietly drunk.

Hunter was on his way out of the office when he stopped. 'I

forgot to tell you,' he said. 'You had a phone call when you were out. From Joe Fenwick, that security man at the Arts Centre. He wants to talk to you. I offered to go but I wouldn't do apparently. He said he'd be at home at his flat in Anchor Street. I told him you'd probably not get to see him tonight but he said he'd wait in anyway.'

'I think I'd better go,' Ramsay said. He liked Fenwick. He didn't want him to wait in all evening hoping for a visit. Hunter shrugged and went back to the control room, to listen for news coming in from the town.

Ramsay put on the overcoat, which was still wet, and went out. The streets were quiet but it was early, not nine o'clock, and any troublemakers would need a few pints inside them before facing the rain.

So, instead of getting drunk at home, he found himself sitting in the steaming basement flat in Anchor Street, listening to Joe's stories of his life in the ring. They drank whisky together and Ramsay made no attempt to hurry the old man. He realized it wouldn't come easy to him to tell tales. When he left the flat at eleven o'clock there was a fire on the horizon and all the cranes along the river stood out in silhouette against the flames.

Chapter Sixteen

The weekend passed in an uneasy peace. There were occasional disturbances which would probably have passed unnoticed if the situation had been less tense. The fire Ramsay had seen on Friday night was in a derelict warehouse close to the river. The arson looked dramatic but the damage was limited. It was rumoured that some lads from the Starling Farm had been paid by the owner to set the place alight. It was well insured and he was planning to redevelop the site with a retail park.

On Saturday afternoon Newcastle United lost 3-1 to Bristol Rovers at St James's Park after a scrappy and uninspired game. The fans were frustrated and angry and there were scuffles at the metro station as they left. The only casualty was a student from the West Country who was jostled and lost his footing when a group of supporters heard his accent. He had not even attended the match and his injuries were superficial. The incident would have been ignored during a normal weekend but the police moved in quickly to break up the crowd and move the boy to safety.

On Sunday, in the early evening, the joy riders returned to the Starling Farm. There was more racing in the street and a spectacular show of hand-brake turns performed to the audience who had been charged a pound each for a grandstand view. The police waited for the crowd to disperse before moving in, thinking that there would be little resistance if the spectators had had their money's worth. The episode ended in good humour and the policemen on the ground began to think that the worst of the tension was over.

Ramsay followed the developments at a distance. On Saturday

morning he drove to Hallowgate police station and haunted the Incident Room, waiting for news. Still no witnesses had come forward to confirm that Gabriella Paston had actually arrived at Martin's Dene, despite a piece in the *Journal* and on local television.

'Sorry, sir,' a young woman DC said. 'It's as if she disappeared.'

'And Lynch's car? The blue Volvo. Did anyone see that?'

The policewoman shrugged. One witness thinks she saw a blue saloon parked on the edge of the hill that day—at the layby where one of the footpaths begins.' She tapped into the computer. 'Her name's Hilda Wilkinson. I'm not sure how reliable she'll be. She's an elderly lady who was walking her dog and she seems pretty absentminded. She can't tell us the make of the vehicle, never mind the age or registration number.'

'Go and talk to her again,' Ramsay said. 'Why would she remember a car? She probably doesn't drive and it would have no interest for her. But she might remember someone she met on the hill. If she's a local she might know if it was a stranger. She might even have tried to engage them in conversation. Don't put ideas into her head but if she comes up with a description like this let me know immediately. . .' He spoke quickly and precisely and watched as the DC wrote in her notebook.

Ramsay went to the CID room and then to the canteen to look for Evan Powell. He needed to re-establish contact. There were still questions to be asked and after the conversation with Joe Fenwick the questions had become more urgent, but he was told by a colleague that Powell had taken the weekend off too. Ramsay tried to phone him at home several times but there was no reply. At lunch time he decided he might as well be at home.

He worked the afternoon in the garden, leaving the kitchen window open so he would hear the phone if it rang. The rain had stopped but the air was misty and damp. He raked dead leaves from the lawn and as he moved rhythmically across the grass the unformed ideas which had disturbed him throughout the investigation grew more substantial. The theory which had seemed possible the evening before now seemed probable, but he felt none of the satisfaction which usually marked the approaching end of the case. He thought he knew what happened but many of the details were still unclear and he took no pleasure in it.

By four o'clock all the light had gone and he went inside. He took a basket of laundry into the living room and ironed shirts as he watched the football results come through on the television. He had no interest in sport but still felt a tribal allegiance to the team his family had supported since he was a child and there was an irrational disappointment when he learned they had lost.

He wondered what his mother would think if she could see him. When Diana had divorced him Mrs Ramsay had wanted her son to move back home so she could care for him properly. His room was still ready for him. She thought it inconceivable that a man could fend for himself. He couldn't tell her that Diana had never ironed a shirt in their married life, that he had usually been the one to cook, that he wouldn't have wanted it any other way. When he had moved to the cottage in Heppleburn, without actually lying he allowed his mother to gain the impression that he employed a woman from the village to help in the house. At least that had put a stop to the phone calls inviting him for meals and the requests for bags of dirty washing. He enjoyed living on his own and he told himself it would be impossible for him to adjust now to anything different. But the evening seemed long and he felt that something was missing.

On Sunday morning he woke early and phoned the police station, where the DC who had taken the first statement from Hilda Wilkinson was still on duty.

'Did you talk to her?' he asked. He needed proof and at present this was the most he had.

'Sorry, sir. I called at her house but there was no reply. A neighbour said she'd gone away for the weekend to stay with her daughter in the Lakes. She'll not be back until Monday. Do you want me to try and get a phone number for her?'

'No,' he said. Some old people disliked the phone, felt flustered by it. 'Wait until tomorrow then. Talk to her in her own home. She'll be more relaxed there.'

In a sense he welcomed the delay. It put off the time when he would have to commit himself, have to say: 'I believe this person is a murderer.' It gave him time to collect his ideas.

At lunch time Hunter called at the cottage in Heppleburn. He stood on the doorstep, his hands thrust deep in his jacket pockets.

'I thought you might fancy a drink,' he said as if it were the most natural thing in the world for him to be there. 'It's all very well the boss saying to take a break but I can't settle to anything while this is still up in the air.'

Ramsay knew that this was no social call. It had never happened before and Hunter had dozens of drinking companions he would choose before the Inspector. They walked slowly through the quiet village to the Northumberland Arms and found a seat in a corner. The pub was busy, full of men enjoying a pint before their Sunday lunch. Hunter got in the first round and Ramsay realized he must want something.

It soon became clear that he was there to lobby for support. He wanted the Pastons' house searched. 'I've been through the records of every lad in North Tyneside convicted of an auto-crime in the last three years,' he said. 'I'm sure that at least six of the boys who went into that house on Thursday have been done for taking without consent. I've the list of names here.'

'If you took a random sample of kids you bumped into on the street in the Starling Farm you'd probably come up with the same result,' Ramsay said mildly.

'But you will support me?' Hunter demanded. 'There's been no real bother on the estate this weekend.'

Ramsay shrugged and went to the bar for another drink. He supposed it would do no harm. He had to keep his options open.

'Well?' Hunter said.

'I think it would be useful to know what's going on there,' Ramsay said cautiously.

That was good enough for Hunter. Having got what he came for he bolted his pint and left, saying his mam would be keeping his dinner for him. Ramsay remained in the pub on his own until closing time. The afternoon stretched ahead of him, empty and uninviting.

He went to bed early and was woken from a deep sleep by the telephone. It had been ringing too in his dream and he was only half awake as he picked up the receiver.

'Yes,' he muttered. 'Ramsay.' The dream had been pleasant, mildly erotic, and he struggled to capture some memory of it.

'Stephen,' a woman said. 'I'm sorry to disturb you. I didn't know what to do.'

It was Prue Bennett.

'How did you get my number?' he asked foolishly. It was the first thing to come into his head. He was ex-directory and he had been certain that it would be a work call.

'I phoned your mother,' she said. 'Not now. Earlier this evening. It's taken me a couple of hours to find the nerve to phone you. I didn't know what else to do. I was frantic and the police station wouldn't give it to me.'

Ramsay looked at the clock by his bed. It was two o'clock.

'What *is* this all about?' he asked impatiently.

'It's Anna,' she said. 'She's missing. She hasn't come home.'

'Have you reported her missing to your local police station?'

'Of course,' she cried. 'Hours ago. But when they found out how old she was they weren't interested. She's an adult, apparently. If she wants to stay out all night with her boyfriend it's up to her. There's nothing they can do.'

'Is she with John Powell?' His voice sharpened. For the first time he seemed properly awake.

'I don't know,' she said helplessly. 'I think so.'

'Look,' he said, 'do you want me to come over? I'm not sure what good it'll do but I'll come if you like.'

'Yes,' she said relieved and he realized that was what she had wanted from the start. 'Please come. As soon as you can.'

When he arrived at the house in Otterbridge he caught a glimpse of her face pale in the street light, peering between the curtains in the living room. Had she been looking out for him? Or was she still keeping a vigil for her daughter? Perhaps she had been disappointed to see him emerge from the car instead of Anna. But when she opened the door to him there was only relief.

'Oh, Stephen!' she said. 'It's so good of you to come.' She put her arms around him. He held her for a moment, astonished that it felt so natural. Her hair smelled as it always had and memories of their summer together came flooding back.

'You look washed out,' he said. 'I'll make you some tea.'

He saw that she was almost hysterical with anxiety. He led her like a child to the kitchen, sat her in the rocking chair, and put on the kettle. The room was still warm but she was shivering.

'Your mother remembered me,' she said. 'After all this time!'

He did not know what to say. He wondered what his mother would have made of the call. She would be imagining romance, wedding bells, grandchildren. He poured out mugs of tea, handed one to her, and sat beside her.

'What happened?' he asked. 'When did Anna leave?'

'This afternoon at about half-past three.' She looked at him over the rim of her mug with dark eyes. 'It seems days ago. We had a late lunch together then we started talking about the play she's in—*The Adventures of Abigail Keene*. There's another rehearsal tomorrow—' She looked at the kitchen clock and corrected herself. 'Today. It all started off quite amicably. We discussed some details of her performance. I heard her lines. She's taken over Gabriella Paston's character and it's a big part to learn in the few weeks before the show. Then it all got more abstract and high-flown. It was almost as if she was trying to pick a fight. She assumed I was critical, that I didn't think she could be as good as Gabby. It was *my* fault, she said, that she couldn't play the part. I'd been too protective. Her childhood had been too cosy. She didn't have the experience.'

Prue paused and looked up at Ramsay.

'I suppose in a way she was right. But I only did what I thought was best.'

'Of course,' he said. 'Did she walk out then?'

'No. Not straight away. I said that it didn't sound like her talking. It was more like Gabby. Or John Powell. That's when she really flew off the handle. What was wrong with John Powell, she said. I'd made it quite clear that I disapproved of him. Didn't I think she was mature enough to choose her own friends? That's when she stormed out of the house.'

'She didn't give you any idea where she was going?'

Prue Bennett shook her head. 'But I had the impression that the whole quarrel was manufactured and that she'd already planned to meet him. She wanted an excuse to go, an excuse to get back at me. But I wouldn't have stopped her going out with John. I don't particularly like him, but she's old enough to make up her own mind. She didn't have to go through all that. I don't know what's got into her.'

'Perhaps she's growing up,' he said. 'Very quickly. After a slow start. Isn't that how teenagers are supposed to be? Moody, confused, rebellious.'

'I suppose so. I can never remember being like that.'

'No,' he said. 'Nor can I. Perhaps we were unusually sensible.'

She smiled for the first time, then her mood changed again suddenly.

'I'm so frightened,' she said. 'Gabby was playing Abigail Keene and now she's dead. What if the same has happened to Anna?'

She looked at him, desperate for reassurance.

'I don't see,' he said carefully, 'how the play could have anything to do with it.'

'Really?' she said. 'Really?' He hoped he could live up to her trust.

'Have you tried phoning the Powells' house?' he said.

She shook her head. 'I never knew John's number. And they're ex-directory too.'

'I know the number. Do you want to ring them? Or would you like me to try?'

'You do it,' she said. 'I wouldn't know what to say.'

He stood in the cold and dusty hall and dialled the number but though he let it ring and ring there was no reply.

'Evan must be away,' Ramsay said. 'I know he's got a weekend off work. If he were there he'd have answered it.'

'That's a good sign, isn't it?' she said. 'That John's not there. It means they must be out together. A party, something like that. At least Anna's not on her own. She's not phoned because she wants to prove she's independent.'

She was brighter. Since Ramsay's arrival she had lost the desperate, haunted look. Now she seemed almost optimistic. Perhaps he was right and it would do Anna good to be rebellious for a change.

Ramsay was noncommittal.

'Look,' he said. 'I think you should get some sleep.'

'No,' she said. 'I couldn't. What if Anna turns up? If she phones and needs a lift.'

'I'll be here,' he said. 'I'll wait until morning.'

At last she allowed herself to be persuaded and left him in the rocking chair, thinking. He tried to make sense of Anna's disappearance. How did it fit in with the theory he had put together over the weekend? It was the last thing he would have expected. Then he saw there was a connection, a common motive at least, even if Hunter would never have recognized it. Now he could see how all the major players in the piece were driven.

Chapter Seventeen

When Ramsay arrived at work Hunter had already persuaded the superintendent to authorize a search of the Pastons' bungalow and was in the process of putting together a team to go. He was triumphant.

'I told the old man I had your blessing,' Hunter said, looking up from his phone. Then: 'By, man, you look dreadful. A night on the tiles, was it?'

'Something like that,' Ramsay said. He wasn't going to tell Hunter he'd spent the night with a murder suspect.

'Do you want to come?'

'No,' Ramsay said. 'I'll be tied up here all morning. I'll leave you to deal with it. But be discreet. We don't want the local lads saying we cocked up an operation on their patch.'

'Man, they'll never know I've been there.'

Alma Paston never missed her cooked breakfast. She thought it set her up for the day. She was sitting at the kitchen table eating a last slice of fried bread when the doorbell went.

Ellen was standing by the sink, running cold water into the frying pan. Her face was flushed with the cooking.

''H' way then, hinnie,' Alma said impatiently. 'It'll be one of the bairns. I heard the cars out racing yesterday. Let's see what they've got for us.'

Ellen left the pan in the washing-up bowl, wiped her hands on her apron, and looked out of the living-room window to see who was there.

'It's a policeman,' she shouted back to her mother. 'Not the tall one that came here. The other one, Hunter, who was at the Grace Darling. What does he want?'

'Well, we'll not find out while he's standing there. Let him in. He'll have some news about Gabby likely.'

Alma heaved herself from the chair and stood, almost wedged in the doorway between the kitchen and the hall to watch what was going on. She thought there was the chance of a bit of banter. She was looking forward to putting the young policeman in his place.

'Come on in, young man,' she called over Ellen's shoulder. 'What'll the neighbours think if they see I've got a gentleman caller?'

'There are three of them,' Ellen said rudely.

'All the more reason to bring them inside, then. I've my reputation to think of.' And she began to laugh so her body heaved and she choked as if she were having some sort of fit.

'Come on in, then, pet,' she said at last to Hunter. She was wheezing, trying to catch her breath. Hunter stared at her with horror. 'And what do they call you?'

He gave his name and nodded to his colleagues—a young woman in uniform and a second detective—to follow him. They all stood ridiculously crushed in the small space of the hall.

'Well now,' Alma said, laughing again. 'This is cosy, like. You'd better come into the front room and tell me what it's all about.'

It was all very different from what Hunter had expected. When Ellen had opened the door to him he had thought it would be easy. He could sense her fear and unease. But Alma's confidence, her jolly good humour, made him wonder if he had made a mistake. He was frightened of making a fool of himself.

'Why don't you put the kettle on?' Alma said to Ellen. 'Take Mr Hunter's friends into the kitchen and make them some tea while I find out how I can help him.'

Ellen stamped away crossly and Hunter found himself alone with Alma Paston.

'I've got a search warrant,' he said.

'Have you now?' She raised her eyebrows and pulled a face in mock horror. 'Do you think that bothers me?'

'I think it'll bother your daughter,' he said.

'Oh, Ellen!' She dismissed the woman. 'She never was up to much. Not like Robbie. Now there was a lad!'

'Is that when all this started?' Hunter said. 'When Robbie was a lad?'

'All what?' she demanded. She looked at him with a theatrical disappointment. I'd thought better of you, she seemed to be saying. I thought you'd have realized I was too canny to be taken in by a trick like that.

He was affronted by her impudence. 'We have reason to believe that you are in possession of stolen goods,' he said angrily. 'We have a warrant to search these premises and I'll ask my colleagues to begin the search now.' He went to the door and nodded through to the kitchen where they were standing awkwardly, watching Ellen make tea.

'Reason to believe!' Alma said. 'Who's given you reason to believe? I hope you've something better to go on than rumours. You can get into trouble making false accusations. You never know, I might sue. For defamation of character.'

Her tone was light but she looked at him intently. He thought he had not misjudged the situation after all. Alma Paston had something to hide and she wanted to know who had informed against her.

'You had a lot of visitors here yesterday,' he said. 'Could you explain to me please the purpose of their visits?'

'Bairns,' she said. 'They were just bairns. They know I can't get out and they came to keep me company.' She leaned forward and thrust her face towards his. 'There's a lot written in the papers about the Starling Farm, Sergeant,' she said. 'You'd think it was a den of wickedness. But they're the salt of the earth, the people on this estate. They look after their own.' She smiled at him, not caring whether he believed her or not.

'Don't mess me about,' he said, losing his patience at last. 'We were watching the house. Most of the lads that came here yesterday were convicted criminals. They weren't here to make your tea and weed your garden. I can give you a list of their names if you like. . .'

There was a pause. He realized that she was intelligent and that she was coming to terms with the fact that he knew more than she had suspected.

'Why not?' she said quietly. 'Why don't you do that, Sergeant? And at the top of the list why don't we put a special friend of mine. Such a nice lad. Well brought up. From such a good family. And bright too. Bright as a button. You'll never guess some of the schemes he's dreamt up to make himself a few bob.' She leaned forward again. 'If you've been watching the house, Sergeant, I'm sure you know who I'm talking about. You'll know his father.'

She laughed triumphantly and he understood now what lay behind her confidence and good humour. She had no anxiety about her own future. She did not care at all what would happen to her if she were caught. All that mattered was that John Powell was brought down with her.

'Is this what all this has been about?' Hunter demanded. 'Revenge?'

'Evan Powell took my son,' she said. 'I've taken his. In a way.' She levered herself to her feet and lumbered to the door.

'You'll find what you're looking for in the loft,' she shouted out to the two police officers who had begun to search her bedroom. 'No need to wreck our home, is there? It'd upset Ellen, you see. She's that houseproud. And the money's in the commode by my bed.' She walked back to Hunter and patted his hand. 'The Red Cross brought it but I never use the thing,' she said. 'I've still got all my faculties.' She laughed again.

'You'll have to come to the station to make a statement,' Hunter said sullenly, withdrawing his hand. He knew he'd been used.

'That'll be a treat then, hinnie. A ride in a police car. I've always wanted one of those. Will you let me start the siren?'

She returned to her chair and stared at Hunter through narrowed eyes.

'I could say that it was all young Powell's idea,' she said. 'That I was just keeping the stuff for him, that he bullied me into doing it.'

'How did you get him involved?' Hunter asked. He knew this

was out of order. He should wait to begin the interview until they were in the station, with the tape-recorder running, a WPC present, but he knew damn fine that Alma Paston would say nothing in front of witnesses unless she felt like it and she was well able to look after her own civil rights.

'He involved himself, hinnie,' she said. 'I'm not a witch.'

'Who brought him here?'

'A friend of mine,' she said. 'A lad from the estate.'

'What's his name?'

She shook her head. 'You'll not expect me to tell you that,' she said. 'I've told you. It was a friend. A good boy.'

'Why did John Powell do it?' Hunter cried. 'A lad like that with everything to lose.'

'It was the excitement,' she said. 'The danger. My Robbie was just the same. I could tell that the minute Johnny was in the house. I recognized the signs. It was like my Robbie all over again. I knew once he started he'd never be able to stop.'

'So you encouraged him to steal cars?'

'I bought what he had to sell,' she corrected him. 'Mostly radios, of course, but you'd be surprised the stuff that gets left in cars.' She shut her eyes and continued in reminiscence. 'I did a nice little line in designer raincoats and jackets for a while: Burberry, Berghaus, you know the sort. You can get a good price for a famous label if it's in decent condition, even secondhand. The lads and lassies around her appreciate quality.'

'How did you sell it on?' he asked. 'You never leave the house. Did the customers come here?'

She opened her eyes and looked at him disapprovingly. 'I'd not be such a fool,' she said.

'Sarge!' There was a shout from the hall. The DC was standing on a short stepladder with his head stuck through a square hole in the roof. 'I think this is what we're after!' He descended, wiping the dust from his hands, and Hunter took his place and shone a torch into the roof space. There, neatly piled in boxes on the floor, was a variety of stolen goods. Most of the boxes contained radios and cassette-recorders, but there were briefcases, ladies' handbags, leather gloves. He could see boxes of wine, jewellery, small electrical household items. Alma was standing at the foot of the ladder.

'It's a canny storeroom, isn't it?' she said with satisfaction. 'That's all Ellen's work. I can't get up there myself.'

'Where did you get the toasters, then?' Hunter shouted down. 'And the booze? The kids'd not have found that in stolen cars. Not all of it at least.'

'No,' she conceded. 'Well, we found we'd saturated the market with in-car entertainment—that's what they call it you know, the radios and cassettes. So we decided to branch out.'

'The ram raids,' Hunter said. There was a grudging admiration in his voice. She had nerve, you had to give her that, and she'd been conning them all for years. 'Was Powell involved in that too?'

He climbed down to join her.

'Oh,' she said, 'I think you can say that Johnny was the leading light behind the ram raids. The moving force.' She touched Hunter's arm conspiratorially. 'The attack on the Coast Road hypermarket on the night Gabby died,' she said. 'That was all his own work. I wasn't pleased about that. I thought the timing lacked respect. But he's always had a flair for organization.'

'You were telling me how you get rid of the stuff,' Hunter said.

'Was I?' She was teasing him, pleased by his interest. 'Perhaps I'll let you work that one out for yourself. We don't want to make it too easy for you.'

'You'll stop mucking me about,' he said.

'I run a sort of franchise,' she said proudly, not intimidated in the least. She had wanted to tell him anyway. 'I suppose that's what you'd call it. I have agents who do the selling for me. I take a commission.'

'That bloke who was in court on the afternoon Mrs Wood died,' Hunter said. 'Tommy Shiels. Was he one of your agents?'

She nodded. 'Not one of the best, though, hinnie. You mustn't think I only deal with the losers.'

'At least he kept his mouth shut,' Hunter said. 'He never let on he was working for you.'

'Oh, they all keep their mouths shut, hinnie,' she said. 'They know that some of my friends are. . .unpredictable.' She touched his arm again with her thick soft fingers. 'You might not believe this, but they're frightened of me!'

She seemed to find the idea hilarious and burst into laughter, rocking backwards and forwards. Hunter, watching her felt suddenly sick and chill. Like Ramsay he could believe her capable of anything.

Before he could settle to the investigation Ramsay phoned Prue Bennett at the Grace Darling Centre. The disappearance of Anna disturbed him, nagged at his subconscious all day. He did not see how she could be in real danger but knew that he would always blame himself if anything happened to her. Prue had been determined to go in to work and had left Otterbridge at her usual time. If she stayed at home she'd just mope, she said. She needed to keep busy. Anna would know where to find her.

'Any news?' he said.

'Yes. I was just going to ring you.' She sounded almost drunk with relief. 'She phoned in to say she was all right.'

'Where is she?' he asked.

'I don't know. She wouldn't speak to me. Her pride, I suppose. Or she'd think I'd just make a fuss, get cross. She left a message with Joe.'

'What exactly did she say?'

'That she was sorry to have worried me, she was fine, and she'd be at the rehearsal tonight. She'd explain it all then.'

Ramsay said nothing.

'Stephen,' she said, perhaps sensing his disquiet. 'You don't think anything's wrong, do you? She *is* going to turn up this evening, full of the adventure?'

'Yes,' he said. 'Of course she is.' There was no point in frightening her.

But as soon as she had replaced the phone he dialled again and spoke to Joe Fenwick.

'That message you took for Miss Bennett this morning,' he said. 'You are sure it was Anna on the phone?'

'Aye,' he said. 'For sure. I knew it was her before she gave her name. There's not much of the Geordie in her voice, y'knaa, and it's very quiet. I'd recognize it anywhere.'

Ramsay replaced the receiver slowly. He hoped to God she was safe.

In the neat terraced house on Martin's Dene Front Street Hilda Wilkinson made tea for the pleasant policewoman who had come to talk to her. Hilda Wilkinson was a widow, spry, independent, energetic. She had just returned from her daughter's and was full of the trip. She had enjoyed her weekend in the Lakes, she said, despite the weather. She still managed a good tramp across the fells.

'It's about the car you saw last Monday,' the young detective said. 'Can you tell us anything more about it?'

'I'm sorry,' Mrs Wilkinson said. It was only mid-afternoon but the windows of the cottage were small and the light was already beginning to fade. The lights were on and she had just lit a fire in the grate. 'It was about two o'clock, I know that, and it's unusual to see cars parked there during the week. At weekends it's different of course. But there was nothing really to catch my interest.'

She poured tea into pretty china cups and handed one to her visitor.

'Did you see anyone out on the hill while you were walking your dog?'

'Not the young girl who was killed,' Mrs Wilkinson said. 'I saw a photo of her in the paper and a description of her clothes. I've rather a good memory, you know, almost photographic despite my age, and if I'd seen her I'd remember.'

'But was there anyone else?'

'Yes.' Mrs Wilkinson sat very still. She wanted to test her memory. She was quite confident in her own ability.

'It was very foggy,' she said. 'In the morning it had been sunny but by lunch time the mist started to come in from the sea. I didn't go very far. I'm not a nervous person but it wasn't pleasant there. . .' She paused. 'There was a young mother,' she said, 'with a child in a pushchair. I almost bumped into her, the fog was so thick. The baby wasn't wearing gloves and I thought it was so irresponsible. His hands must have been freezing. I almost said something but she hurried away.'

'Anyone else?' The policewoman looked out of the window. She supposed the inspector must know what he was doing but this seemed a waste of time. She nibbled a piece of shortbread, stretched her hand towards the fire, and thought she might as well make the most of the rest. It had been a busy weekend.

'There was Eleanor Darcy,' the old woman said, 'but I don't suppose you'll be interested in her. She walks on the hill every afternoon. She'll not have remembered anything. She's rather confused, poor dear. Still on the committee of the WI but not really up to it, I'm afraid.'

'I'll take her address,' the policewoman said. 'Just in case.' She jotted the information in her notebook and stood to go.

'Wait a minute!' Mrs Wilkinson said. She was suddenly excited. 'There was someone else. Not actually on the hill but on the road close to where the car was parked. Now, let me think. . .' She shut her eyes and then began a detailed description which tallied almost exactly with that given to the policewoman by Stephen Ramsay the day before.

Chapter Eighteen

By early evening the news of the Pastons' arrest had spread over the Starling Farm estate. Neighbours who hadn't seen Alma Paston in the open air for years described her departure in the police car.

'Man, you'd have thought she was the Queen, waving and bowing. Ellen held an umbrella over her so she'd not get wet. And the size of her! They tried to squeeze her into the back of the car but she wouldn't fit and in the end she had to go in the front beside the driver.'

It started as good-natured gossip. There was little resentment. Most of the people in the street had guessed what the Pastons had been up to and thought they had been lucky to get away with it for so long. They'd had a good run for their money, the neighbours said. You couldn't blame the police for doing their job. Alma Paston had never been popular. They were too frightened of her.

It got nasty later. When the trouble was over they blamed Connor for that. He'd always been a hot-head, a firebrand. They'd never taken him seriously but he had too much influence over the kids. They could only guess at his motive for stirring up resentment. Perhaps it was political. He was always talking about the revolution. Perhaps he believed it would finally start on the Starling Farm estate. Or perhaps he had his own personal reason for wanting to cause trouble for the police—he had always been close to Alma Paston and had supported himself for years by supplying her with stolen goods. Whatever his motive, everyone agreed that without Connor the evening would have ended quietly. It was a cold and wet Monday evening—not the night for taking to the streets. It took Connor's rhetoric to start the kids off.

He got the news in the Community Centre on the Starling Farm in the afternoon. A boy who had bunked off school to play pool passed on the information almost casually, as if it were a joke.

'Old Ma Paston's been arrested!' he said. 'The cops took her away at dinner time.'

It was Connor who called the arrest harassment. He made the unemployed teenagers switch off the music and stood in the middle of the Games Room lecturing them.

What right did the police have, he said, to take the two ladies from their home? What harm could they be doing? How would they feel, he demanded of his audience, if the police came and dragged their grans into the police station for questioning? It was a vendetta against the Paston family, he said earnestly. Robbie was dead, Gabby was dead, and now Ellen and Alma were in custody. He was so eloquent that the boys almost believed that the police were responsible for Gabriella Paston's death.

'It's Evan Powell,' he said at the end. 'He's behind it. He's never liked the Pastons or the Starling Farm estate.'

'What are we going to do about it then, Connor?' one of the lads asked.

'We'll show them,' he said, 'who's in charge here.'

At the police station Alma Paston was remarkably frank despite the tape-recorder and the policewoman sat in the corner. Ellen seemed so confused and frightened that she was almost incoherent and Hunter soon gave up on her. He'd never been known for his patience. But Alma told them everything they wanted to know. Ramsay sat in on the interview and watched her dominate the conversation.

'Oh yes,' she said. 'I can give you names. It was John Powell, hinnie. He brought in most of the stuff and he was behind the ram raids too.' She repeated the boy's name at every opportunity like a talisman or a chant, looking at the machine on the table as she spoke to make sure it was recording.

Later Ramsay sought out Evan Powell to tell him of the allegations made against his son.

'I tried to phone you yesterday,' he said at first. 'You must have been away.'

'Yes,' Evan said. 'Jackie's been off-colour lately. I thought we could do with a weekend on our own. I took her to a place we know in the dales.'

So the house had been free for John and Anna, Ramsay thought, but he said nothing. The boy's illicit night of love-making with a girlfriend hardly compared with the other things Evan would have to accept. Evan looked tired and drawn and Ramsay thought that the weekend could not have lived up to expectations. He had expected a romantic second honeymoon and had been disappointed.

'How can I help you?' Evan said. He spoke warily but without hostility. Perhaps he thought Ramsay was there to apologize for the bad feeling between them on Friday night.

'Hunter arrested Alma and Ellen Paston this morning. Their house is full of stolen goods. Apparently they've been dealing for years.'

'Why are you telling me?' Evan said, though he must have guessed what it was all about.

'Their statement implicates John.'

'No!' Evan cried. He leaned forward across his desk. 'Don't you see? It's their way of revenge. They're lying to pay me back for Robbie's death.'

'I don't think so,' Ramsay said. 'It was revenge of a sort. They encouraged John to get involved. They knew that would hurt you more than anything. But he *was* there. Hunter saw him. And he was seen by Joe Fenwick in Anchor Street on the night of the Co-op ram raid driving a car similar to that used by the thieves.'

'That's impossible,' Evan said. 'He was home all night.'

'Are you sure?' Ramsay said. 'Couldn't he have left the house without your knowing?'

Evan said nothing.

'We'll have to talk to him,' Ramsay said. 'You do realize that? Have you seen him today?'

Evan shook his head. 'He'd left for school before we got home.'

'He's not in school,' Ramsay said. 'We've checked.'

The news that John was absent from school seemed to affect Evan more than the possibility of his arrest. He had put all his faith in his son's academic success. He saw it as a passport to a brilliant future. Now he put his head in his hands and shut his eyes. All the fight had left him.

'He'll be at the rehearsal at the Grace Darling tonight,' he said. 'If you don't pick him up during the day you'll find him there. Whatever happens he'd not miss that.'

'You don't know what plans John had for the weekend?' Ramsay asked. 'Did he mention a party? Friends he might visit?'

Evan shook his head. 'He told me he'd be working,' he said. 'And fool that I am, I believed him.'

'Yes,' Ramsay said. 'I see.' He would have liked to offer some comfort to Evan but knew that kind words would only make things worse. 'I'll check at your house first,' he said. 'Just to make sure John's not gone back there. You don't mind?'

'No,' Evan said. 'I'd be pleased. You can talk to Jackie. She might know where he is.' He paused. 'I'd rather she heard about all this from you than from the press.'

'You could come with me,' Ramsay said. 'Take some time off to be with her.'

'No,' Evan said. 'I can't face her. Not yet. I'd lose my temper. Say things I'd regret.' He looked up at Ramsay. 'You *will* go yourself?' he said. 'I'd not trust anyone else.'

Ramsay nodded but when he got to Barton Hill the house was empty and there was no reply when he knocked at the door.

Over the weekend Gus Lynch thought with relief that at last Jackie was getting the message that their affair was over. During the week following Gabby Paston's death there had been no peace from her. She had phoned him almost continually. At home he had switched the telephone to the answering machine and at work he refused to take her calls. Joe Fenwick was usually on the switchboard and had come to recognize her voice. She never gave her name.

'It's that woman again,' he would say.

'Tell her I'm busy,' Gus would shriek. He thought she was mad.

She would ruin everything. 'Tell her I'm in a meeting and I can't be disturbed.'

'She won't believe you're still in a meeting.'

'I don't care what she believes.'

On Wednesday night she had come to his flat. He had seen her car pull up in the street below and had switched off all the lights and bolted the door so even though she had a key she could not get in. She must have known that he was there because she stood on the wooden steps in full view of the street banging on the door and shouting through the letterbox, threatening to tell his secrets to the trustees, the press, the whole bloody world. He had stood in the kitchen, out of her view, shaking, thinking how easy it would be to let her in and keep her quiet for good.

Then, over the weekend everything went quiet. There were no calls from her on his answerphone, no sight of her car parked on the quay. On Sunday morning when he went into Hallowgate to buy the papers he felt that at last the worst was over. For the first time he thought there was no danger he would be followed. In the new year he would leave the area to begin his new job and he could leave the nightmare of the last few months behind. He even allowed himself a little optimism and excitement. There were FOR SALE posters stuck in the windows of his flat and he saw them as a symbol of change. They proved that the episode at the Grace Darling was a temporary aberration, and soon he would take up his life properly again.

The phone calls started once more on Monday. The first one came when Gus Lynch was out of the Centre, having a sandwich and a pint in the Anchor at lunch time, determined to maintain the old routine. Joe Fenwick put it through to Prue, who couldn't persuade the caller to say what she wanted.

'There was some woman on the phone for you just now,' she said to Lynch when he returned. 'She was in a phone box somewhere and wouldn't leave a message but she was really upset, almost hysterical. I said you'd be in all afternoon.'

'Oh, thanks!' he said. He wondered how she could have been so stupid. 'That's just what I need!'

Prue ignored the sarcasm. She was still thinking about Anna.

Then the optimism of the weekend re-asserted itself and Gus thought that Jackie could do him no harm. He refused to let her phone calls threaten him or undermine his confidence. If she went public it would be an embarrassment of course, but who would take her seriously? Who would believe a middle-aged neurotic woman who had been jilted by her lover?

He sat in his office and concentrated on preparing a press release to advertise the performance of Abigail Keene. He was determined that the production would be a success. He wanted to go out with a bang. His phone rang.

'It's that woman again,' Joe Fenwick said cautiously. He was expecting Lynch to be angry and was surprised by the director's reaction.

'Tell her to piss off, Joe,' he said cheerfully. 'Tell her I want nothing to do with her. It's one of the problems with being famous, old son, being pestered by women you've never met in your life.'

He replaced the phone, feeling pleased with himself, and shouted through to Prue to come into his office. He wanted to talk about costumes. They'd need to find the money from somewhere to hire them. This time he wasn't going to have it done on the cheap.

'I'll not have it looking like a school play,' he said. 'There'll be no jumble-sale cast-offs for us.' Then, noticing for the first time how tired and tense she looked: 'What the hell's the matter with you today?'

'I'm worried about Anna,' she said. 'She went out with John Powell last night and didn't come home.'

He laughed unpleasantly.

'Good for Anna!' he said. 'I never knew she had it in her. She's fancied him for ages, we could all see that. Now that Gabby's out of the way. . .'

'That's a dreadful thing to say,' Prue snapped. 'Anna was Gabby's friend. She wouldn't have done her any harm. . .'

'Of course not, pet, but it's not done Anna any harm either, has it? She's got the leading role and her man. Good luck to her. I only hope they get off the nest long enough to make it to rehearsal.'

And he laughed again.

Chapter Nineteen

The disturbances on the Starling Farm got out of hand because nobody was expecting them. It was a rainy Monday evening and the weekend had been quiet. The possible trigger to trouble—the arrest of the Pastons—no longer seemed to apply. The women were given bail in the late afternoon and delivered home by a kind constable. He accepted Alma's offer of tea and stayed and chatted to her for half an hour before returning to the station. On his way out of the estate he saw a group of lads gathering in the car park of the Keel Row. They jeered at the panda car and threw a few stones but that was par for the course on the Starling Farm estate. He had a feeling that the gathering was more purposeful than usual, that the kids might be waiting for someone, but when he reported the incident back at the police station no one took any notice. It was five o'clock. Trouble usually started later when the pubs closed.

By five o'clock in Hallowgate police station Stephen Ramsay thought he knew who had killed Gabriella Paston and Amelia Wood. He had motive and opportunity and the description of the person Mrs Wilkinson had seen in Martin's Dene was more accurate than he could have hoped. But he had no proof, no forensic evidence. At this stage there was definitely not enough to convict. He discussed the problem with his superintendent.

'Should we go for an arrest?' he asked.

The superintendent sat behind a desk stacked with paper and was deeply troubled.

'Think of the publicity,' he said. 'It'll be a media circus. Could we guarantee a fair trial after that, even if we get enough to bring charges?'

'Not here,' Ramsay said. 'But the trial could always be moved out of the area.' Besides, he thought, that's not our problem. My problem is to find the evidence to convict and I'm not sure an arrest would help. A confession's not enough. Not these days.

'What about searching the property? Would that be any use?' The superintendent looked up from his papers. He looked suddenly tired and very old.

'I think it would. We've the forensic report on Lynch's car back now. There are some unexplained fibres on the driver's seat. I'd be happier if we could tie them in with something belonging to our suspect.'

'Yes, I see.' He paused, seemed to be considering all the options. 'Not a pleasant job,' he said. 'Never is.' He looked at Ramsay with some sympathy.

'Will you go yourself?'

Ramsay stood up and walked to the window. He looked out at the rain. A buoy flashed on the south side of the river.

'No,' he said. 'I think I should go to the Grace Darling Centre.' The drama had started there, the week before, and he thought that was where the thing would be concluded.

'How long then,' the superintendent demanded, suddenly alert and awake, 'before it's all over?'

Ramsay turned to him sadly. 'We'll get it finished tonight,' he said. 'One way or another.'

Ramsay drove to the Arts Centre through the centre of Hallowgate. The shops were still dark and shuttered, the streets almost empty. A squally wind blew litter across the pavement and made the branches of the big Christmas tree outside the shopping centre sway crazily. The large coloured bulbs which were its only decoration scattered light on to the wet streets and the blank shop windows. As Ramsay stopped at a junction a car drove up behind him very fast and overtook him, jumping a red light, almost causing an accident. It sped off at great speed before he could take the registration number and left him with a sense of shock and unease which remained all evening.

At the Grace Darling Centre everything was much as it had been the week before. It was the quiet period before the evening rush. Joe Fenwick sat behind the desk in the lobby, his legs stretched in front of him, his eyes half closed, resting.

Gus Lynch's sense of elation had persisted. He paced about his office, with his door wide open so his voice carried through the building, speaking on the telephone, trying to drum up advance publicity for *The Adventures of Abigail Keene*. He used the murders shamelessly.

'Look,' he said to friendly reporters, 'the girl who died was actually playing the lead. You can't get more topical than that. . .'

And he replaced the receiver satisfied that they would have all the publicity they could use.

Prue Bennett tried to work but she was distracted by Gus Lynch's voice and her anxiety about Anna. It was not only a concern for the girl's safety which made it impossible for her to concentrate on the report to trustees she was trying to prepare. Gus Lynch's insinuations that Anna had benefited from Gabriella's death remained with her, persistent and alarming, and other incidents, things Anna had said, took on a new and disturbing significance.

This is mad, she thought. It's caused by exhaustion and worry. If Anna were here, so I could see her and talk to her, I'd realize it was all nonsense. But still she could not settle to her work and finally she went to the cafeteria and waited there, drinking coffee after coffee, trying to clear her mind of all her suspicions.

At six o'clock Ellen Paston turned up for her shift in the cafeteria. She nodded to Joe in the lobby on her way through as she always did, leaving her soaking raincoat on a hook behind the counter and put on her nylon overall. The place was quiet and she had time to fill all the sugar bowls before the customers arrived. Prue came to the counter to order another coffee but Ellen said nothing of her ordeal of the morning. She kept the humiliation of police questioning to herself, and brooded on it as she worked.

Half an hour later members of the choral society and the writers' group began to arrive. They talked with ghoulish curiosity of the tragedy that had occurred the week before and spent longer over coffee than they would usually have done.

'Come on, then,' one said at last. 'We'd best get started. I think we're all here. Except Evan. He said he'd be able to make it this week too. Oh well, if he were coming he'd be here by now. We'll have to manage without him.'

And they went to make music without giving Evan a further thought.

When Ramsay arrived at the Grace Darling Prue was still in the cafeteria, sitting in the corner where she could watch the door, waiting for a glimpse of Anna. As soon as the inspector came in she got to her feet and hurried to meet him, knocking a coffee cup off the table with the sleeve of her jacket in her haste.

'Why are you here?' she said. The colour had drained from her face. 'Is there any news?'

He shook his head. 'You've not heard any more from her?'

She tried to hold back her tears.

'She'll turn up,' he said. 'I promise she'll turn up.' He wanted to take her into his arms and comfort her.

At six o'clock news began to come through of disturbances on the Starling Farm. The news hit so quickly because the television companies had been warned in advance by an anonymous phone call about what would take place. The reporters were in position in the grounds of the nursery school which had been left untouched by previous looting. They watched a gang of youths smash the windows of the school and break down the door. They did nothing to assist the caretaker, an elderly man, who tried to stop the destruction, but they turned to each other and called it 'good television.'

The mob who had broken into the school ran off with a television, a video recorder, and an aquarium full of newts, but it seemed that they were more interested in provoking a reaction from the police, in bringing them on to the estate, than in what they could steal. When the police arrived to find a road block of burnt-out cars outside the school the crowd cheered and pelted the officers with rocks, bricks, and beer cans. They lobbed petrol bombs like grenades. It was all more organized and serious than the policemen had expected. They retreated and waited for reinforcements.

The police who arrived in the next wave were so anxious not to be overwhelmed by the crowd that they over-reacted. They were aware of the criticism of delay levelled at them after the Meadow Well riots, and decisions were hardened because the television cameras were already there. No one wanted pictures of riot and disorder to be seen again in living rooms throughout the country. The north-east had a bad enough image already. The officer in charge of the operation was insecure, temperamentally unsuited to taking responsibility. He panicked. He thought it was better to have the reputation of coming down hard on troublemakers than going soft. All the political comment in recent months had reinforced his attitude. He was not prepared to wait, to be seen as a coward, a laughingstock.

His men arrived in armoured buses, wearing riot helmets, carrying shields and batons. They were greeted by an even louder cheer from the crowd and that seemed to provoke the officer in charge beyond endurance. He told his men to go in hard, immediately, and the young people behind the road block, many of whom were only there as spectators and stood laughing and drinking beer were surprised by the attack. It was over very quickly and brutally. The riot police weighed in without proper supervision or preparation. They seemed to lose control, hitting out with their batons, tramping over bodies already knocked to the ground in the rush to escape. It was perhaps fortunate for the officer in charge that only one incident—the beating of a twelve-year-old boy—was captured on television. It could have been worse. The rioters retaliated aimlessly, set the school alight, then scattered on foot and in stolen cars.

At the Grace Darling Centre Gus Lynch eventually agreed reluctantly to cancel the rehearsal. Anxious parents who had seen pictures of the violence on the local early evening news phoned in and said that they would not let their teenagers out. Still there was no information about Anna, and Prue Bennett grew more anxious and withdrawn.

'Where the hell is she?' she cried. 'She should have been here by now. I can't stand this waiting.'

Ramsay said nothing. His work was all about waiting and he was used to it.

A police car on traffic patrol on the road from Newcastle to the coast was parked in a layby close to the Co-op hypermarket which had been raided earlier in the week. From there the driver could look down on the Starling Farm estate. He saw the flashes of petrol bombs and the huge bonfire which had once been the nursery school. He heard the screech of sirens.

'If any of them come this way,' he said to his partner, 'we'll get the bastards.'

In the opposite direction two fire engines and an ambulance went past at speed. They turned off the main road. The policemen in the car were frustrated and watched the disappearing blue lights with envy. They wanted to be involved. They had friends hidden behind helmets and riot shields. But they had been ordered to keep their position on the Coast Road until they were needed.

The radio crackled and the message had begun almost before they had realized, while their attention was still on the scene below.

'Blue Sierra. Registration number: Alpha 749 Romeo, Tango, Golf. Two occupants wanted for questioning in relation to Starling Farm disturbances. Moving west towards the Coast Road.'

'That's it,' the policeman said. 'They're ours.'

He switched on the engine and sat, tense, over the wheel, just as John Powell had sat watching the races on the estate.

They heard the car before they saw it. Its exhaust had no silencer and it roared like a jet plane up the slip road to the dual-carriageway. They switched on their siren and followed.

'Bloody young fools,' the older policeman said uncomfortably. 'They'll kill themselves.'

But the driver was caught up in the excitement of the chase and said nothing. The speedometer rose to a hundred miles an hour.

'That old banger will fall to bits if they go much faster,' the older policeman said, but still the driver made no attempt to moderate his speed.

The road was busy still with commuter traffic. On the opposite carriageway there was a tailback from roadworks and temporary traffic lights and as they approached the town the cars ahead of them were moving less freely.

'Slow down!' the policeman shouted but the driver seemed not to hear him.

Ahead of the Sierra a Mini indicated and pulled out carefully to overtake a bus. The middle-aged woman driving must have seen the Sierra behind her but had misjudged its speed. The Sierra swerved wildly to avoid it but clipped the back of the Mini, so it swivelled to face the oncoming traffic, then crossed the central reservation and smashed into the stationary cars on the opposite carriageway. The Sierra hit with such force that the chassis crumpled and the stationary vehicles were bounced like billiard balls across the width of the road. The driver of the police car slowed down automatically and came to a halt, then stared at the wreckage with astonishment. It was as if he had just wakened from a dream and couldn't believe the reality in front of him.

The Grace Darling Centre was quiet. The Writers' Circle and Choral Group finished early and rushed away to watch the violence with a vicarious excitement on their television screens. Ellen was sent home.

'Can't we give you a lift?' Prue said. 'It might be dangerous out there.' But Ellen refused the offer firmly, without explanation, and they stood in the lobby and watched her plod across the square, her back more stooped than usual, until she disappeared down Anchor Street. Only Prue, Gus, Joe Fenwick, and Ramsay were left.

Ramsay could sense Prue's tension. He knew she would wait there all night for Anna if he let her. 'I'll drive you to the police station,' he said. 'If there's any news of Anna they'll have it there.' He turned to Gus. 'You might as well go home too, Mr Lynch. I need to talk to you but I can do it just as well in your flat. You will be in all evening?'

'Yes,' Gus said. 'I'll be in. But I can't think what this is all about. I'd have thought you had better things to do with all these disturbances. It's all a matter of priorities, surely.'

'My priority is to complete a murder investigation,' Ramsay said quietly. 'I'll be coming to talk to you tonight.'

Behind his desk Joe Fenwick was almost asleep. The doors were already locked and he stretched as he got up to let the three of them out. Outside it was still raining and the bare chestnut trees in the square glistened and dripped. There was a faint smell of burning. Ramsay and Prue waited at the top of the steps to say goodbye to the old man and Lynch went ahead of them into the street. He stopped and turned towards Ramsay.

'You people have still got my car,' he grumbled. It was another grievance. 'I've had to hire one. This time I've left it in the street where I can keep an eye on it. I hope you intend to pay me back. It's costing me a fortune.'

He stepped out into the road to cross the square.

From the corner of his eye Ramsay saw the headlights of a car move around the square. They seemed to be picking up speed, to be moving much too fast in the enclosed space.

'Look out!' he shouted and Lynch threw himself on to the pavement as the Renault hurtled past. It mounted the pavement, missing Lynch by inches. Its wing hit a lamppost and the car came jerkily to a stop. In the orange street light they saw Jackie Powell, her head resting on the steering-wheel.

Ramsay went to the car, opened the door, and helped her out. He told her gently that he was arresting her for the murders of Gabriella Paston and Amelia Wood. As he stood on the pavement to radio for help he saw a small, bedraggled figure walk across the square from Anchor Street. It was Anna Bennett. She saw Prue and ran into her mother's arms.

Chapter Twenty

They sat in the kitchen of the house in Otterbridge. It was almost midnight. Ramsay had sent them back in a police car and promised to come later to explain it all to them. Anna was wrapped up in a towelling dressing-gown in the rocking chair. When Ramsay arrived Prue made a fuss of him, took his wet coat, offered him tea, a drink.

'Whisky,' he said. 'If you've got it.'

'Anna's been explaining what happened,' Prue said. She couldn't take her eyes off her daughter. She sat on the arm of her chair and stroked her as if she needed to make sure she was really there.

'Perhaps you'd better tell me,' Ramsay said to the girl. 'If you can face going through it again.'

'I think it was a kind of madness,' she said. 'I don't know what got into me.'

'You met John Powell?' he said.

She nodded. 'We went to the Starling Farm,' she said. 'The kids there race stolen cars. . .'

'And you?' he asked. 'Did you take part?'

'Not the first time,' she said. 'The first time I just watched but when I went on Sunday afternoon I joined in. John was driving. I just sat beside him. I had my eyes closed most of the time but it was so exciting. . .'

'And after the racing?' Ramsay said flatly. 'What did you do then?' He wanted to tell her that she was a stupid fool, that her mother had been frantic with worry, but he knew that Prue wouldn't have wanted that.

'I asked John to take me home,' she said defensively. 'But he wouldn't. He was going with some friends to a sort of party in one of the boarded-up houses on the estate.'

'You could have phoned me,' Prue interrupted. 'I would have come for you.'

'I know.' Anna paused. 'It was pride, I suppose. I couldn't bear phoning up, begging to be collected. Like a child. And I wanted to be with John.'

'So you went to the party with him?'

She nodded. 'I didn't enjoy it much. It lasted all night. I just wanted to go to sleep. John drank himself senseless and was in no state then to take me home.'

'What happened in the morning?' Ramsay asked.

'I said I should go to school but they all laughed at me. What did I want with school, they said. I told them I'd have to phone my mother. She'd be frantic. She'd have the police out looking for me and it would only cause trouble. So John took me to the Community Centre and I used the phone there.'

'You were still in the Community Centre when Connor got the news that the Pastons had been arrested?' Ramsay asked.

She nodded. 'Connor told John to run away. He said the police would be on to him like a shot. They'd cause a disturbance to distract them, and give John a chance to get away. But John said he wasn't running anywhere. I think in a way he would be glad to be caught. He knew he was out of his depth. It had all got out of hand.' She looked directly at her mother. 'I tried to leave then,' she said. 'But Connor wouldn't let me. He said I would only give them away. I was a sort of hostage, until it was all over.' She shivered. 'I think he must be mad,' she said. 'I heard him plan it all—the petrol bombs, the looting. He phoned some friends from Newcastle to join in.'

'Did you go out on to the street with them?'

She nodded again.

'How did you get away?'

'When the police came it was dreadful, chaotic. I don't think Connor had expected it to happen like that. They weren't interested in me by then. I walked up to the Centre. I knew Mum would be worried.'

'Of course I was worried,' Prue cried. 'I was worried all night.' But she put her arm round her daughter's shoulder and there was no anger in her voice.

'What will happen to John?' Anna looked at the policeman.

'You don't really care?' Prue interrupted. 'After all he's done. . .'

'There was an accident on the Coast Road,' Ramsay said. 'The stolen car which John and Connor were driving was being followed by the police. It was speeding. John was the driver. As you say he didn't seem to care what happened to him. He hit a Mini and was spun into the oncoming traffic.'

'Is he dead?'

Ramsay shook his head. 'He's very ill. They think he's got spinal injuries.'

'And Connor?'

'He was killed immediately.'

There was a silence. Anna stood up as if she were exhausted and said she was going to bed. The adults watched her leave the room.

'I suppose the police will be blamed for that as well,' Prue said bitterly. Ramsay looked at her, surprised. It must be a new experience for her to consider herself a champion of the police force.

'We've got the disturbances under control,' he said. 'There was a danger that they'd spread when news of Connor's death got out, but there were only a few skirmishes on the Starling Farm. There was worse trouble in the west end of Newcastle but that's all quiet now too.'

Prue stood up and brought the whisky bottle to the table.

'So the murders of Gabby and Amelia Wood had nothing to do with joy riding after all,' she said.

'No,' he said. 'Not directly.' Yet there was a link, he thought, between the crimes of Jackie Powell and her son. They were motivated by the same sense of dissatisfaction, the same inability to live in the stifling atmosphere of conventional family life.

'Why did she do it?' Prue cried. 'What could she have against Gabby?'

'Jackie Powell was Gus Lynch's mistress,' Ramsay said. 'You never guessed?'

'I knew there was *someone*. He made jokes about her. The little woman, he used to call her. The bored housewife who needed his attentions to bring her a bit of excitement. She's been more demanding lately but I never realized it was so serious.'

'Oh,' Ramsay said, 'she took it very seriously. She saw it as an escape. She couldn't stand the thought of being on her own with Evan after John left for university. She thought that when Gus moved out of the area he'd take her with him. Of course he never had any intention of doing that.'

'How did you know?' Prue said. 'You weren't surprised, were you, when she went for Gus? You were looking out for her.'

'Yes,' he said. 'I thought she must be desperate by then. She hadn't been home all day. I guessed she would try to see Lynch. That's one reason why I spent so long at the Grace Darling yesterday evening.' He poured himself another whisky. 'I didn't expect violence, though. I should have realized that was a possibility.'

'But how did you know she was having an affair with Gus? He didn't tell you?'

'No,' Ramsay said. 'Joe Fenwick told me. He asked me to his flat on Friday night. He'd seen them together once in the Centre and when she started phoning he realized who she was. He didn't realize, of course, how important the information was, but he thought I should know.'

'I still don't understand,' Prue said, 'why she would want to hurt Gabby. They can't even have known each other. Not well. I know she'd met Gabby at the party at Barton Hill but they had nothing to do with each other.'

'Jackie Powell was protecting Gus Lynch,' he said. 'Gabby was blackmailing him. She was worried she might not get a grant for drama college. She used the information she had to get money out of him.'

'She knew about the missing funds?'

He nodded.

'Did he set Jackie up to it?' she cried. 'What a bastard!'

'No,' he said. 'Really. I don't think so.' He found it strange to be defending Gus Lynch.

'What happened that lunch time?' Prue asked. 'Do you know?'

Ramsay nodded. Once Jackie Powell had begun to make her statement there had been no stopping her. The tension of the previous week had been released in a stream of words. But before he gave Prue the details he wanted to explain why he made so many mistakes during the course of the investigation.

'It took me so long to work out what happened because I had the perspective all wrong,' he said. 'I knew the thing had been planned in advance—the fact that the table at the Holly Tree had been booked the day before proved that. But I thought the murderer had planned it. In fact of course Gabby set it all up, using the name of Abigail Keene. She sent Jackie a letter inviting her to lunch—if you're going to try blackmail it's best, I suppose, to do it in a civilized setting, and she'd expect Jackie to pay. The reply came in the envelope we found in Gabby's drawer.'

'So Gabby knew about the affair too?'

'She knew everything that went on in the Grace Darling through Ellen.'

'Yes,' Prue said. 'Of course. Did Gabby blackmail Jackie about her relationship with Gus?'

'No. Jackie wouldn't have worried too much about that being made public. It was the missing money that was the subject of the blackmail. Gabby realized she'd got all she could expect out of Gus, and she knew Jackie wouldn't want him to be charged with fraud and sent to prison.'

'Tell me what happened,' Prue said.

'Jackie had no transport. Evan's car was in for a service and he was using hers. So she borrowed Gus Lynch's car. She had the keys—he'd given her a spare set so she could get into the flat. She met Gabby at the bus stop and they walked over the hill towards the Holly Tree. It was foggy that day if you remember. They were very close to the road but no one could see them.'

'But they never reached the restaurant.'

'No,' Ramsay said. 'They never reached the restaurant. Gabby was taunting Jackie about the affair—she was there of course at the party at Barton Hill when it all began. Then she began to talk about the missing money. Gus had told Jackie that there had been administrative irregularities at the Centre and he had come under pressure from Amelia Wood to sort them out, but she didn't know the extent of his fraud. It must have come as a terrible shock. Gabby was threatening to expose him and all Jackie's dreams of escaping Hallowgate would be ruined. Gabby was walking over the hill ahead of her, full of herself, full of the information she had, mocking Jackie for making a fool of herself with a thief. Jackie lost control. She went up behind her and strangled her with her scarf. She says it wasn't premeditated and I believe her.'

'Why didn't she leave the body there, on the hill?'

'She panicked,' Ramsay said. 'Someone was coming. The fog was very thick, but she could hear voices coming over the hill. She pulled Gabby back to the car. It wasn't far and she was terrified. She lifted Gabby back into the boot. Gabby was tiny, wasn't she? There was nothing to her. Then she realized that Gabby's bag was still on the hill. She flung it over the wall into the nearest garden.'

'So that was a coincidence,' Prue said. 'She didn't mean to implicate Amelia.'

'It was a coincidence,' Ramsay said. 'The only one.'

'Then she returned the car to the Grace Darling Centre,' Prue said. 'She must have been mad. Why did she do that if she was trying to protect Gus?'

'She didn't know what else to do,' Ramsay said. 'She wasn't thinking rationally and she couldn't face moving the body again. And she was Evan Powell's wife. She had a naïve and rather pathetic belief in the English justice system. She didn't think it possible that an innocent man would be found guilty of murder. She cleaned the car as thoroughly as she could and returned it to the Grace Darling in mid-afternoon when it was quiet. No one saw her. I suppose if Gus Lynch was ever found guilty she would have come forward.'

'So it was all a dreadful muddle,' Prue said, 'and not planned logically at all. Did she tell Gus Lynch what she'd done?'

Ramsay shook his head. 'She went to his flat later that evening but she didn't tell him. She didn't want him involved. She thought she was being terribly brave to cope with it by herself. She's really infatuated with him and saw it as a sort of romantic sacrifice.'

'Didn't he ask her if she'd taken his car? He must have known she had access to his keys.'

Ramsay shook his head. 'Apparently not. He made some joke about it—a policeman's wife as a murder suspect—but he thought she was just weak and silly. It never occurred to him that she would be capable of taking his car without telling him.'

'Where did Amelia Wood come into it? Did she see Jackie in Martin's Dene on the day Gabby died?'

Ramsay shook his head. 'No, it was nothing like that. Jackie knew that Gus had applied for a job out of the area. It was her great hope. She thought she could escape Evan and the tedium of Barton Hill and start a more glamorous life with Gus. John would be leaving home anyway and wouldn't need her any more. On the day after Gabby's death Gus had a phone call from his agent, pressing him to sign the contract and make the move public. But the night before he'd had a visit from Amelia Wood. She'd made it clear that she wasn't going to lose him from the Grace Darling without a fight. If he persisted with his intention to move she'd make his theft public, and who would want him then? Lynch didn't know what to do. He told me that he went out into Hallowgate to meet Mrs Wood from court, intending to plead with her again to release him. But just as he was about to approach her she was called back by the usher. He went home without speaking to her.' Ramsay paused. 'He was depressed. He phoned Jackie Powell for comfort, sympathy. He got rather more than that.'

'She went out and killed her!'

Ramsay nodded. 'Again, I don't think it was terribly well thought out. Gus Lynch had told her where Amelia Wood lived and that she was on her way home. She parked in the same place as she had the day before and walked over the hill to the back of the

Woods' house. She intended to go in and confront Amelia Wood but while she was waiting there, trying to make up her mind what to do, the woman came out with the dog. By that time Jackie Powell was under tremendous stress and in her unbalanced state she saw it as a sign, an answer to her prayers. She followed Amelia into the dene and killed her in just the same way as she'd strangled Gabriella. The dog barked and there must have been a struggle, but there was no one on the hill to hear.

He paused and poured himself another drink. 'She left the body where it was. It was dark and there was no one on the hill to disturb her this time. She walked back to her car. Nobody saw her.' He paused again. 'Then she drove on to the supermarket and did the week's shopping. I can't imagine the state she was in. She needed to explain her absence from the house, I suppose. When she got back to Barton Hill her son was there, and her husband decided they should go out for dinner at the Holly Tree. She must have been frantic, having to go back to Martin's Dene, knowing Mrs Wood's body was still on the hill. Even I could tell she was unhappy but it never occurred to me then that she might be involved. She was just Evan Powell's wife.'

'Perhaps that was the problem all along,' Prue said. 'She wanted to be more than a policeman's wife. I can understand that.'

'But you wouldn't have committed murder.'

'No,' Prue said. 'I wouldn't have committed murder.' She paused. 'Did Lynch suspect what she'd done?'

'I don't think so for a moment. He wouldn't have the imagination. Wouldn't consider his little woman capable of it. All he could think about was himself. And if he *had* suspected I think he'd have come to the police. He'd not want to be implicated in murder.'

She looked at him over her glass. 'You never thought it was me, did you? Or Anna?'

He shook his head sadly. 'No,' he said. 'I never thought it was you.' He realized that wasn't quite true and at the beginning of a murder investigation he suspected everyone. He wasn't a good judge of character, especially of women, and he couldn't afford to trust his instincts.